LAST TRAIN TO NOWHERE

AN INSPECTOR THOMAS SULLIVAN THRILLER

K.C. Sivils

"The price of freedom is eternal vigilance."

Thomas Jefferson – 3rd President of the United States

I want to thank my precious wife Lisa for all of her patience and encouragement.

I would also like to thank Ann Smith and June Poleski for all the time and effort they spent reading the rough drafts and finding my numerous errors. Any mistakes you find are all mine.

My mother-in-law Dona Green deserves my heartfelt thinks as well for her patience and encouragement.

CONTENTS

I watched Sarah as she stared out into the frozen, snow-covered countryside as the archaic train sped toward our destination. Annoyed with Josephson for our chosen mode of transportation, I glanced at my watch, noting time was wasting.

"Tell me again why we are taking the train? Is there a slower way we could have traveled," I growled at my partner, Sergeant Detective Josephson. He shrugged indifferently, confirming what I suspected.

"You don't like to fly." I snapped. Josephson, fresh back from medical leave, let his head drop in response. "Valuable time is being lost at the crime scene."

"Yes sir," the humbled youngster replied, drawing Sarah's attention. The mysterious, aloof doe eyed beauty glared at me, frowning as she shook her head in disapproval.

Not wanting to damage an already fragile relationship, I swallowed before explaining the source of my frustration.

"Look, you know every minute lost hurts our chances of solving the murder. If you have issues with flying, you should have booked a flight for Sarah and me and taken the train yourself."

"Yes, sir. It won't happen again, Inspector Sullivan."

I settled back into my seat, casting a glance at Sarah whose gaze had returned to the frozen countryside. Looking out at the snow and ice covered plain; I closed my left eye and adjusted the vision in my right eye, the cybernetic one. Doing so eliminated the "snow blindness" effect of the light reflected off the snow, allowing me to view the

1

scenery with perfect vision as it sped by.

I considered the purpose of our journey and grew even more worried. An officer in a Shore Patrol detachment attached to a company of Space Marines had been found murdered. That wasn't what disturbed me, though any time a Space Marine dies is troublesome. No, it was the fact the officer in command had specifically requested my assignment to the case.

Typically, in such a situation, the Shore Patrol would handle its own investigation. Calling in civilians was bad form, and a fight over jurisdiction was inevitable. For me to be requested by name raised my normal level of paranoia even higher.

It could mean only one thing. Somebody knew about my past as a Sergeant in the Shore Patrol during my hitch in the Space Marines.

I smelled a rat.

◆ ◆ ◆

Annoyed with Sully for chastising Josephson, Sarah focused her attention on the beautiful scenery as the train sped through the rolling, snow-covered white hills. The chilling winds from the west buffeted the train, enhancing its gentle, comforting rocking motion as it rolled along.

Ignoring Sullivan, her new employer, Sarah took a quick peek at Josephson. He'd donned the special glasses most humans needed to not suffer snow blindness in the open spaces of Beta Prime. Sullivan would just close his left eye and use his cybernetic eye to scan the countryside.

Sarah did not need the special glasses but had accepted a pair of regular sunglasses from Sullivan. Feeling for the glasses stored in the inner pocket of her new coat, Sarah recalled the knowing look from Sullivan as he'd handed her the glasses.

"Better nobody learns about your eyesight. Don't attract attention by not wearing these."

2

Sarah's cheek touched the cold plastiglass, returning her attention to the present. Most trains were maglevs. The high tech design relied on magnets built into the track and the train. Each set of magnets repelled each other, creating a frictionless electromagnetic buffer for the train, allowing the train to travel at speeds otherwise not possible due to friction.

Worlds like Beta Prime did not permit the use of such technology. The extreme cold required levels of power that made the use of the maglev technology impractical. The centuries old earth design, steel wheels on steel rail, proved to be the most efficient method of moving large amounts freight and people under the planet's extreme weather conditions.

Sarah sensed Sullivan was worried. Not just about the murder of a Space Marine, a sensitive issue for any Space Marine. Sarah had learned in her short time with Sullivan there was no such thing as an ex-Space Marine. They simply were no longer on active duty.

No, something else was bothering Sullivan. Sarah was certain. If it bothered the Inspector, it was serious.

Something about the assignment was more out of the ordinary than the Inspector was letting on.

◆ ◆ ◆

Looking down at the dead, frozen body, the young Marine wished his watch would end soon. Each time he checked his chronometer it seemed like time was moving backward. A layer of white frost had collected on the blue and red uniform of the dead Shore Patrol officer.

Typically, like any Marine, he wouldn't have felt any emotion other than irritation at the presence of the military policeman. Seeing the frozen, lifeless form made the young guard feel something entirely different. The SP was the first real, dead body he'd ever seen.

On his first deployment following basic, the Marine had been relieved his first tour would be a boring one on Beta Prime. It would give him a chance to adjust to life in the Corps on active duty without worrying about getting killed.

Now he wasn't so sure. SPs were invincible. They fearlessly broke up bar fights, arrested Marines and manhandled them into the brig if necessary. Marines viewed SPs with respect even though they disliked them. Mainly due to the fact SPs were armed to the teeth and knew how to take down Marines. Application of brute force and weaponry being two things all Marines respected.

Sneaking another glance at the dead SP, the guard noticed for the first time the dead man's eyes were open. The eyelids drooped slightly; giving the appearance the dead SP had been struggling to stay awake when he died. His imagination began to get the better of him; giving the young guard the impression the dead man was watching him.

Another strong gust of freezing wind with ice particles mixed in slammed into the guard. He decided the body wasn't going anywhere, being as it was dead and frozen stiff, and retreated around the corner of the building the body lay next to.

Snow drifted as another gust of wind blew, depositing another fine layer of flakes on the body. Lying on his back, the dead man's tired, unfocused eyes stared up into the blue sky, never blinking as white clouds moved overhead.

◆◆◆

Still feeling the sting of Sullivan's rebuke, Josephson slumped further down in his seat, pushing his shades up to rub the bridge of his nose. His fear of flying had clouded his thinking. The Inspector was right. He should have been honest and booked passage by air for his boss and Sarah and taken the train with their luggage.

Josephson shifted position again, his new hip still stiff despite the months of rehab. His new skin grafts itched like crazy. Sullivan had promised the genetically neutral tissue grown specifically for skin grafts would stop itching after a couple of weeks. Josephson was starting to think his boss had lied to him.

He stole another glance at the strange new team member sitting across the aisle of the coach from him. She wasn't a partner, or even a real law enforcement officer for that matter. Sully had informed Josephson while he was still in the hospital that Sarah, the young woman's name, would be their assistant.

Upon his first few days back he'd learned Sullivan was paying this Sarah out of his own pocket, which raised more than a few eyebrows. Somehow, Chief O'Brian and Captain Markeson had not objected, leading Josephson to expect Sullivan his partner had something on the two.

He was undecided about the new addition to their team. Mainly how the girl's presence would change his position with Sullivan. There were, however, two things Josephson was certain of when it came to the enigmatic Sarah.

Sarah was easy on the eyes.

That and her mere presence made Sullivan uneasy.

◆◆◆

I went through my mental checklist. We'd arrive at Brownstown in an hour, providing the train didn't breakdown or derail. Sarah seemed distant, but that wasn't unusual. I just needed her to stay close enough I could keep an eye on her. That and I wanted to be able to pry her observations from her without the usual verbal sparring required.

Josephson, the puppy dog, was going to be more trouble now than when first assigned as my partner. Coming off medical was hard for anyone. Already lacking in confidence, Josephson was a bit more fragile than normal. I'd have to be watchful of my sharp tongue.

He was a good kid and might make a good detective in time.

Murder is serious business in my book, this murder even more so. SPs were tough to kill.

I ought to know. I used to be one.

Keeping my two partners safe while solving this would be a challenge ordinarily. This case was going to be more difficult. Somebody wanted me here for a reason.

And I didn't as yet know what that reason was.

CHAPTER TWO

The Major brushed a snowflake off the lapel of his coat, annoyed by the constant dusting of snow the brisk wind applied to his uniform. He glanced again at his chronometer, the act of which did nothing to hasten the impending arrival of the noon passenger train.

Alone on the station platform, the others, waiting to either catch the train or greet travelers, remained in the waiting room of the train station. He needed to be alone when he met Sullivan.

It had been a lot of years since they had last spoken. Hopefully, those years had taken off some of the edge to Sullivan anger. Anger the Major's former Sergeant had a right to feel.

He was counting on the fact Sullivan was a professional. That and the Inspector was straight as an arrow when it came to matters of law enforcement.

He'd changed a lot since the incident. Changed for the better. Losing nine good Marines, SPs no less, in what was an avoidable incident could have been a career ender. His mother's connections and father's wealth had saved him and in the process destroyed the military career of the real policeman. Time and a lot of guilt and reflection had shaped him into a good officer.

Not good enough to ultimately overcome the silent stain of the fix that had been put in to save his career. But good enough for him to rise to the rank of major in the Corps and earn another chance at a real combat command.

It had been hard, but Kilgore had paid the price. Transferring from the police arm of the Space Marines, the

7

Shore Patrol, to the regular infantry had cost him. He'd had to go through infantry school again as well as combat officer school. But Kilgore saw the sacrifice as necessary. He had nine lives and a career to atone.

◆◆◆

Chief O'Brian looked at the report for the seventh time since dispatching Sullivan and Josephson to Brownstown. With that strange woman Sarah in tow no doubt. Sullivan had violated an untold number of protocols by hiring her. Earlier, when confronted, Sully had bluntly told both him and Markeson there was nothing immoral going on. He needed an assistant, and she would not be involved in actual police work.

Sullivan was a straight enough arrow he might be on the up and up about the immoral stuff, but O'Brian was certain Sullivan wasn't on the level with him about something regarding the girl. Markeson had just smiled when Sullivan departed after the testy exchange between the Inspector and his superiors.

"Let'em do it, Chief," Markeson had mumbled. "You know, give him enough rope, and we'll be rid of him."

O'Brian had glared at his Chief of Detectives. "Yeah, like you thought we'd be rid of him with that hearing."

He'd enjoyed the speed at which the grin on Markeson's face disappeared at the mention of the disastrous Internal Affairs hearing months earlier.

"How was I supposed to know Sully was that smart? Everything indicated he was a screw-up."

"You're supposed to be the best detective on this planet," O'Brian grunted back. "Nothing should surprise you."

Markeson frowned and stood up to depart. "He got lucky. Sooner or later Sullivan's luck will run out." To emphasize his point Markeson disrespectfully slammed the door to O'Brian's office when he left.

Something was up with Sullivan. That much O'Brian was sure of. The military, particularly the SP's, never requested civilian help in solving a crime involving one of their own. Yet, the officer in command of the unit had requested Sullivan by name and insisted he be placed in charge of the investigation.

"Sullivan, so help me, trouble just seems to follow you," O'Brian mused aloud. "See to it you make sure it stays your problem and not mine."

O'Brian shifted in his standard issue office chair to get slightly more comfortable. The chair creaked loudly in protest, making O'Brian wonder again just how was it Markeson had a comfortable, custom chair and he, the Chief of Police of Beta Prime has a standard issue government chair.

Putting all thoughts of Markeson aside, O'Brian focused his attention again on the limited details provided about the case he'd just assigned Sullivan on. O'Brian's cop sense told him it was a bad deal all the way around.

Military bases were few in number on Beta Prime and its two moons Serenity and Persephone. Brownstown was a mining town trying to masquerade as an up and coming tourist destination. Besides a little seasonal activity from the local farms and loggers, the only other source of income for the town was the military base.

The fact Markeson had taken an interest in the case, albeit a casual interest, told O'Brian he'd sent his best detective to disarm a time bomb.

He hoped Sullivan was up to the task.

◆ ◆ ◆

I stumbled as the swaying motion of the train suddenly lessened as the screeching sound of brakes being applied filled the coach. Sarah and Josephson stood up and began putting on their long, military styled great coats before retrieving their carry-on luggage from the racks over their seats. I pulled down my own backpack and slipped the right strap over my shoulder like school kids have been doing for centuries.

Sarah pulled on her backpack, using both straps to secure her load. Josephson struggled with his large suitcase, as the brakes released for a moment, causing him to stumble into me, earning him a frown in the process.

I moved past Josephson to get a view of the station as we approached. I was irritated enough with him already. Sometimes it was just better if I didn't say anything.

The train continued to slow as it passed through a sharp curve to the right. In the distance, I caught my first glimpse of Brownstown. Judging by the rail facilities coming into view, there couldn't be much to Brownstown.

As the locomotive pulled through the long curve, it began to obscure my view of the freight yards located to the eastern, or left, side of the train. From what I had been able to see the freight facility was primarily dedicated to the transfer of minerals and ore to freight cars. A small container transfer facility passed from my view while the train entered a section of straight track as it entered the edge of the town.

I adjusted my right eye to take in all the detail possible as the train continued to slow its approach to the passenger station. Unlike the large passenger facility we'd departed from in Capital City, this depot was not covered. An open platform greeted the passengers on the train, promising a cold reception before they rushed to what I hoped was a warm waiting room in the station.

A lone man stood waiting on the platform. I didn't need my cybernetic eye to recognize him as the train approached. I'd know the man anywhere, the posture, the way his mere stance conveyed his sense of superiority.

The Space Marine uniform didn't hurt either.

"Hey, you two," I growled softly, turning to see if Josephson and Sarah had heard me.

Their silent looks of expectation told me they had.

"See that Marine?"

They both glanced through the window and then back at me, nodding they had.

"Don't talk to him. If he asks a question, give a non-answer. If he presses you, refer the matter to me. Have I made myself clear?"

Again, the pair nodded.

"Sarah, you stay with me when we get off the coach. Josephson, you get our equipment and then find me."

Sarah remained silent. Josephson just nodded, not wanting to irritate me further. The other passengers began standing up and collecting their possessions as the train smoothly rolled to a stop. The door in the vestibule at the end of the coach opened automatically, extending steps down to the platform. I stood still, letting the other passengers in our coach bound for Brownstown get off first.

I watched my old CO scan the passengers as they hurried to the waiting room door. He stood still with his hands in the pockets of his greatcoat, moving only his head slightly as he surveyed the individuals passing by. He waited patiently, glancing down the platform.

I descended the steps and marched over to my old CO. I noted the oak clusters on his collar designating he'd made major since we'd last seen each other.

"Major," I snapped brusquely.

He turned slowly to look at me.

"Inspector I believe," he replied evenly, holding his gaze as he examined my face. His own showed signs of having aged, which was to be expected I suppose. What I hadn't expected was the lines around his eyes, the sadness that seemed to emanate from his arrogant blue eyes.

"You requested my presence."

"You haven't changed Sullivan," he sighed. "Which was exactly what I was hoping for."

CHAPTER THREE

Silence blanketed our walk to the crime scene. There wasn't anything I wanted to say, and the Major wasn't talking. Sarah followed in total silence. When I turned to sneak a glance at her, I wasn't surprised by what I saw. She moved gracefully, carefully leaving the least noticeable trail in the snow blown on the sidewalk by the constant, bone chilling wind from the west. Sarah was also taking in every detail as she moved, no doubt planning her escape if necessary.

I was still irritated with Josephson for booking passage by train when we could have flown. So I let him struggle with his suitcase and the several boxes of forensic tools we'd brought with us.

Our path followed a rail siding traveling due west. After nearly a kilometer's walk, I began to wonder why the Major had arrived alone and without a hovercar. He must have read my mind.

"I wanted to meet you alone Sullivan," Kilgore said evenly. "Don't worry about covering for me, because in case you're wondering, that's not why I insisted you be assigned to the case."

"Don't worry, Major," I replied with my best sarcastic tone and smile. "It will be my pleasure to see you escorted to the brig if at all possible."

I was disappointed when he didn't even flinch at my response. In the past, any snarky, disrespectful comment would have rated a ten-minute tongue-lashing.

"Sullivan, I need to keep a lid on this," he replied in his monotone. "Something's going on, and it scares me."

He stopped and turned to stare at me, pausing for a few

seconds before speaking again.

"I'm not the same officer. Let's leave it at that. This isn't a simple murder. I need an outsider to find out what happened. I don't want a military cover up. Both of us know how those work."

◆◆◆

Father Nathan watched as the assorted street urchins ate their hot breakfast. In the past few months, their number had grown to nearly two dozen. The faces changed from day to day, but the number remained steady. A warm place to sleep and a hot breakfast had a way of doing that.

In minutes they would make their way out into the cold, mean streets of Capital City. Away from the warmth and safety of the dormitory on the grounds of the Anglican Church where he served as vicar.

"It's one way to grow a parish."

He turned to see Alice, the waitress who usually waited on him and his friend Inspector Sullivan when they ate their evening meal together at *Joe's*, the local tavern and restaurant.

"Yes, Alice. It is. Though I don't think this approach is what the Archbishop had in mind when he installed me here."

"People are noticing, Father. Give them time. It's not like the people in this city are a religious bunch."

Alice's kind words made him laugh.

"They'd notice more if I could get the little hoodlums to stop picking their pockets.

◆◆◆

Grimacing from the cold, the engineer pulled his head back in and closed the cab window. Slapping his hands together repeatedly, he raised them to his mouth to blow into them in a vain effort to warm them.

"If you'd quit opening that blasted window, we'd be warm."

Turning to look at the brakeman, the engineer laughed.

"You want to be wandering around out in that? Be my guest. It's your job, not mine."

"Okay, you got me there" the brakeman complained. "When we get back, I'm booking off this run. This military stuff gives me the willies. No using comm devices and having to pass hand signals. If the union knew about this, they'd red flag this branch."

"Naw, you know how it is. Union boss got his from whomever, so we got to do the run. Never mind how dangerous this is. Snow, ice, no comm, passing hand signals. That stuff was outlawed, what, four, maybe five hundred years ago?"

The sound of boots clambering up the ladder to the door of the locomotive silenced the pair. Freezing cold air with a flurry of snowflakes exploded into the cab as the conductor opened the door and hurried in, shutting it behind him. Covered with tiny specks of ice and snow, he stomped his feet to loosen the snow. Rubbing his gloved hands together he finally extended his arms and gave his entire body one big shake.

"We got the all clear. Time to go. Remember, no lights and no horn till we reach the mainline."

◆◆◆

Rumbling sounds filled the air as a powerful diesel-electric engine revved up. I stopped and looked in the direction of the sound as did Sarah and Josephson.

"This is part of what is strange," the Major said softly. "That's a freight train. The siding over there runs to the military base where my Marine unit is attached. Look, tell me what you see that's strange."

I looked in the general direction Kilgore pointed. In the distance my right eye detected a huge, dark mass moving at a walking pace. Without gaining speed, more of the short freight train appeared from behind buildings in the distance, moving across what seemed to be a snow-covered field. The locomotives plow tossing the powdery snow aside like the bow of a boat cutting through water.

"No running lights," I said aloud without realizing I'd even thought of the answer to his question.

"Highly illegal," Josephson blurted out. "All trains in motion must..."

The quickly raised hand of the Major silenced Josephson's outburst. Kilgore motioned for us to follow as the rumble of the train grew distant.

In a few minutes, we approached an out building located close to the now visible track. Lights a few hundred meters away pierced the growing darkness, indicating the location of the military base.

Crunching snow alerted us to the presence of a lone Marine guard. He came to attention and saluted the Major.

"Has anyone been here in my absence Private Alphonse?"

"No sir, Major."

"Very well. You are relieved. Make sure Sergeant Maxwell has another sentry posted by 1900 hours. I will remain on location until then."

The private nodded, happy to be relieved of guard duty early. As he secured his weapon, he gave me a quick once-over and then Josephson. Like all Marines, he took his time examining Sarah, giving her a smile and a wave, which she ignored, as he departed in the direction of the base.

"Where's the crime scene?"

"It starts inside. I didn't touch anything. There have

been two guards posted. The one you just saw and another private before him. Punishment detail of sorts."

"Who found the body?"

"I did," Kilgore answered. "A private went missing at roll call yesterday morning. I have a small detachment of SPs. I sent two of them looking. Within an hour one of the SPs was back with the private who is now in the brig for going AWOL."

"How long before you noticed your SP was missing?" I asked.

"I got worried after another two hours passed. Couldn't raise him on his comm. We have great comm gear. I got worried and went looking for him myself. The door was open. I found him and then I requested you."

"Does the base commander know?"

"She does now. I gave you a six-hour lead before I informed her. I didn't realize you'd be traveling by train."

"Yeah, well, about that..."

"I know Sullivan. Bureaucracies everywhere try to pinch pennies."

I let it go at that, noting Josephson's look of relief.

"Is the body inside?"

"No, the door got my attention, but when I looked, there was nobody inside. The snow had been disturbed, not that you can tell now with this insufferable wind blowing. The body is over here. I put up a wind screen to force the wind around the body."

I nodded in response to the Major and walked with him along the side of the building toward the now obvious windscreen.

"Sure enough, one bona fide dead Shore Patrol officer," I muttered to no one in particular.

"Two shots center mass and one to the head," I noted. "He was dead before he hit the ground."

I stood over the corpse and turned the body on its side. "How long have you known this SP?"

"Not long," the Major answered. "He appeared with papers less than a week ago. I hadn't requested any additional SPs. We didn't need him. I thought at first it was a punitive assignment for screwing up, you know, sending him to this frozen hell. But his record was blank."

My mental paranoia kicked off into overdrive as I stepped away from the body, gently lowering it back to the ground as I did so.

"Sarah!"

I turned to see my mysterious female assistant running away. Josephson, who had called her name, chased after the surprisingly fleet woman.

"She's never seen a dead body before?"

"She's seen plenty, Major. She's seen plenty," I said grimly.

"Something spooked her."

I looked at the Major, trying to get a read on his thoughts. "Probably the same thing that frightened you."

From a distance, we could hear Josephson pleading with Sarah to return. With both arms folded across her chest and a determined side-to-side shaking of the head, it was evident I was going to have to find out what had spooked my already jittery assistant personally.

I left the major with the body and took my time walking in the ice-crusted snow. The sun had gone down for the evening, and the temperature was plummeting. If I was going to get anything out of Sarah, I had to keep my temper and control my tongue.

Not the easiest of tasks for me.

"I'm not going back over there," Sarah said with firm defiance.

"You don't have to," I replied. "But you are going to tell me just what spooked you so bad."

"Nope. Am not. Sully, you promised me this job would be pretty safe."

"Sarah, the guy's dead," I answered; annoyed Sarah had picked this moment to have one of her sometimes bizarre displays of stubbornness.

"I can see that," she declared, her body language that of a defiant teenager.

Josephson stepped back, giving the two of us more space. The expression on his face indicated he clearly did not want to become collateral damage.

"Look, Sarah, I have a job to do."

"I know you do. But this was not what I signed on for when I agreed to work for you."

I had to count to ten. I don't do well with women in general, and stubborn ones really get under my skin.

"Just tell me what spooked you. Then I will have Josephson escort you to the hotel we're staying in."

"Nope. I'm going back to Capital City on the next train or hoverplane. Whichever leaves the soonest."

"Uh, Sarah, unless you plan to walk back, you're going to have to stay with us tonight," Josephson said in an apologetic tone of voice. "Nothing leaving until mid-morning, either way."

If Sarah was scared before, she became more so at Josephson's announcement. Shaking from fear, not cold, Sarah ran to me and clutched my great coat with both hands.

I watched as Sarah frantically looked all around, looking for the source of her sudden terror. Still gripping my great coat in both of her hands Sarah looked up at me, eyes pleading.

"There will be a hunter here," she whispered.

"A hunter?"

I thought back to her ramblings the first time we'd ever talked. Fear was Sarah's constant companion.

"You mean?"

"Sully, the dead man's a clone. Just like me."

19

Dead bodies generally don't bother me. I've seen enough of them. But some of them stick with you. Can't be helped I suppose. You just can't unsee some of the horrors I've seen. The helpless victims always bother me. So do children.

There was nothing particularly gruesome about the dead SP. He'd died almost instantly, limiting the amount of blood loss. Beta Prime's frigid temperatures had frozen the dead SPs body quickly enough. We'd have to get the corpse back to Capital City for Bones to give an accurate time of death.

I was taking the good Major's word for the approximate time of death.

What troubled me was Sarah's reaction to seeing the body. She was hardly a stranger to death and violence. Major Kilgore didn't raise an eyebrow when I informed him of Sarah's suspicions. He just stood silently in the cold, scanning the area near the crime scene.

"Sarah, please come here," I shouted, motioning vigorously for her to return. She responded like a spoiled child, not the adult she physically appeared to be. By stomping her right foot, folding her arms across her chest again and providing another stubborn display of head shaking from side to side, Sarah did a fantastic impression of being an overgrown five-year old.

"That tears it," I muttered.

I used every centimeter of my long strides to move quickly to where Sarah, still accompanied by Josephson, was throwing her tantrum.

"I don't believe you."

"Believe what you want, Sully."

"There is no hunter. That SP just stumbled across a drug deal he shouldn't have or maybe a black market dealer buying weapons from someone at the base."

I wanted to take the words back as soon as they left my troublesome tongue. Sarah looked away, trying to disguise the hurt in her eyes. With just a few words, what trust I had built with her evaporated into the frozen air.

"Just prove it to me, and I'll believe you," I snarled, trying to bail myself out.

"About the hunter?"

"About all of it. Prove to me our victim is a clone. Because Sarah, I can't tell."

Casting her glance at Josephson for support, Sarah only received a noncommittal shrug from my official partner.

"Okay, but you have to draw your weapon. And Josephson has to draw his and keep a look out while I show you. The Major too," Sarah answered, oozing petulance.

It seemed like a fair enough compromise. I was cold, angry and growing more paranoid by the minute. Sarah spooked easily. But given her crazy claim, I had to give her a chance to prove it.

Looking around, I adjusted my right eye for the weather and light conditions and did a 360-degree sweep, searching for movement, texture variation, and heat signature. I made a show of doing so, hoping it would calm Sarah enough to get her back to the corpse. All I got for my troubles was a hateful glare.

"Draw your weapon," she demanded. "The hunter won't be in the open and will be wearing shielded clothes."

I pulled my .50 caliber chemically powered kinetic energy weapon, an old school revolver. Nothing like a large lead projectile slamming into a human body to do

22

massive damage to anyone I felt like doing extensive damage to.

Josephson hurriedly pulled his phase pistol, to which I shook my head. Losing his hip and going through the painful replacement, skin grafts and physical therapy hadn't been enough for him to realize a lead projectile didn't just kill the bad guy; it knocked him down in the process. Phase weapons just burned away tissue and bone till somebody fell.

Appeased for the moment, Sarah grabbed me by my left elbow and hurriedly pulled me toward the waiting, frozen corpse.

◆◆◆

As the rumble of the locomotive's engine lowered, the brakeman opened the door and peered out into the cold. Without speaking to the other two crewmen, he turned and climbed down the ladder from the cab. A few minutes passed before the door to the cab opened again.

"What's the problem?"

The brakeman shot a nasty look at the conductor. "Frozen switch."

"Should have taken the de-icer with you."

Responding with the centuries old universal gesture informing the conductor to reproduce with himself, the brakeman pulled the heavy device from its storage locker and pulled the thick straps over his shoulders, allowing him to carry it like a pack.

Again he ventured out the cab door and down the ladder. The engineer and conductor watched the orange glow in the distance as the brakeman melted the ice from the track, allowing him to move the lead rails. Ignoring the prohibition against using his comm, the brakeman informed the engineer the train could pull onto the main.

Setting the control in a higher run notch, the locomo-

23

tive's prime mover began to rumble louder as the train began to move onto the mainline slowly. In just a few minutes the short train, consisting of only three flat cars with standard shipping containers tied down on them, was on the main line.

"I hate this," the engineer mumbled. "No running lights, no train orders, no dispatcher's clearance. This is a wreck waiting to happen."

"It's okay," the conductor said calmly. "Nothing is moving till tomorrow morning."

"Still, I don't like it. I'm with Ed. I'm booking off this run when we get back to Capital City."

"No, you're not. And neither is Ed," the conductor sternly replied. "We all took the money."

The comm buzzed again, indicating the short train had cleared the switch. Another couple of minutes passed before the brakeman returned, his face red from the cold, his breath coming quickly from the exertion. He stored the de-icer in silence and again ventured out into the cold, walking to the rear of the train to lead it while it backed down the main line toward the Brownstown yards. It would be another ten minutes before the crew could safely tie down for the night, nobody the wiser about the clandestine switching operation.

◆ ◆ ◆

"Show me," I said firmly. "Make me see it too."

Sarah didn't say a word. Taking both hands, she felt gingerly on the back of her skull. Dividing the long hair as if intending to part it, Sarah suddenly bent at her waist, letting her long, dark tresses fall to either side of her head.

Uncertain of just what it was I was supposed to see, I leaned over and adjusted the vision in my right eye, zooming in and enhancing the image. I stood up quickly and took a step back.

"Are you sure you shouldn't have a doctor look at that?"

Standing up and finger combing her hair back into place at the same time, Sarah responded with another hateful glare. Her response to my question, a legitimate one I thought, was to unfasten the belt of the new great coat I'd given her as an advance on her pay. Opening the coat, Sarah promptly pulled up the several thin cotton shirts she wore, displaying a flat, smooth, muscular abdomen. Right in the middle of the toned midsection was a belly button.

A perfectly normal looking belly button.

"They do it surgically. I was a week old when the surgeon gave me a bellybutton."

Suddenly, I understood what it was Sarah had shown me.

I turned our dead SP on his side again. A quick glance at the exit wound in the back of his skull showed a small, but identifiable indentation in the scalp. Exactly like the one Sarah possessed.

"He was tank grown like me," she explained. "Some of us are grown inside a human mother. The rest of us are grown in tanks. The ones grown in a human mother take nine-months and then have to grow up like a regular human."

"Let me guess, tank grown clones hatch full grown, whatever that means, when you're born."

Sarah nodded. "I don't know why they use human mothers. It's a lifetime before the clone is fully grown. It only takes three months for a tank grown clone to reach full development. The only way you can tell is what's left of our umbilical connections."

"Why the head? Why not your abdomen where the nutrients need to go?" a bewildered Josephson asked.

Sarah shrugged. "I'm just a clone. I don't have any idea why they do what they do."

25

Cold air hit a crown on one of my molars, letting me know my mouth was hanging wide open. I shut my mouth and looked at the young woman before me. Her infantile behavior and uneven social skills suddenly made sense.

"How old are you Sarah?"

Busy buttoning her great coat back up, Sarah didn't look at me as she answered softly.

"I can appear to be as young as my early twenties or as old as mid-to late thirties."

"How old are you," I said with greater firmness.

Sarah looked up at me with her big brown eyes, her expression one of deep sadness.

"I'm five, almost six. But I'm a woman," she insisted. "I can have children, just like a regular human female. I feel all the emotions an adult woman can feel. I can't help the fact I've only been out of the tank for five years."

CHAPTER FIVE

I made my way across the empty street. It didn't matter which direction I was walking; it seemed like the night wind was blowing directly in my face, seeping down my jacket, freezing me to the core.

I am never going to get used to living on Beta Prime.

Turning down the road toward the military base, I stopped to scan the shadows. Who or what I was looking for I wasn't certain. Annoyed with myself, I shook my head, pulled the collar of my great coat up and headed into the icy wind. I had about five minutes before I was supposed to meet Major Kilgore.

I just couldn't shake the sensation someone was watching me.

This time, I stopped in the middle of the street and turned a full 360-degrees, using all the capability my cybernetic right eye possessed. Nothing.

"This is stupid. Sarah's got me looking for things that aren't there."

When this case was over I was going to insist she talk to a professional about the constant fear she experienced. There had to be an explanation and a solution to her constant need to be ready to flee, to never trust anyone.

In order for Sarah to agree to stay the night, I had the hotel cancel the single room Josephson had booked for her and move a cot into our double room. A cot she had instantly designated as Josephson's.

When I left the pair, Sarah had just finished dragging Josephson around in the cold, scouting every possible escape route from our room and the hotel complex, such that it was.

I couldn't blame her I suppose. It's not like I didn't have an advanced security system I'd custom installed myself in my apartment building.

After one final visual sweep, I turned back into the wind. I'd have to hurry to arrive on time for my meeting with the Kilgore.

◆◆◆

Sitting in his usual booth, Markeson watched the cute waitress bring his second drink of the evening. She smiled while leaning over, letting her blouse fall, giving him as much of a view as he wanted.

"Your meal will be coming right out, sir," she informed him in her best flirtatious manner.

Markeson watched appreciatively as the waitress walked away, adding just a little more roll to her hips than usual for his benefit.

Vibration in his jacket pocket broke his concentration. Pulling out his comm, Markeson realized it wasn't his work comm vibrating. He returned the first comm and pulled out the second device.

Glancing at the Caller ID, he was surprised by the lack of any information. Very few individuals knew how to contact him with this comm. Truthfully, the fact there was no ID information caused him a bit of alarm. Curiosity finally got the better of Markeson, and he opened the link.

"Who is this?"

"Why Detective Markeson, or should I say Captain Markeson, is that any way to greet a new friend," a sultry female voice purred from the device.

"Well, it is a bit rude," Markeson answered with his usual charm. "For someone to block their ID information when that person calls this comm."

"But Captain, a lady must have her secrets," the voice

replied.

Markeson grinned, enjoying the banter. "Yeah, but I don't usually associate with a proper lady."

"Perhaps it's time for you to seek out a new, higher class of lady to consort with."

In the corner of his eye, Markeson saw the cute waitress approaching with a broad smile on her face, carrying his meal on a tray. He smiled at her as she laid his meal out before him. Noticing he was using his comm, she left without saying a word. She did, however, glance over her shoulder as she sashayed away to give him a flirtatious wink.

"Yeah," Markeson mumbled, still watching the waitress wiggle her way back to the kitchen. "I'm not so sure I want to do that. Now, you called me. Unless you expect me to break this link, you need to tell me who you are and what you want."

The voice sighed over the link. "Has anyone ever told you, Captain, that you can be quite rude."

He laughed. "Yeah, they have. I'm breaking the link. Goodbye."

"Stop! You've made your point."

Markeson listened to the voice sigh, giving away a hint of tension.

"I'm afraid I can't identify myself over a comlink. But I do want to arrange a meeting," the voice paused seductively. "A business meeting."

"And why should I agree to meet you, assuming it's you I'll be meeting?"

"Because you have skills, and information, I need. And because my good Captain, you need money. Or at least you want money," the voice told him with an assuredness Markeson found irritated him in its arrogance.

"Where then, just where am I to go to meet a stranger who is nothing more than a voice on my unlisted, secure comm?"

"Brownstown. By tomorrow morning."

"Brownstown! Why there? It's more godforsaken and frozen than Capital City?"

"I couldn't agree with you more Captain Markeson. But the location has far too many positive aspects to overlook, simply because it's, as you say, godforsaken and frozen."

He sat and thought for a moment. Markeson might be a bent detective, but he was still a detective, and when motivated, a very good one. Like all good detectives, he did not believe in coincidence.

"This has something to do with one of my Inspectors," he stated simply, listening for a tell from the voice.

"Right you are, Captain, but not in the way you think," the voice cheerfully replied.

"Seriously," the voice continued, growing business like and cold. "I will compensate you for your time, regardless of whether or not you accept my proposition. How does the price of a first-class ticket on the morning flight and a thousand credits, hard money, sound for a consultation?"

Markeson thought for a moment. He had nothing pressing that couldn't be handled for the coming day. Looking down at his cooling meal, he noticed a small white card next to his plate. Turning it over, he noticed the cute waitress had written her name and the time she got off work along with her comm number.

His habit was expensive. But then, women always were.

"Make it two thousand credits, any form you like, and I'll meet you."

"Very well, Captain. Your ticket will be waiting for you. I will have my associate greet you at the airfield and take you to lunch so we can discuss business," the voice answered cheerfully.

"Good, now, please, tell me how I will recognize my new," he paused for effect, "how shall I say this...my new, high-class lady friend?"

"Oh, don't worry," the sultry voice whispered. "You'll

30

know it's me when we meet."

◆◆◆

Sullivan did not seem to be overly bothered by the cold the man thought resentfully. He had to remind himself. If this operation weren't so important for the future, his future; he wouldn't be in this frozen, forgotten town on this miserable planet.

Sticking to shadows and often scurrying for cover, the man followed Sully, keeping enough distance to avoid detection. He stopped to adjust the earpiece he wore, the cold making the device uncomfortable to wear. Not daring to remove it for fear of not picking up any conversation Sullivan might engage in, the figure tried to ignore the irritating sensation.

Emerging from the shadows of the building where the dead SP had lain was a Space Marine, an officer by the looks of his bearing and manner in approaching Sullivan. Neither man spoke, much to the frustration of the watcher.

Ignoring the cold wind, both men vanished inside the building and stayed for several minutes. Sullivan exited and stopped, waiting for the officer who had stopped and turned to shut and secure the door, making sure it was locked.

Still without speaking the pair started walking again, this time making their way to the snow covered rail line, following it with little trouble. After waiting several minutes, the watcher moved out from the shadows and hurried down the icy sidewalk, slipping and sliding clumsily on the slippery surface. Moving to the road to avoid a nasty spill, the man rushed to catch up with the pair before losing them. An earlier search of the area told the watcher the rail line paralleled the road he was on.

Slowing to take a glimpse between two buildings to his

right, the watcher caught a glimpse of Sullivan and the officer, walking quickly down the rail line. The shadowy figure scurried to take cover by the building, stepping on the sidewalk to avoid detection. A quick check of his listening device confirmed the pair still had not spoken to each other.

Staying in the shadows, the watcher seemed to vanish from sight as he silently followed the unwitting pair.

◆◆◆

I'd been up over twenty-four hours, and I was tired. I was also not about to let the Major know I was tired. Not when he had to have gone without sleep for what had to be close to forty-eight hours.

Making our way along the rail spur to the military base, it was evident there was no indication if the dead SP had walked along the rail line to the small building where he'd been murdered. Any trace he'd used this route had been covered by the fine, misty powdered snow the cursed wind swept over the barren, frozen roadbed.

As we neared the now visible perimeter security fence of the base, I stopped looking for any signs of how the dead SP had traveled.

"He could have been transported there some other way," I said out loud, more to myself than the Major.

"How do you mean," Kilgore asked.

"Hovercar. The train that passed. The victim could have been on it when it made the run to the base. Any number of ways."

Kilgore just nodded and said nothing.

"You didn't give me a lot of time with his file. What's the SP's name again?"

Kilgore just laughed once without humor.

"John Brown. But I doubt it matters what his name is... was."

I didn't like this bit of news.

"John Brown? Really? You'd think the military could be a little more creative in coming up with a new identity when they wipe a guys record."

"Unless he was only a couple of weeks old."

I stopped and turned my back to the wind, motioning the Major to do the same. He glanced at the sentries at the post entrance we'd been heading for and slowly turned as well.

"You don't really believe this Brown is a clone do you, Major?"

Kilgore's cheeks moved as he ground his teeth in silence, thinking. Turning his head to me slightly, Kilgore squinted as he spoke.

"What do you think Sullivan? You saw the body, up close before we had it moved to the town morgue."

I didn't know what to think, and I wasn't ready to let the Major know that. Not until I knew more about what was going on. And not until I knew I could trust the man who'd destroyed my military career.

"I know Sarah; my assistant believes he's a clone," I admitted.

I did not share the fact she healed unusually fast and could deal with extreme temperatures that would kill an ordinary human. Oh, and things like she could hide in plain sight, move like a cat and sense things a regular person couldn't.

"She should know," Kilgore said quietly.

I laughed, hoping to draw something from the Major. "What makes you say that?"

This time, it was Kilgore's turn to look paranoid by doing a 360-degree scan of the area before leaning close and whispering, "because she's a clone herself."

"What?" I exclaimed, hoping to get Kilgore off that idea. "You think because she has a scar on the back of her head she's a clone?"

"No, I believe she's a clone because she's not affected by the cold like we are. She's unduly observant Sullivan. It gives her away. Instead of focusing on staying warm, she watches everything, never looks down to avoid the wind."

"So Sarah likes cold weather. That's not proof she's a clone."

Kilgore smiled knowingly.

"You don't believe in charity cases, Sullivan. I know you. That girl doesn't have a clue about police work. You would never have hired her as your assistant unless she was trained, had at least studied criminology. She's never been to school. I'd bet a month's pay."

I didn't say anything.

"You hired her to keep an eye on her."

Grimacing to display a sense of irritation, I replied sarcastically, "I did no such thing," trying to stay calm, not letting Kilgore see he was right.

"Sure you did. You only need that young detective they saddled you with to carry stuff. He might be a promising detective and I'm sure you'll do a good job training the pup, but you work better alone. You always have."

"Seriously, Major. None of that is evidence that will hold up in court."

"No, Sullivan, it isn't. But I'm willing to bet you've seen something unusual. Like the fact she heals faster than she should."

"And how would I see something like that?"

Kilgore suddenly looked tired, bored with our verbal game.

"Sullivan, your lovely little Sarah is a clone. Just like her sister Maria was."

CHAPTER SIX

Markeson watched the waitress to the door of her building. Typically he would have pushed things by walking her to the door. Not tonight. He was worried about the strange conversation earlier in the evening. Worried enough he'd decided to cut the night a bit short. Shauna, the woman's name, turned and smiled as she waved before slipping through the door into her small apartment. Like so many others in the southwest part of town, a converted shipping container from when the planet's first colonists arrived.

Relieved, despite being a little disappointed, to call it an early evening, Markeson shifted a bit to get comfortable in his hovercar. He did a quick U-turn and accelerated back toward the raised hoverway to return to the northwest, the nice part of the city.

With no traffic on the hoverway that early in the morning Markeson sped home at over 200 kph. He parked his craft in its assigned space in the parking garage and walked quickly to his apartment. Markeson pressed his palm against the pad over the locked keypad. The device took his biometric readings while scanning his palm print. Leaning closer to the door frame and looking down, giving the appearance to the casual observer he was straining to look at the lock's keypad, another device scanned both of his eyes, checking the scan of his retinas against the scan on file.

A tiny green diode in the keypad flashed once, indicating he could now enter the code into the lock's keypad. It buzzed once, clicked, and the door opened a centimeter. Markeson stepped inside and leaned against the door, causing it to shut behind him.

"Lights on," he commanded. The entire apartment lit up, allowing him to scan the open space without moving.

"Signs of biological life," he asked the computer.

"You are the only current biological life form inside the residence, Captain," the computer monotoned.

"Have I had any visitors while I was gone?"

"Yes."

"How many?"

"Your maid Margareta came and cleaned as per her usual schedule. There was also an unidentified male who entered your residence at 1611 hours. The individual moved through your home quickly and departed in less than six minutes."

"Did the individual plant any devices of any kind?"

"Unable to state with certainty."

"Did the individual remove anything?"

Unable to state with certainty."

Markeson opened his jacket and eased his phase pistol out of its holster. "What good is having a military grade security system if it can't tell you what you need to know," he mumbled under his breath.

"It is not any shortcomings with my programming or logic," the computer replied, sounding almost irritated. "The fault lies with the lack of the necessary number of sensors strategically installed throughout the residence for me to be able to gather sufficient data to make an accurate assessment of the situation. We have been through this before Captain."

Taking a step forward into the living area, Markeson ignored his computer. He'd deal with the petulant AI later. If necessary, he'd threaten to wipe its memory, the threat of which generally got his computer's attention for a few months.

Markeson moved slowly and with stealth, clearing each

room one at a time. With only his bathroom remaining, Markeson eased into the space.

Holstering his phase pistol, he spoke firmly, "Shower, hot water on."

He stood and watched as steam filled the space, fogging up the mirror. Clear as Beta Prime's atmo on a sunny day was the message written by the male intruder.

"Be careful who you trust."

♦♦♦

I just stared at Kilgore, speechless.

"I have connections still Sullivan. I've followed your career since you left the Corps."

I couldn't help myself.

"Feel guilty?"

Kilgore didn't flinch.

"You won't believe me, but yes."

"You have a funny way of showing it."

Kilgore looked away, his jaws working again.

"Now is not the time, Inspector."

"Sure it is," I growled. I felt an almost overpowering need to hurt this man like he had hurt me. Hurt those dead SPs his incompetence, his stubbornness, had killed.

"Sarah was part of a somewhat successful experiment. Not by the military but by a private contractor."

"Somewhat successful? Sarah's odd, but you might be too if you were in her shoes," I told him. I needed to defend her. I also needed to find out what the Major knew and how he'd learned it. "Just what's wrong with her?"

"Not Sarah. She's the one everyone wants."

Kilgore sighed as he shoved his hands in his pockets.

"You couldn't have known Inspector, but you shouldn't have brought her here."

"Then why didn't you say something when you first saw her? There was time for me to get her out of here."

"No there wasn't, nothing moves in Brownstown unless it's scheduled to move. Besides, I wasn't sure until she showed you her umbilical mark."

Paranoia began kicking in. I ramped up the works in my right eye and scanned the area, doing a full sweep, recording as I slowly turned. I took my time and then watched the replay, letting Kilgore wait.

Something seemed out of place near an outbuilding with snow drifted against the northwest corner. I couldn't place what was setting my nerves on edge. I replayed the scan of the building, sweeping through all the spectrums of light my eye could see. I checked the heat scans, everything. I finally brightened the view, creating more contrast.

Then I saw it, the faintest movement of a mere shadow crossing from the building to the snowdrift.

I pulled my revolver from its holster and moved slowly; setting each step down gently and slowly letting my mass sink my foot down into the snow. As luck would have it, the wind had decided to stop blowing, allowing the sound of snow crunching beneath a footstep carry.

Taking aim, I eased the hammer back till it locked, ready to fire. I took my time using my right eye to aim, utilizing my new upgrades from my last hospital stay to calculate angle, wind drift and drop due to the effect of gravity on the round as it traveled. I slowed my breathing, gradually increasing the pressure on the trigger right to the point of pulling it. Taking a final breath, I squeezed the last bit, firing my .50 caliber round into the snow drift.

Momentarily deafened by the explosion of sound from my gun, I couldn't hear anything. Snow began to twirl in little whirlwinds as the wind again whipped up; as if it was pleased I had done something so violent.

Moving with caution and my firearm at the ready, I approached the snow drift carefully, Kilgore next to me, his own sidearm drawn and at the ready. We separated and approached the snow drift in a pincer like movement. I approached from the north and Kilgore from the south.

I finally cleared the sightline of the drift. There was nobody there. Kilgore lowered his firearm and approached the drift slowly. I covered him as he carefully scanned the area. He motioned to me. I approached with caution certain somebody was observing us.

"You grazed somebody," he whispered, pointing at a drop of blood quickly freezing in the snow.

◆ ◆ ◆

Josephson's breathing was slow and rhythmic as he slept. Otherwise, Sarah would have kept him awake so she could listen. Sitting with her back against the wall in the corner of the room, Sarah hid behind the second double bed. Slumped over she could just see the entrance to their hotel room while not being readily visible herself.

Hidden from view, Sarah fingered the knife she had lifted from Sullivan's boot without him noticing. She listened to every sound, the wind, a couple arguing in a room several doors down, and the sound of powdered snow drifting, sorting the sounds out, listening for someone approaching.

An irrational sense of unease had filled Sarah when Sullivan departed to meet with the Marine Officer, leaving her alone with Josephson. The sleeping detective caused Sarah no fear. He was not capable of harming her.

Things she couldn't control caused Sarah's anxiety, things like Sullivan's dislike for the officer. Seeing the dead clone had almost sent her into a panic driven flight. Angry with herself for relaxing her guard in Sullivan's presence, Sarah fought back the fear and anxiety telling her to run.

Somewhere in Brownstown was a hunter, a shadowy

figure determined to take her back. Sarah knew she could evade the hunter and make her way back to Capital City. The cold would make things hard, but the wind and snow would help too. Providing her with a natural cover to fade into and not be seen.

Keeping Sarah in place was the knowledge her sister Ellie was still somewhere on Beta Prime, possibly in Brownstown. With a hunter close, Sarah would need Sullivan to find Ellie, keep her sister safe. Long enough for Sarah to figure out what to do.

Sullivan frightened Sarah. He was a towering individual, two meters tall and thickly muscled. His facial scar and often blunt manner intimidated people who did not know him. Then there was the Inspector's propensity for violence. She had seen it personally. Seen him beat a monster to death with his steel hand and the remains of a mutilated but human hand.

Sullivan also made Sarah feel safe. Cared for in a way she had never experienced. Before he had convinced her to work for him, Sullivan had let her stay in his apartment when she wanted relief from the cold or was hungry enough to take advantage of his offer to eat the food in his apartment.

She didn't know which Sullivan scared her the most, the tough, brutal cop or the man who wanted her to be safe and well cared for. It was all so confusing. Sarah knew men desired her. Monsters in her past had made that lesson painfully clear. Sullivan had never once tried to touch Sarah that way. If anything, it seemed to her the big man did everything possible to avoid touching her at all.

Sarah was certain of one thing, Sullivan wanted something from her.

CHAPTER SEVEN

Kilgore sat down a cup of hot chocolate before taking a seat on the other side of the interrogation table. I took a sip and let the sweet, hot liquid run down my throat, warming my insides just a touch.

"What do you want to know," Kilgore asked evenly. "I can only tell you so much, but I'll tell you what I can."

"Sarah said she was made for a particular client who was dying. The template, as she called this person, passed away before Sarah was born."

"True. I can tell you that much, but I believe Sarah is slightly misinformed."

"How so?"

"The template funded the process of cloning the three girls. After that, she was no longer needed."

"I see." These were ruthless people. I would have to be a little more patient with Sarah and her fits of paranoia. People, even crooks, usually don't kill their source of income. Not unless they see the potential for a better deal somewhere else.

"Who is after Sarah?"

I watched my former commanding officer think, filtering through what he could tell me and what he couldn't.

"Several different groups I guess is the best way to describe the situation. Our military but not for the reasons you might think."

"What reasons do I think?" I wanted to know as much as possible.

"To keep others from getting the technology Sarah represents. The Alliance agrees with the ban on human cloning. It's a can of worms the military would like to see kept shut."

"Okay. I might buy that. I might not. Who else wants Sarah?"

"The Confederation and probably the Caliphate would be my guess as to who the military groups are."

I thought for a moment. It made sense. The Confederation, the rebel group of planets who'd started the civil war within the Interplanetary Alliance, had taken horrific losses in the war historians now called the Intergalactic Wars.

The Caliphate, planets settled by Islamic groups from the Old Earth had been showing a desire to expand. History told stories of suicide attacks hundreds of years ago by the factions that had later formed the group of settlers that became the group of colonies known as the Caliphate.

"Makes sense. Quick way to raise an army if you're the Confederation and a source of suicide squads, if the stories from history are true, for the Caliphate."

"They don't scare me as much as the other groups Inspector," Kilgore said grimly.

I took note of his expression, and it chilled me, making my legs feel weak like I'd just finished a long run on an empty stomach.

"How so?"

"For profit breeding. Assassins for a single, one off job, organ harvesting, illegal human research and even raising expendable mercenary armies for corporations. The possibilities for abuse of the process are limited only by the greed and evil of the individual."

The urge to get Sarah, and Josephson for that matter, out of Brownstown began to feel like a compulsion. Like the kind I used to have when I was hitting the bottle. The urge to take another drink.

"This is more than just a murder of one of your SPs."

"Sullivan, it is indeed that. I'm going to level with you. I'm not just in the Space Marines."

Kilgore let his words hang in the air like pieces to a puzzle. He wanted me to fit them together.

"I see," I told him. It was clear now, or at least I thought it was.

"How long have you been the Marine commander at this outpost?"

"Five months."

"What goes on here?"

"Normal military stuff. Mainly, we patrol the wastelands around here. Keep an eye out for bandits and act as a ready defense force if Capital City comes under attack."

"Yeah," the cynical part of me replied, knowing full well Kilgore was telling me the truth. The part of the truth the Alliance military didn't care if anyone knew. "What actually goes on here?"

"Sullivan, I wish I could tell you."

I hated all this back and forth. I like simple, direct communication.

"Stop it with all this top secret stuff. Either tell me or don't. I want to get the body and the evidence back to Capital City and file my report. The odds are your shooter was whoever it was I winged, and he or she is long gone."

"Sullivan, I'm not playing games. I don't know. I was sent here to find out. This much I can tell you. The base, like most on planets similar to Beta Prime, is also a research facility. What's more, the security to enter that part of the base is the best I have ever seen. I don't have clearance to get in."

I had to decide if I was being played. Kilgore owed me. He knew I hated him for what he'd done to those other SPs and me. He also had a job to do now. Military Intelligence in the Alliance military drew from all of the branches. They were a secretive bunch on a good day.

Kilgore was taking a calculated risk bringing me in, a risk that made sense. He didn't know whom he could trust. A civilian cop he knew, possibly trusted, might be worth the risk. Catching the killer might shake something loose. I thought in silence for a while. Partly to try to make sense of the jumble of facts and partly to see if I could get Kilgore to fill the silence by talking, giving away something.

He didn't say a word after some time passed. He just smiled at me. I shrugged. He had been an SP once and as such, familiar with interrogation tactics.

"You think the base might be the source of the clones?"

Kilgore didn't speak. His eyes did though.

"You think the SP was cloned here."

More silence.

"Rogue unit?" I mouthed, suddenly paranoid about recording devices.

"Inspector, I've kept you far too long. You have got to be exhausted. After you've returned to Capital City and gotten some rest, please send me a copy of your preliminary report. I've made travel arrangements for you and your assistant to fly back with the body and evidence. The young detective will be traveling back on what the railroad refers to as a mixed train. Part freight and part passenger. He'll be awhile."

I smiled. Kilgore had picked up on my irritation with Josephson. The long, boring trip might teach him a lesson. If it didn't, the military's way of trying to get your attention by causing harmless pain wouldn't hurt the young pup.

◆◆◆

Brownstown didn't look as small from the air as Markeson thought it would. The airfield was relatively large, but the presence of the military base had a lot to do with that. Mining activity had led to the development of the large rail complex for loading ore, and containers of equipment from off planet transferred to freight hauling hover vehicles.

Circling the growing town, Markeson had seen the tourist development. Several medium sized hills had been developed for an old fashioned ski resort. He'd laughed at that idea. It would take a lot of marketing to get him to learn to slide down a hill in the freezing cold with a pair of sticks on his feet. But,

44

there were plenty of stupid, gullible people out there willing to part with their credits.

Lining up for the approach to land, the hover craft passed over the working class part of town. Converted space freight containers, used by the mining companies to bring the first loads of equipment to the site, made up the bulk of the housing. Like most mining towns, there was the main street, dotted with shops and offices of the few professionals who'd hung out their shingles.

He could see why Sullivan had been requested. The cops in Brownstown handled drunks from the mines on payday and vandalism by the high school kids on weekends. There wouldn't be a decent investigative detective on the force.

Not that he cared.

Chief O'Brian was responsible for the police force on Beta Prime, a big job, but primarily concentrated in Capital City. As far as Markeson was concerned, assigning a detective to Browns-town would be a form of cruel and unusual punishment.

As the hovercraft finished banking and began its final descent, shedding speed and altitude, Markeson tried to concentrate on his meeting. He hated surprises and liked not being in control even less. Still, for two thousand credits, he could listen. Information was critical in his many enterprises, and he'd learn what he could and if possible, give little to nothing away in return for the credits, first-class ticket, and lunch.

A gentle bump followed by the shifting of the craft as it settled on its landing gear signaled the end of the flight. Markeson stood up, smiled at the attractive flight attendant and made his way to the exit of the craft, not waiting for the obligatory and infuriating message to remain seated until the pilot gave the all clear.

Flashing his badge at the crewman, Markeson waited in silence for the hatch to open. Icy cold air seeped in as the seal was broken, reminding him of how much he'd grown to hate the climate on Beta Prime. Walking through the causeway connecting the hovercraft to the terminal reminded him just how

45

backplanet everything was on Beta Prime. Modern terminals on upscale worlds in the Interplanetary Alliance allowed hovercraft to dock directly with the terminal. No causeway was required.

Waiting for him in the terminal was a tall, impressive male who had the air of a professional soldier. If the man was not currently serving, Markeson concluded, he had either served in the past or was a mercenary. Without showing any emotion, the man approached the detective, stopped and bowed slightly.

"Captain Markeson?" he asked in a monotone.

"Yeah. In the flesh."

"If you will follow me, please. My superior is waiting for you in the only restaurant in this town worthy of being called such. Do you have any luggage we need to retrieve?"

Markeson shook his head no, and the man turned without speaking, evidently expecting Markeson to follow. A short walk through the concourse and past security took them to the exit for ground craft. A long, black hovercar sat waiting. Markeson's escort approached the passenger door in the back, opened it and waited for Markeson to enter the car.

Curious, and always ready to enjoy luxury, Markeson climbed in and seated himself, fastening the safety restraints. The grim escort shut the door and walked around the front and opened the door to the driver's compartment and climbed in. Separated from the front by what Markeson was certain had to be weapon proof glass of some sort, the escort turned driver did not speak as he pulled out and drove away from the airport.

As promised, the drive was short. Stopping in front of what indeed appeared to be a new, upscale establishment, the hovercar stopped, the escort exited, opened the door for Markeson and waited for the detective to climb out, shutting the door behind him.

"My superior awaits inside," the escort informed Markeson, chilling him for some reason with the words.

Walking to the entrance quickly to escape the cold, Markeson stopped and looked back. The black luxury hovercar was already gone. He shrugged and took the last few steps to the entrance, which opened automatically.

Upon entering, he saw no one. The restaurant appeared to be empty. No hostess or maître de to greet customers, no waiters or for that matter, customers. He removed his coat and draped it across his left forearm and adjusted his jacket, giving himself a chance to make a quick, nonchalant check his sidearm was ready in its shoulder holster beneath his left arm.

"Captain Markeson, prompt I see. I like that in a man."

Turning to identify the owner of the sultry voice from the commlink the day before, Markeson was surprised by the creature who stood in the entranceway to the dining room located on the right side of the entrance.

Long red hair cascading in perfect waves down past her shoulders, contrasting with perfect pale white skin the color of ivory was what first caught his eye. Being male, it didn't take long for his gaze to descend downwards, noting the other desirable female attributes his mystery hostess possessed.

Dressed in an immaculately tailored black two-piece pants suit appropriate for the weather of Beta Prime while making a striking, albeit conservative, fashion statement. Razor sharp creases in the slacks caught Markeson's eye as he moved his gaze upwards from the black, pointed, high heel ankle boots. Pleats at the waist hid hips just wide enough to give the woman a pleasing shape, a shape complimented by a somewhat narrow waist and a chest the jacket could not completely hide.

He remained silent, watching the striking creature evidently responsible for his presence. She smiled, comfortable in the silence and allowed him to observe her, take in all that he wanted.

Markeson noted her makeup was minimal and well placed. Her slightly thicker than fashionable waist indicated a strong, well developed muscular core. The nature of the clothes was nothing most people would find too unusual, simply the dress of a conservative and successful businesswoman. To Markeson, it screamed of military background.

"I'm afraid you have the advantage on me," Markeson opened with his first gambit, smiling his most charming smile.

47

"How so, Captain?"

"I'm afraid I don't know your name, but you know mine."

The red-headed creature smiled, a big smile, exposing a mouth full of perfect, white teeth.

"As I said before, a lady has to have her secrets."

"Well, I don't deal well with people who keep things from me, Ma'am. Or is it Colonel? General?"

Gone in a flash to be replaced by a scowl was the brilliant smile.

"It's Colonel, or rather it was."

"Very well, let's compromise," Markeson smiled, having scored a point. "I'll settle for Colonel for now."

He looked around the restaurant and gestured with his arms. "It would appear the establishment is not open for business."

"I convinced the management to remain closed for the breakfast service. It was a light business for them, and I compensated the staff appropriately. We have some time to discuss business before the lunch service commences." She smiled dangerously at Markeson, as a wolf smiles at a lamb before it strikes.

"Then we can enjoy that meal I promised you."

◆◆◆

Father Nathan shivered as he crossed the street, looking for one of the charges he'd take under his wing. Spotting the young Jaliel spying from behind a parked hover truck making a delivery, the priest briskly approached the lad, striking from behind. Lifting him up by the collar of his new coat, the priest felt the boy relax as he dangled from the big man's grasp.

"Father."

"Jaliel."

"I'm sorry. Payday is coming, and the Boss Man was angry last time. Says we aren't clippin' enough."

"Who is this Boss Man?"

"Father Nathan, there's a lot o' things I'd tell you, but that ain't one of 'em."

48

"Wallets and the two watches."

"Father Nathan, please."

"Jaliel, what is the Eighth Commandment?"

"Thou shalt not steal," the boy answered somberly, producing the purloined items and holding them up with his left hand. Father Nathan calmly took the things and released his grip, allowing the boy to drop to the ground. Without looking back, Jaliel sped away.

Shaking his head in frustration, the priest turned to find the owners of the stolen items.

He thought of his words to his injured friend, the Inspector Sullivan. If Sullivan did not find this boss, he would. Father Nathan's face darkened at the prospect. He'd turned away from his violent past. But this, this he couldn't let this continue.

CHAPTER EIGHT

Relieved at not having to fly back with Sullivan and the pouting Sarah, Josephson watched as the hovercraft took off to return the pair to Capital City. Making the trip with them was the body of the deceased SP and all the trace and forensic evidence. Sullivan had conducted the few interviews of possible witnesses himself.

Glancing at his chronometer, Josephson made his way to the greasy spoon eatery familiar to most hoverports to get something to eat. Hoping to find something to quell both his hunger and ease the turbulence in his stomach, Josephson slipped into line. Glancing about, Josephson decided to engage in one of Sullivan's skill development games. He watched every person within visual range, trying to determine as much as he could by just observing.

Catching his eye was a tall man. Well dressed and neatly groomed, the man stood out. Not so much because of his height or dress. It was the man's bearing. The quiet strength and intimidation the man projected as he waited. Josephson wished Sullivan were there so he could share what he observed, to learn if his conclusions were on the money.

Watching people take a wide path around the man, who made no physical signs of intending to harm anyone convinced the young detective there was something unique about the patiently waiting stranger.

Without warning the stranger turned and looked directly at Josephson, almost as if he was aware of being watched.

"Hey, you want somethin' or not?"

Relieved to be called, Josephson hurriedly turned around and stepped up to the counter. "Muffin, bran with raisins."

"Sheesh, a health nut," the woman groaned, taking a fresh piece of wrapping material and moving off to retrieve Josephson's breakfast. Cautiously, he glanced over his shoulder for another peek at the stranger.

Marching toward the exit, matching the stranger step for step was Captain Markeson.

◆◆◆

Sitting at his desk, Kilgore glanced out of the symbol of power and status awarded to the officer who commanded the Space Marine detachment at the base. He smiled at the silliness a simple window could cause. Two colonels, one Air Force and one regular Army, had protested when he'd arrived and assigned the office. Their noses out of joint because a lowly major had been billeted in one of the few offices with a window.

The seriousness of the situation he found himself in returned his usually grim expression to his face. He hoped he'd not signed Sullivan's death sentence by involving the Inspector. He just knew he needed someone he could trust with the skills required to find out what was going on.

A dead SP was always a serious matter. He'd taken heat in the past. Involving a civilian had infuriated the General in command of the base. Kilgore had let the woman vent before explaining his reasoning. He'd concluded with the excuse Sullivan wasn't really a civilian. He was a Marine. A former SP and the best investigator Kilgore had ever known. Claiming to suspect the killer was military, he justified the need to bring Sully in.

Regular Army to the core, the general had given him her most hateful glare before sighing and laughing.

"You Marines are something. No longer on active duty is the phrase I think the Corps uses."

"Yes, General. We never leave the Corps. The Inspector is simply no longer on active duty," Kilgore had responded, relieved interservice rivalry had raised its head, making his decision seem like more a case of not looking outside the boundaries of the Space Marines than breaking actual military protocol.

Kilgore leaned back and thought about what little he knew about his situation. Military Intelligence had sent him to find out what exactly was going on in the research facility. Now he had a dead clone on his hands. One with a fake military background so poorly done Kilgore wondered if it was meant to raise a red flag.

Sully had wounded somebody spying on them while they'd talked outside the perimeter. If it was the killer or not, Kilgore had no idea. Whoever it was, he was certain the individual was a professional. Nobody could move and not be seen, or take a wound like that in silence, without professional training and equipment.

Complicating matters was the fact Sullivan had not only found but also brought with him the one clone alive just about every military, mercenary and criminal organization in the galaxy wanted to get their hands on.

Another glance at his chronometer reminded him of the fact he'd been without sleep for nearly three days. Sleep was a weapon. Deny it to the enemy, and you gain an advantage. Make certain you get it when you can, and it can give you an advantage.

Nothing would change until Kilgore heard from Sullivan. He pulled the shade down over the weapon proof pane of glass embedded in the plastisteel wall with exterior armor appliqué. He secured his door, entered his encrypted code to secure the lock and pulled a chair up against the door.

Within minutes of lying down on the humble couch in

his office, Kilgore was asleep.

◆ ◆ ◆

My ticket was for the window seat. Sarah's was for an aisle seat on the other side of the aisle. She hadn't spoken a single word to me since I'd returned to the hotel. I'd found her sitting on the floor in the corner of our room, brandishing one of my knives. I replayed the strange events from early this morning, using the video from my cybernetic eye.

I started with entering the room and securing the door behind me. Noticing Sarah and not wanting to wake the boy wonder sleeping on the cot, I quietly walked over to where she sat and simply held my hand out. Sarah frowned, reversed the weapon, and gave it to me. Cold, exhausted and sore, I sat down on the end of the bed and pulled off my boots, setting them next to each other.

I took my .50 caliber revolver from its holster and set it carefully on the bedside table between the two beds. I patted my pockets, checking for my other weapons and decided to sleep in my clothes, great coat and all. Pulling my comm from my pocket, I set the alarm, giving myself two hours to sleep. I set it next to my pistol and turned the light on the table off.

The digital images flickered for a moment causing me to squint to improve the image. A habit, not that it would help. The image cleared and I was rewarded with a view of the ceiling of our room. A hazy darkness filled the image as I fell asleep and my eye stopped recording.

Minutes before the alarm went off I'd awakened, as oft was my habit. Still on my back, I rolled on to my left side and started in surprise. Lying next to me on her right side was Sarah. Both eyes wide open, two brown gems surrounded by pools of transparent white. She blinked once, making me notice the frown she still wore on her face.

Arms folded across her chest, she was completely dressed, including I noticed upon looking, her boots.

Without speaking, she'd gotten up and vanished into the bathroom. After a few minutes the sound of water running filtered into our room, waking the still slumbering Josephson.

"Once Sara's done, however long that is, I'm gonna take a shower," I told Josephson. "Fifteen minutes max. Then you have twenty. I'm going to check on our tickets. Kilgore said they'd be at the desk. You're going back via mixed train."

My young charge had simply nodded and laid his head back down, waiting for his turn to clean up.

Airborne and homeward bound, I glanced over at Sarah, sitting in my window seat. I was okay with that. At my size, I hated window seats. In fact, I hated flying in tubs as small as this one.

Maybe I'd been too hard on Josephson. Traveling by train had been more comfortable and civilized. I decided to tell him in the future, if time were not an issue, we'd travel by train.

I thought about the day ahead. We'd deliver the body as soon as we arrived. Bones would be waiting with a bus, and I'd requested some uniforms as well. He hadn't asked why, but I'd have to have a few words with Bones in private. He was too smart not to realize what he had in his morgue.

The Chief would have to settle for a phone call.

The evidence was going to stay with me. The uniforms could take the equipment back with them.

Then whether or not she wanted, Sarah was going with me to get something to eat at Joe's and then we were having a talk. Once that was done, however long it took, I was going to get some sleep.

Depending on how our conversation went, Sarah was coming back with me to be kept under lock and key in my apartment, or I'd let her do whatever she wanted. Knowing Sarah, slipping away into the mist and fog of Capital City and vanishing for a day or so would be high on her agenda.

My military days harkened. The flight would be short. I needed sleep, and none of the few passengers on the aircraft looked like a threat. Sarah had made it more than clear she had no intention of talking.

Sleep when you can.

CHAPTER NINE

Born and raised on Beta Prime, Josephson loved the planet's perpetually cold weather. Rather than wait inside the depot with the handful of other passengers who would be traveling on the late morning mixed train, the detective stood on the platform. He watched with interest as the train crew eased the long line of freight cars back toward the two passenger coaches sitting at the boarding platform.

Harkening back to his youth, Josephson counted the freight cars and identified each car by the cargo it hauled. Mainly made up of loaded ore cars, the string included several container flats carrying unsealed containers, indicating they were empty and being returned to Capital City. A pair of tank cars between the ore cars and containers flats completed the train.

Standing as close as he dared, Josephson watched with fascination as the brakeman checked the automatic couplers between the last freight car and the first passenger coach before connecting the brake controls and communication lines. Fascinated by old technology, the trains on his home planet were among one of his favorite subjects of study.

The train's conductor appeared and glanced about nervously before talking to the brakeman who whispered his response. Odd behavior for men who worked in a heavy industry under dangerous conditions Josephson thought. Clear communication would be critical when operating with masses the size of what they handled.

Nodding after the conductor whispered a reply, the

brakeman climbed the steps to the first coach and disappeared. Noticing Josephson, the conductor smiled and approached in a friendly manner.

"Will you be traveling with us today, sir?"

"Yeah. Going back to Capital City."

His response elicited a short laugh from the conductor.

"Picked the slowest way to make the trip. This is a mixed train. Basically a freight train with a pair of coaches coupled on the end to squeeze out a bit more revenue for the stockholders."

"That's okay. I find trains like this to be fascinating. It's a curious form of technology."

Glancing at his watch the conductor nodded his understanding. "Except for the weather and the pay, this is the greatest job in the universe."

Passengers began to filter out of the depot, and the conductor greeted them with a smile.

"All aboard," he called, indicating it was time to board the train. Taking the opportunity, Josephson stepped back and allowed the dozen fellow travelers to board before him, providing an opportunity to observe each passenger. None looked particularly impressive, let alone any type of threat.

Finished observing, he picked up his heavy suitcase and recalled Sullivan's rather pointed lecture about traveling light when on a case. Waiting until the passenger before him finished boarding the last coach, Josephson hoisted his baggage up and placed it on the floor of the coach's vestibule and climbed up the steps. Wanting to see as much of the train as possible, he picked a seat toward the rear of the coach and stored the heavy suitcase in the luggage rack overhead.

Wasting no time, the conductor closed the doors on the coach's vestibules and began the process of checking tickets. Finally reaching Josephson, the railroader smiled as the detective held up his comm to have it scanned for his ticket.

"Hope you enjoy the ride today. Not a lot of stops to switch today so we shouldn't be too far behind the scheduled arrival time."

As the words left the conductor's mouth, a loud bang sounded as a powerful impact rocked the coach forward. Startled, Josephson was thrown forward with the rest of the passengers as the impact pushed the coach forward nearly two decimeters.

"What was that?"

"Just coupling a few more cars to the rear of the train. Nothing to worry about," the conductor announced for the passenger's benefit. The brakeman made an appearance shortly afterward and nodded at the conductor while making his way toward the front of the coach, vanishing as he passed through the door to the vestibule.

Two long blasts from the locomotive's air horn in the distance sounded and seconds later the coach eased into forward motion as the train got underway. Puzzled by the odd addition of cars, Josephson stood up and made his way to the rear of the coach to peer out the window. A quick count indicated three container flats had been added, each containing a sealed container.

Seeing nothing else really unusual, Josephson sat down, settling comfortably in his seat, leaning against the cold window to watch the train as it made its way toward Capital City.

◆◆◆

Markeson sat in silence, staring at the striking creature sitting across from him. After ten minutes of polite sparring, the "Colonel" as he'd come to call her was no closer to telling him precisely what it was she wanted from him. Nor in the process of their back and forth banter had the detective learned any more about his mysterious host.

"Pardon me, Colonel," he interjected, weary of the game and desirous to learn what was expected of him or to be paid and sent on his way. "Could we get to the matter at hand?"

"You're no fun," the redhead purred back before pouting, a delicious pout. Her lips pressed together, head tilted somewhat to the right, her right shoulder elevated ever so slightly higher.

The detective's silence indicated he was willing to be labeled no fun. It was time for business. She sighed, the fun at hand having been spent. "Very well. It would seem there has been an unfortunate murder near the military base here in Brownstown. A fact I'm certain you already know."

She paused, glancing out the window before continuing. "A member of the Shore Patrol no less. Needless to say, that sort of thing not only upsets the military in general, but it really tweaks the other SPs and the Marines."

Glancing back at Markeson, she smiled her practiced smile and brushed a stray lock of fiery red hair back into place. "But then you know that already. A Major Kilgore is the officer commanding the Marine detachment. This puts him in control of the SPs and all of their law enforcement responsibilities."

"We can agree that's been stipulated to."

"The Major has done something unexpected."

"He sent for my Inspector Sullivan."

"Yes, most unmilitary of him. Why do you think he did that?"

"Sullivan, who for the record I don't like personally, is one of the best investigators I've ever known. I respect him professionally. He's also ex-military. Served in the Space Marines, an SP himself to be exact. I don't recall the exact specifics of his service record, but it's possible Sullivan served with Kilgore at some point in their careers in the Corps."

"That, my dear detective, would explain why he picked Sullivan. It does not explain why he went outside his own Shore Patrol unit to investigate the homicide."

Annoyed someone as capable as the "Colonel" had summoned him to answer a question with such an obvious answer, Markeson was unable to hide his irritation.

"Really? That's what you summoned me for?"

"Yes, a bit childish of me, isn't it Detective. Apparently, Major Kilgore doesn't trust his own investigative unit, or he suspects the murder is related to something going on at the base's ultra-secret research facility."

Shifting her weight in the overstuffed chair, the woman uncrossed her legs and recrossed them. Surprised Markeson's eyes had not followed her movement; she made a note to herself to wear a skirt the next time she met with the detective.

"It's the goings on in the facility that you're interested in," Markeson observed dryly. "You want to know what you're up against in Sullivan. You also want to get an idea of the price it will take for me to sell him out to you if it comes to that."

"My, you must be in a hurry to return to Capital City. Who is she?"

"Speaking of that, why did you have some one break in-to my apartment? Leave me a message I might not have found warning me to be careful of who I trusted?"

All signs of feminine charm and seductive airs vanished at his words, replaced by a coldness that chilled the cynical Markeson.

"It would seem my competitors are involved. Well then. I'll get to the point. I have an idea of what goes on in that facility, an excellent idea. What I don't have a good handle on is who is funding the research and production. I know when but not where the shipments are going. Most importantly, I don't know who is receiving the ship-ments."

Sensing an opportunity for a tidy consulting fee, Markeson leaned forward in a conspiratorial manner. "What, my pretty lady, just what might that merchandise be?"

◆◆◆

Chief O'Brian leaned back in his creaky chair and for the umpteenth time, that day reminded himself to order a new chair. One like Markeson's. He looked down at the comm on his desk.

Sullivan had checked in, giving him a quick summary of the case in Brownstown. Of course, Sullivan had left out as many details as he could. Apparently, his best Inspector wanted the Captain of Detectives to know as little as possible about the case. He decided he could live with that for now.

Grinning, the Chief picked up his comm and typed in the number for the best office furniture outlet in Capital City.

◆◆◆

Barely half an hour into the autopsy, Bones stopped his recording device. Removing his latex gloves, he made his way back to his office and fished around in the bottom drawer of his desk. After nearly a minute of looking, he found what he wanted, an older model, portable recorder for fieldwork. A quick check showed the battery still held a good charge.

He returned to the autopsy room and donned a new pair of blue gloves. Sitting the tiny recorder down on the autopsy table near the victim's head, the Head Coroner of Beta Prime shook his head before pressing the record symbol.

"Sullivan, what have you gotten us into this time,

bringing me a clone to autopsy?"

Thinking back to his stint in the Navy as a flight surgeon during the Expansion Wars, he shuddered at the memories of the slaughter he'd witnessed. Particularly toward the end when the Confeds had grown desperate and started using poorly engineered clones as cannon fodder.

It had been pointless. The clones were of such poor design many could not function even as basic foot soldiers, getting in the way of the few well trained Confeds remaining, leading to the deaths of many of them. Other clones had grown psychotic, turning on their masters in a blood thirsty, blind rage.

The outcome of the pointless exercise, a desperate last gasp of a losing government in a bloody war it had no hope of winning, had been for the practice of human cloning to be banned throughout the human occupied universe. The Confeds themselves had proposed the ban and enacted the harshest punishments for anyone caught breaking the ban.

Pressing the record symbol, Bones began his observations. "The deceased is a human male clone. The height and weight recorded in the official report. My best guess is the deceased is at most, three weeks old. Fully grown and developed. I have no means to determine the mental state of the deceased prior to death."

Ten minutes passed as Bones continued his inspection. He paused only to stop recording with his portable device and to restart the official autopsy recording. Picking up a scalpel, he hesitated before making the Y-incision to begin the examination of the victim's internal organs.

◆ ◆ ◆

Exhausted, I marshaled the last of my energy as I dried my hands. Alice and Joe both were sitting with Sarah in my regular booth. It was time to have a talk with Sarah and get to the bottom of a few things.

Stepping into the restaurant, I immediately looked at my booth and relaxed. Alice was sitting next to an anxious Sarah while Joe waxed poetic about something or another, pointing at one of his many posters of classical bands proudly displayed as part of the décor of his restaurant. Following the direction of Joe's emphatic pointing, I couldn't help but smile. Like Joe, I have a weakness for the band once billed as *The World's Greatest Rock 'N' Roll Band*, back when humans only occupied the planet Earth. The print was a reproduction of artwork for their classic work *Exile on Main Street*.

"Carrying on again about your fascination with *The Rolling Stones*?"

Joe grinned, knowing I was a fan of the classic group of musicians.

"Fascination," Alice laughed. "More like obsession." Standing, she stood up and touched Sarah on the shoulder, smiling at the anxious girl.

"Whatever," Joe complained, standing on cue to leave me alone with Sarah, the job of keeping her from fleeing over.

I sat down across from the moody child-woman. She glanced at me and then back at the plate that held her barely touched sandwich.

"Sarah, we need to clear the air."

She looked up at me and nodded in agreement.

"Not here though. Somewhere my secrets can't be heard by anyone."

Usually, her insistence on being secretive would have rankled me a bit. Not now. Not with a dead clone lying on the slab in the morgue and someone sneaking around the military base. My former commanding officer, with whom I'd parted on bad terms, had requested my presence on the case.

Sarah was right.

"I have devices that can sweep for bugs in my apartment and create background white noise for any listening devices across the street. You know as well I do the place is secure, as secure as it can be made."

She thought about it for a moment. "Okay. But if I need to go, you'll let me?"

"When we're done. When I'm satisfied the air has been cleared."

After a moment of silence spent looking out the window, she looked back at me. "Okay. But I want the door to the balcony open. Just in case."

I answered by standing up and tossing a couple of hard credits for Alice on the table. Joe ran a tab for me, so Sarah and I left.

We had a few things to talk about.

CHAPTER TEN

Sitting and watching the train could only hold Josephson's attention for so long. Once the mixed train had left the Brownstown area and the few indigenous trees that grew in the area, the scenery was a bland, dull white with a few rolling hills. It was a beautiful day without a cloud in the sky, a rarity for the planet.

Rather than don his glasses to avoid snow blindness from the bright light reflected off the white landscape, Josephson decided to busy himself going through the notes he frequently took in his attempts to learn as much about the detecting business as he could from his boss Sullivan.

One of Sullivan's mantras and that of several of the older detectives kept playing itself over and over in the young detective's mind. With near maddening clarity, Sullivan's voice kept repeating the detective's proverb over and over; *I don't believe in coincidences.*

Remembering seeing his supervisor, Captain Markeson in the airport in Brownstown, departing in the company of the man he was certain was ex-military, if not currently serving. Josephson realized his subconscious had made a connection. There was no reason for the Chief of Detectives to be in Brownstown, not having just sent his best team, with Sarah in tow no less, to investigate the murder.

It was strange, but so was Sarah's claim the dead SP was a clone. It was also strange the military had requested Sullivan handle the investigation. Josephson decided it was all strange and beyond him to figure out.

He pulled out his comm and began typing in a message. Knowing Sullivan would chide him for the delay in letting him know about Markeson's appearance, Josephson included as much detail as he could from memory about the stranger who'd escorted Captain Markeson out of the terminal.

Josephson hit send and settled back in his seat for a nap. Between the cot and the fact Sarah had scared him half to death with her odd behavior, he'd not slept well. With any luck, the train would be late, and Sullivan would have calmed down about his delay in messaging about Markeson's puzzling appearance in Brownstown.

◆◆◆

Walking through streets the average person would not venture down out of fear of being mugged was nothing new for Father Nathan. A big man and still fit despite the streaks of gray at his temples, the priest's collar did little to send a message of weakness to any would be thieves looking for easy prey. Given his mood at the moment, Father Nathan seemed to convey the opposite vibe, that he, in fact, was the predator seeking prey.

He'd lost three of his charges months ago to the streets. Every day in his morning prayers he begged for God's forgiveness for failing Toby, Lucy, and Anna. For not getting them off the streets before a bigger animal on the food chain found them.

The Father had focused his efforts on the string of pickpockets who worked the working class neighborhoods around his parish church. He'd managed to convince nearly two dozen of them to take advantage of the vacant dormitory space the parish had to get out of the cold at night. Built for just this reason, the vicar before him had done nothing to reach out to the needy, and those who lived on the streets and the dorm space had gone unused.

In fact, the vicar before Father Nathan had not done much of anything in advancing the Kingdom of God in the

Southeast Quadrant of Capital City. As a result, the Archbishop for that region of the galaxy had seen fit to install the priest no other diocese wanted as the vicar. It seemed to be a good solution to the problem of what to do with Father Nathan.

God may forgive a man's sins and forget his past; people had a much harder time living out the concept of grace. If Father Nathan failed, at least it would be in a parish that had no congregation to speak of.

He'd known all of that when told of his assignment. Knowing he was expected to fail had made the fledgling priest all the more determined to succeed. He had to succeed. God might have forgiven him, but he hadn't forgiven himself.

Despite providing a haven and a warm breakfast each morning, despite the growing bonds of trust between him and the street urchins, Father Nathan had not been able to discover the identity of "the Boss Man" who seemed to possess some unbreakable hold over the kids. If his kids wouldn't tell him, he would find the man himself.

◆◆◆

I handed Sarah a glass of lukewarm water. She looked at it and then me, her long brown hair hung in front of her face. Sarah looked a bit worse for the wear and her hair, in particular, showed it. Despite living on the streets most of the time, I'd never seen her hair disheveled like it was at the moment.

"You need to drink more water, Sully. You can dehydrate in a cold environment like this just as well as a hot and humid one."

She cut her eyes at me, watching me through her hair as I made my way around my apartment, checking for bugs of any type. I didn't expect to find any, but I also didn't want Sarah flitting out the door to the balcony and disappearing. Finished with my sweep, I put my device away and retrieved a really nifty device I had picked up when I first entered civilian police work.

It generated white noise, a series of signals across just about every frequency imaginable that could be used to eavesdrop, audio or video, in my apartment. I set it up on its tripod near the balcony and made a show of adjusting it before I activated it. Sarah observed every movement I made, her demeanor not changing.

I sat down and looked at the source of my current misery. Her expression wasn't quite a pout, though Sarah did have her lips pressed together causing them to protrude slightly. Furrows were present in her brow, just visible through the long locks of brown hair still obstructing my view of her face.

Sarah had finished her glass of water and set it aside. Still dressed in her warm, black leather trench coat, I had little doubt she would make good on her threat to flee if she didn't like the way our talk went. So much so, she'd gone to the trouble to make a show of placing her backpack, with all of her few possessions, right by the open door to the balcony.

"It's cold in here," I told her.

"So," was her petulant response.

"I'm going to close the door to the balcony."

"I'm leaving then," she said flatly, rising quickly to prove she meant it.

"Not all the way, just enough to stop the wind from forming ice on the walls of my place. Do you mind?"

Sarah thought about it for a moment and then strolled over to the exit, watching me over her shoulder to see what I would do. I let her walk.

With a firm tug, she managed to slide the heavy door over, closing off most of the opening but leaving enough room for her to slip through and easily make good her escape.

Not saying a word, Sarah sat back down, placing her forearms on the table. She shook her head from side-to-side once, moving the hair from in front of her face.

"Do you believe me now?"

"The part about you being a clone?" I watched an expectant look form in her eyes. My answer was important to her. More so than I had realized.

"I'm not sure." It wasn't the answer she wanted to hear, and her sour expression let me know it.

"I am positive you believe you are a clone, and, let me say this, I believe other people think you are a clone. I'm just not sure what to think, okay?"

"I showed you my umbilical scar," she protested.

"Plastic surgery could explain that easily. Just like the plastic surgery, you claim was done to give you a regular belly button."

"I'm leaving. Don't expect me to be back for awhile," Sarah announced spitefully, standing up to leave.

"Sit down," I ordered in my best Space Marine sergeant's voice. The booming sound echoed in the confines of my apartment, startling Sarah. Her mouth open, she sat down quickly, using her right hand to brush the hair behind her ear.

"We're not done," I said harshly. Too harshly, I realized as Sarah suddenly looked like the five-year-old child she, in some ways, really was. I made myself count to ten. Then I counted to ten a second time.

"That was harsh," I said through gritted teeth, struggling to keep my temper in check. "I apologize."

I had to count to ten a third time. Women and I have a long history, and it's not a good one. I've been manipulated too many times and done too many stupid things because of a woman. The waterworks in her eyes were on the verge of starting, and it angered me.

Of all the weapons in the arsenal women possess, crying is the one I can't stand the most. It just leaves a man defenseless.

"I also believe you when you say there a hunter, or hunters, are looking for you. They certainly think you're a clone."

Sarah wiped her eyes dry and made a pass at her runny nose with one of my dishtowels that I'd left on the table.

"I need to know more, Sarah. If that SP was murdered because he really is a clone, or the killer thought he was a clone, I need to know what you know. Tell me why you're so valuable? Why is Ellie so valuable?"

My words gave her pause, making Sarah look down at the table, in the process letting her long hair cover her face from my view again.

"Maria was simple. Not retarded or anything like that, just simple. She was happy. I learned to read and do math, stuff like that. They didn't send us to a real school, didn't try to educate us. Maria wanted to learn, to be able to teach herself book learning, but I couldn't teach her to read. Neither could Ellie."

I thought for a moment about what Sarah had just shared with me. "You taught yourself to read?"

She nodded sadly. "Ellie was smart. Book smart but not street-smart like me. Maria was simple. She was happy so long as they weren't doing stuff to us or yelling at her because she couldn't play the games they wanted."

"What kind of games?"

"Puzzles. Find the fastest way through a maze, putting stuff together, looking at pictures and seeing which ones were different or similar."

"Once they realized Maria was simple, they started doing mean things to her."

"Can you explain," I asked. "Mean things is a pretty broad range of activities."

"They made her do things," Sarah screamed, startling me this time. Tears ran down her cheeks, leaving black streaks through the dirt on her face.

"I got it," I said calmly. "You don't have to explain."

It took Sarah a few minutes to calm herself, and I remained silent to let her do so.

"Ellie and I are different, but we're not simple. We all look exactly the same, but we're different. Ellie is quiet but not like me. She'll talk to people. Maria, she liked people, liked talking to them."

"Just like regular sisters," I said gently.

"I think they want Ellie for organs. To put them in other people who are sick. Me? The military wants me. I heal fast. I can stand heat or cold other people can't. I can go without food for extended periods of time."

Sarah looked at me carefully. I got the feeling she was deciding if she could reveal one of her deep secrets.

"I can hide in a crowd, there one second, gone the next."

I didn't say anything. I was pretty sure Sarah could do just that. It wasn't like it had been easy for me to find her. More like dumb luck intervened.

"Do you believe me," she asked, voice quivering.

"Yeah, I do. I'm pretty sure I've seen you do it." I smiled at Sarah, hoping to reassure her. "I mean if what you say is true, I can't really see you vanish. You just sort of disappear."

She thought about it for a moment and then decided to continue.

"I've told you my senses are much better than the average person."

"Yes, and I believe you." I did. She could hear things nobody else could, of that I was certain.

"I have a sixth sense. I can tell things. Like when a hunter is on my trail."

I nodded in agreement. I'd seen her fear first hand, and Sarah'd been justified to feel that way in the past.

Tears ran down her face again, this time Sarah let them. She seemed to be less burdened somehow as if telling me just one or two of her secrets had lifted a weight from her. Or maybe it was because I believed some of what she had told me, even if I couldn't bring myself yet to believe she was actually a clone.

"It's not fair," she said to me. "I'm a woman. I can have babies. I like being around people I can trust." She paused to give me the evil eye for a moment. "People like Ellie, maybe Miss Alice and Ralph."

After a few seconds, Sarah continued. "I like men. I've never had a real family, but I know what one is. I like being able to do what I want, but I'd like to not be in fear all the time. Not have to be ready to run at a second's notice."

"Nobody should have to live like that," I said softly.

"Ellie shouldn't have to be cut up for organs. They belong to her! Not some sick person with money or power. I shouldn't be a test subject for some military experiment. Did you know the ban on clones says if any clones ARE created, we're property! We have no rights as individuals!"

Angry now, she stood and began to pace. "I can't be a citizen. I'm just an object. Stupid military. I might volunteer if I could be a person with rights. A citizen. I should be able to make my own choices. I don't belong to anyone but myself!"

My heart went out to my mystery girl. It was no wonder she didn't trust anyone.

"I have to find Ellie," she stated calmly. When she turned and grabbed her backpack, I wasn't surprised. I got up and shut the sliding door behind her. She'd be back when she was ready.

CHAPTER ELEVEN

There was no doubt the chef could cook. Markeson made a note of it. If he ever had to return to Brownstown in the future, this was where he'd eat, but only, if he had to make another trip.

His hostess still had not answered his questions. She liked to play games far too much for the detective, bent as he was. Still, she was easy on the eyes, and Markeson enjoyed a redhead as much as he did a blonde or a brunette.

"Colonel, I have to be getting back. I'll trouble you to have my consulting fee deposited into my account. I'm sure you have the details."

He stood to go and looked about for the hard looking man who'd brought him.

"You are just no fun," the redhead complained. "Very well, business it is. Please, sit back down."

Despite his better judgment, the lure of easy money was too much. Markeson sat down.

"I cannot tell you at this moment the what. I can tell you I'm going to come into possession of some very valuable property."

Markeson looked at the woman with renewed interest. She was leaning forward, her chin resting on one hand as she smiled at Markeson. A smile only a woman bent on sinning with a man could smile. He ignored it.

"You need a way to move this property off planet."

"See, wasn't that easy," the redhead laughed, clapping her hands once in merriment.

"No, it isn't that easy. If it was, you wouldn't need me. I take it you would like to not have any issues with customs, on this planet or the next."

"That goes without saying."

"You'd like to avoid problems en route. No questions asked by those hired to make the delivery for you."

"Again, that goes without saying."

"It won't be cheap. The bigger the package that needs delivering, the more it will cost."

"I would assume that would be the case."

"How big is the package?"

"Does it matter right now?"

"Of course it matters," Markeson sighed, growing weary of the game playing. "Any particular conditions, does the package need to be kept at a specific temperature, does it need oxygen, food, water, anything like that?"

Reaching into her jacket, the Colonel pulled out a small information chip and slid it across the table. Markeson reached for it. The woman slipped her hand over his and grasped it firmly.

"All the specs you require are there."

Frowning, he withdrew his hand, taking the chip with it.

"I'll be in touch with an estimate."

"Oh, about that," again the woman reached into her jacket, this time withdrawing a comm. "Encrypted. It can only call my comm."

Markeson pocketed the device.

"If there's nothing else, I'll be leaving now."

"Actually, there are two things. First, this Inspector Sullivan, he makes me nervous. Take him off the case."

Markeson laughed, irritating his hostess. "That's the last thing you want. If I pulled him off the case, it'd make him so suspicious he'd take leave to devote all of his time and attention to it. Trust me; it's best to let him do his job and eliminate evidence that could be problematic before he gets wind of it."

The redhead pushed her luscious lips together in a pout, making it obvious the advice was not what she wanted to hear.

"What was the last thing you wanted," Markeson asked, standing up and adjusting his clothes, brushing off an imaginary speck from his suit coat before running his hands through his perfectly groomed hair.

"Captain, you are always in such a hurry," the Colonel complained. Standing up, she moved closer to the bent detective and draped her arms around his shoulders. "We could go to my quarters. You have plenty of time before your flight."

Markeson smiled his most charming smile as he gently removed both of the offending hands from his shoulders.

"Mixing business and pleasure is never a wise idea. I'll be in touch."

Before he could turn to leave, the Colonel stroked his cheek with the back of her fingers of left hand.

"Your loss." She smiled her wicked smile again, just to let the idea take hold in his imagination. "But there's always the future."

Markeson didn't say a word. Didn't flinch. Didn't smile. He just turned and left, slipping the chip into his pocket as he made good his escape by heading for the entrance.

Moving from the shadows nearby, the tall, hard man moved silently next to his employer and waited.

"He is a very cool customer," the Colonel said dryly. "I believe we have selected well."

"Indeed," the hard man agreed. "It takes a strong man to resist the lady's charms."

◆ ◆ ◆

I walked to Joe's. It was early evening, and I needed to eat. Not wanted to eat, but rather needed to. Sarah wasn't going to be back. Not tonight. What worried me was she might not come back at all.

I gave a nod to Giganto and Baldy, the two bouncers who worked the night shift when Joe's family dinner morphed into Joe's Tavern, bar really. The two toughs gave me a respectful nod as they went about their business, in this case checking a trio of tough looking young men for weapons.

After I'd become a regular, I learned nobody had ever gotten the best of Giganto and Baldy until I came along. I had a feeling this trio of toughs wasn't going to join my exclusive club.

Sitting down in my regular booth, I looked outside at the dreary street, watching the workers coming and going during the evening shift change. Sarah was not going to make an appearance, and I knew it.

Alice came by and smiled, knowing I had troubles on my mind. She didn't say much, just asked if I wanted my regular dinner. I nodded, and she left to turn in my order. Joe caught my eye and nodded from behind his bar.

Josephson should have reported in by now. The kid could frustrate me at times. He was reliable for the most part, but occasionally had mental lapses that boggled my mind. Of course, he was traveling by train and Kilgore had told me his ticket was for a mixed train, mostly freight with a couple of passenger coaches coupled on the rear.

I pulled out my comm and looked at it. Dead battery. Alice was returning with my soft drink and noticed the scowl on my face as I shook the stupid comm.

"Dead battery Sully?"

"Yes."

"Here, let me take it and get it charged real quick for you."

Alice didn't wait for an answer.

Before I could complain, Ralph, her cab driver husband, slipped into the seat across from me.

"Rough day I hear."

"You could say that," I mumbled.

Ralph looked around for a moment like he was worried.

"Ralph," I sighed, "Are you in trouble? Does Alice know?"

"No," he moaned, shaking his head before glancing around again.

"Then what is it?"

"It, it's the Father."

"Father Nathan?" I was a bit concerned now. Ralph had done a stretch and didn't scare easily.

"Yeah, you know Alice, and I have been helpin' the Father with the street kids."

I nodded.

"He's not makin' any headway with findin' out who their boss is."

Just what I needed. I'd promised my friend I would handle that little task when I got out of the hospital. By the time my hands had healed, and I'd been released, he'd not brought it up again, and I got busy.

Solving murder cases has a way of distracting me.

Still it was no excuse. I had made a promise to one of my few friends on Beta Prime. The good Father had warned me too. Told me if I didn't take care of it, he would.

"You think he's looking for the Boss Man himself."

"He has to be Inspector. Father Nathan is never around anymore. I mean he's at the church when the kids show up at night. He's there when we get 'em up to feed 'em. But last few days he hasn't come by to eat. Alice is worried, and so is Joe. If something happens to the Father, the kids will just go back to what they were doin'."

I understood what my friend the priest was trying to do. He was fighting an uphill battle with these kids. Most of them, despite his efforts, would probably wind up in prison. Still, I knew the man felt compelled to make an effort.

We'd had more than one disagreement about the subject.

He'd just smile in a way that irritated me to no end and mumble something about redemption, forgiveness and that it was possible to change. Then, just before he'd leave me sitting there simmering, Father Nathan would invite me to services next Sunday, smile and leave.

One thing was certain. Father Nathan was slowly making a difference in his parish. Not that the average person would notice. But those who were really down on their luck noticed and I suppose those are the people that count when it comes to these things.

"You want me to look for Father Nathan?"

Ralph looked around again.

"No. Father Nathan can take care of himself. That's what worries me."

"You've lost me."

"Father Nathan, well, it's not my place to tell you. But if you don't find that Boss Man, something bad is goin' to happen."

I nodded. It made sense. I'd long suspected my friend the good father had a past. Ralph was wise to what the Father was capable of, and I should have been too.

"I'll look into it."

Ralph nodded and looked up as his wife Alice returned, giving him a knowing look as she sat down my food and then fished my comm out of her pocket.

"All charged up, Inspector. Come on, Ralph. Let the Inspector eat his meal."

I picked up my comm and turned it back on. Waiting for me was a message from much earlier. Josephson had spotted Markeson in the terminal after Sarah, and I had departed on our morning flight back to Capital City. A man my partner described as being ex-military had greeted Markeson, and the pair had left together. It could be a coincidence, but he knew what I thought about coincidences.

My fingers moved quickly as I sent the young pup a message.

◆ ◆ ◆

Watching the tall man dressed in black approaching, the shorter of the two muggers grinned and nudged the bigger thug.

"Do you see what I see," he whispered.

"I'm not sure I believe my own eyes," the bigger more muscular thug chuckled. "I'd heard they existed. Even saw a picture of one, but I never thought I would ever see one for real."

"C'mon," the shorter thug said. "Easy pickings."

Strutting toward Father Nathan, the pair crossed the street without looking, making a direct line toward the priest. Noticing the pair, Father Nathan sighed. Two young predators who had not the sense to realize they were in danger.

"What can I do for you," the priest chirped, taking his hands out of his pockets.

"You can give us your money, that fancy cross looking thing you're wearing and anything else you have," the shorter thug growled, doing his best to intimidate the big man dressed in black.

The smile vanished from Father Nathan's face.

"No," he said with a polite firmness.

"I don't think you understood what my partner here told you," the larger thug said, stepping up closer, puffing his chest out. The wind blew, blowing the tails of the two thugs black great coats back.

"I understood him just fine. The problem is, you and your friend didn't understand me."

The two thugs looked at each other in surprise. Long ago in their lives, the word no had ceased to have meaning. A nod from the smaller thug was all it took. The pair lunged at the priest.

Expecting to be attacked, Father Nathan stepped quickly out of the way of the smaller thug, leaving his foot behind, tripping the kid. Stepping inside the haymaker, the bigger thug threw at his head; the priest moved close to deliver a brutal uppercut, slamming the punk's mouth shut and turning his lights out with one blow.

Before the second attacker hit the ground, the priest latched on to the lapels of the smaller man with both hands, lifting him up. Pivoting hard as he stepped back on the sidewalk, Father Nathan slammed the shorter thug into the steel wall of the prefab building.

"Apologize."

Wide-eyed in terror, the thug did the only thing he could do. He apologized.

"Now that we understand each other," the priest said firmly, "I have a few questions, and you're going to answer them."

The little punk stretched his toes in hopes of touching the ground and kicked futilely.

"Stop squirming."

A quick glance at his partner sprawled on the icy ground stopped the squirming.

"You know priests are supposed to be do gooders. I'm trying to help a gang of pickpockets from winding up like you. Do you know the kids I'm talking about."

A quick nod from the punk confirmed he did.

"They have a Boss Man. I need to meet him. Is that clear?"

Again, the punk gave a quick nod.

"You and your friend seem like you could be nice enough young men. In time. Tell the Boss Man the priest would like to talk to him. Can you do that for me?"

"Yeah, I can do it priest man."

Father Nathan sat the terrified thug down and smoothed his greatcoat. "Now, just one more thing."

"Sure, whatever, just say the word."

"Every Sunday at the Church, you know, the building with a really steep roof? I have services at 0800 and 1000. It would be a good thing if I saw you and your friend on a regular basis."

Father Nathan smiled at the bully and made a point of turning his back. As he walked away, he listened to the terrified bully pleading with his friend to wake up. He was certain his message would be delivered. There was even a possibility the two might show up one Sunday.

CHAPTER TWELVE

Praise from Sullivan, though not impossible to receive, was rare enough it always made Josephson feel good when his boss gave it. Sullivan agreed with him. Something was not right about Markeson being in Brownstown.

It wasn't the only thing that wasn't right that day, but it was the one thing the idealistic and inexperienced detective had noticed. Oddly enough, the other thing was something only he would have thought odd. Sullivan would never have.

Bored, Josephson checked his chronometer again. The conductor had been misguided in his assessment of how long the day's run would take. It could have been a result of the switches that were frozen shut, and the ice had to be melted to switch out the empty container cars and exchange them for loaded ones at one industry. The process had to be repeated at another mine where more loaded ore cars were picked up.

Probably it was the long spell spent sitting "in the hole" as the crew had called it. Sitting on a siding waiting for the two passenger trains, one northbound and one southbound, to pass the mixed train as it sat waiting for the mainline to be clear for its use.

Either way, the mixed was running late. Frustrated, but not surprised as he knew a bit about how the railroad operated, Josephson settled back in his seat to try to catch another nap. It was likely to be a long night once he returned to Capital City. Sullivan would want him to report and who knew what the situation was with Sarah or the case.

His nap would have to wait.

A sudden series of loud bangs sounded, followed by the locomotive engineer setting the brakes on the train hard. Hard enough to produce a loud squealing sound as the coach lurched suddenly due to the sharp reduction in speed.

"What was that?" a panicked woman passenger cried, clutching her two small children to her.

"It's okay," Josephson volunteered. "It sounded like a torpedo. It's like a really big firecracker railroaders use when they need to warn a train and get it to make an un-scheduled stop. They put them on the rails, and when the locomotive runs over the torpedoes, you get that loud sound, one right after the other. Then the engineer knows to stop the train."

Relieved the woman leaned back, whispering to her children, soothing their fears. The other passengers were satisfied with Josephson's explanation and set about grumbling about yet another delay.

Curious to know the cause of the delay, and not seeing a crewman, Josephson stood up and pulled his great coat on. It took only a few steps to reach the door at the end of the coach. He opened it and stepped into the vestibule, letting the door close behind him. After fiddling with the latch on the vestibule door, it opened inwards, allowing him to lean out into the frigid air and cast a hard glance at the now long line of loaded and heavy freight cars the two coaches were coupled to.

A blast of air and the hissing sound of its escape combined with the grunt of heavy steel shifting against heavy steel immediately behind the coach drew his attention. Something was not right, and Josephson knew it. There were no sidings here and thus no reason to uncouple any cars.

Jumping out of the coach and landing hard in the snow,

he turned and carefully pulled his phase pistol from its holster. It was then he remembered how odd it was to have the coaches coupled into the train instead of on the very end. The three container flats and their loads attached on the end would complicate any switching of cars during the run.

Mixed trains always put the passenger coaches at the end of the train. That way they could be uncoupled and allowed to safely sit at a distance while all the switching was done. It was then an easy matter to simply back the train up and couple the coaches on again.

As glad as he'd felt about sending the message to Sullivan about Markeson, Josephson felt stupid for not noticing the odd change in operations for mixed trains. Something he actually knew more about than Sullivan possibly could have.

Looking under the wheels of the coach and the adjacent freight car, the young detective noticed three darkish gray greatcoats with black jackboots like Sullivan's protruding. Two long blasts of the locomotives air horn indicated the train was about to start. In seconds it eased forward, leaving the three container flats and their loaded containers behind.

The locomotive must have hit a patch of ice on the rails or possibly a taller than normal snowdrift. After moving only a few meters, it skidded to a stop. Josephson ran through the gap between the last coach and the first freight car, pistol ready.

Working quickly to open the seal on the first container, the three men failed to notice Josephson. Without stopping to think, he shouted loud enough for the men to hear him.

"Freeze! It's the law! Stop what you're doing and lay down on your stomachs with your hands behind your heads!"

For his efforts, two kinetic projectiles whizzed past his

ears, heating the air in the process hot enough for him to feel it for a mere microsecond. A hot blast of plasma at his feet kicked up dirt, rocks, and ice.

Josephson fired three times, hitting one of the men in gray dead center in the chest. Not waiting for another round of kinetic projectiles to be fired in his direction, Josephson jumped back through the gap, grabbed the handrail on the coach and pulled himself up on the steps just as two long blasts of the horn sounded again and the train bucked forward, this time staying in motion.

Slamming the vestibule door shut, Josephson peered through the small window in the door at the end of the coach. He pulled his comm out and used the device's tiny camera to record the two men rolling the dead body out of the way and returning to their efforts to open the first container.

As the train picked up speed, it kicked up a fine powdery mist of snow and ice, obscuring the view of the stolen freight cars.

As he dropped his comm back into a side pocket, the interior door behind him opened. Josephson turned around to see a red faced, angry conductor glaring at him.

"Just what do you think you're doing," the man shouted indignantly.

Josephson started to shake. It was the shaking that drew the angry conductor's eyes down to the right hand that still held the phase pistol. A faint wisp of black smoke curled up from the recently discharged weapon. Reaching into his greatcoat, he pulled out the leather case that contained his detective's shield and flipped it open.

"I'm the law. Sergeant Detective Josephson. Conductor, would you mind telling me why three men back there shot at me?"

◆ ◆ ◆

My ceiling had not changed. Not one bit since my last sleepless night. I got up and went to the kitchen and looked at what was available for a snack at this time of the night. Or was it morning? I left the sandwich I made on the counter and sat down at my table to think.

I thought about the mess things were in. I hadn't been able to save Maria, but I had saved Sarah, for the moment at least. Hiring Sarah as an assistant, a massive ethics violation at work, hadn't kept her safer, I'd taken her directly to the source of danger it seemed. My old CO appears to have gotten past our issues. I hadn't. The pup, who'd just gotten medical clearance, had almost gotten himself killed in a shootout on the train back home. A train I should have been on or at least I should have made Josephson face up to his fear of flying.

Then Ralph tells me Father Nathan was prowling the streets looking for trouble. I had a feeling my friend would find it. That collar didn't fool me. Nathan had a past. Just like I had a past. Like Ralph had a past. And most assuredly, like Joe had a past. I just didn't know what that past was yet.

The thing keeping me awake was it was all my fault. I was supposed to keep my friends safe, all of them. Instead, I'd had a hand in placing all of them in danger. Well, not Kilgore. It just bothered me he could look past our beef with each other to get the job done professionally, and I was having trouble with the idea.

Sarah didn't just worry me anymore. She scared me. I was certain the way she had lifted my knife and handled it anyone who messed with her was likely to get sliced up. That scared me too. I wasn't scared of her hurting me. She couldn't. The most she could do was add a couple more scars to my collection.

It scared me how she upset me. I hate it when a woman cries. It's a weapon they use. In the past when that weapon came out of the arsenal it was the end. I cut 'em loose.

Now I was worried sick about Sarah. I was worried I wouldn't see her again.

This clone business, I'd lied to her.

Sarah was a clone. I knew it. She knew it. The people hunting her knew it.

And I didn't know what to do about it.

◆◆◆

Sitting atop the building by the church made Sarah feel better. It was one of her favorite places. She'd disabled all the CCTV cameras with possible coverage of her spot, allowing her to feel a sense of privacy.

Nobody knew about her spot, and she liked it that way. Not even Sully knew about it, and that pleased her too.

The spot was good because it also let Sarah watch her part of town. From her vantage point, she could see Joe's where her new friends worked and usually ate their meals. If she leaned out over the ledge a little bit and looked around the wall where the building went up another level, Father Nathan's church and its buildings were visible.

Leaning back against the wall by the building's ledge, Sarah could see the balcony of Sully's place. It was her third place and the one that confused Sarah the most. Joe's was warm, and so long as she was careful, nobody noticed her presence. Sully paid for the meals she ate there which made her feel better. Stealing made her feel bad, and Miss Alice was kind to her. Plus, Joe looked out for the neighborhood, though he'd never admit it. The dorm at the church was nice too. On the nights it was too cold even for her, it was a place she could sleep with no questions asked. Father Nathan looked out for people, not that she needed him to look out for her.

Sully's place was the best, but it scared Sarah to go there. He kept food just for her. There was a big, cushy pillow on the couch and Sully kept two thick survival blankets folded and draped across the back of the sofa. Sarah liked having her own key so she could come and go.

That was the best.

Why did the dead man have to be a clone?

Sarah picked up a handful of snow and compacted it into a hard ball of ice. Without aiming at anything specific, she threw the ball of ice in frustration as hard as she could.

Seeing the dead clone reminded Sarah the world she was making for herself wasn't as safe as she'd let herself believe.

It was Sully's fault Sarah decided. The big man had not been able to save Maria. She was simple and trusted everyone. Even the men who hurt her. It was better for Maria this way. Sarah had decided that long ago.

Sully had saved Sarah though. Saved her from a monster she might not have been able to escape. Made her feel safe for a while. Given her a job so she didn't have to steal what she needed to survive.

Pulling up the thick, lined collars of the warm greatcoat Sully had given her as a "signing bonus" the first day she'd gone to work for him, Sarah decided her current situation was Sully's fault.

His and the hunters who had come for her.

◆◆◆

They always came after the violence. It never failed. Father Nathan looked at his hands as they shook. There was nothing he could do to stop the tremors. They would pass as the adrenaline cleared out of his system. He looked up from the pew where he knelt and fixed his gaze on the cross behind the altar.

Lowering his head, Father Nathan closed his eyes. He felt the tremors stop. Without speaking aloud, he cleared his mind and began the comforting words of prayer, *Our*

Last Train To Nowhere
Father, Who art in heaven...

CHAPTER THIRTEEN

"What do you mean," the tall redhead's icy response demanded. "He's dead? Just how did that happen?"

She listened to the explanation with a stony silence. "I see. Are you certain?"

More details came through the secure comm.

"Well, if he says so."

The voice on the other end of the link continued.

"Yes, take care of it. Make it look like a work accident."

More talk by the voice on the other end of the link.

"So long as the product is undamaged. Do what you must."

Cutting the link, she turned to face the tall, well-groomed man sitting down in the chair on the opposite side of her desk. She paced for several minutes, red coloring her face as the anger inside boiled.

The man sat patiently. When she reached a decision, he would be ready to carry out her instructions, whatever they might be.

"We have secured the product."

"Yes, Colonel."

"There have been complications."

"It would seem so from what I heard of the conversation."

"I need to talk to Markeson. That man is beyond difficult."

The tall man sat in silence for a moment. "Pay him more. He has expensive tastes."

"Fly to Capital City. Arrange a meeting there. Some place nice, with class."

"Yes, Colonel."

"Reserve a suite for me at the Mayaran Resort. Make sure you have a room nearby. I want our people in place at my lodgings and the meet."

The tall man nodded. "The accident you mentioned..."

"Yes?"

"Would you prefer I handle it?"

She thought for a moment. "No. It is a simple enough task. Let's see if they can do the job properly. I need you for more important tasks."

He stood, nodded, and took his leave.

◆ ◆ ◆

I looked up from my tablet at the sound of footsteps entering the detective's bullpen. The lack of privacy to think and work was something that was going to have to change and soon. I made a mental note to myself to complain to Chief O'Brian about the issue again.

The footsteps turned out to be none other than my missing pup, Josephson. He sat down, looking as tired as I felt, but not too much worse for the wear.

"Tell me about it," I ordered.

He started at the beginning, in the terminal. Josephson did the best job he could describing our mysterious possible ex-military man. He finished with the trip back after the hi-jacking of three freight cars.

"Describe the three cars one more time," I instructed.

I listened carefully. Josephson's description was a good one. I was going to have to link up with Kilgore as soon as possible. The three cars the train robbers took had to be the same three we'd seen being moved on the spur to the military base.

"Did I screw up by coming back here first?"

"No, the containers are gone and so is the guy you

shot."

Josephson nodded and sat looking down at the floor.

"It was you or them. What's more, you warned them."

The pup nodded.

"One more thing."

Josephson looked up like the puppy he was, expecting another smack on his nose for being a bad dog.

"You did the right thing. But you have got to quit carrying that phase pistol."

"Sir," he replied, confused, thinking I wanted to disarm him.

"We're getting you a proper sidearm. Let's go. You're going to fly for the first time."

I grinned as I walked past him. Anything I might have said to Josephson that he thought was some kind of chastisement was forgotten. He'd thank me later.

He had to get over his fear of flying sooner or later.

◆ ◆ ◆

He knew them by sight and their pitiful reputation as wannabe thugs, but not by name. It was evident to anyone who paid the slightest attention the pair had been traumatized, particularly the shorter of the two.

"A priest did this to you?"

"Yeah, see, the guy isn't what he looks like," the taller thug said. "Nobody has ever knocked me out before. I never saw what hit me."

"Yeah, yeah," the shorter thug said hurriedly. "This guy is a bad dude. He's working some kind of angle or somethin' you know. We're just deliverin' the message, that's all."

"I see," the man replied. "Why would you do that?"

"Because," the small thug answered nervously, "we talked it over. We figured you might take it into consideration. Better you know this guy is lookin' for you than for him to get the drop on you. I mean if we'd known he could handle himself, we woulda done things differently."

Unwilling to agree with the pair's logic, the Boss Man sat in silence, observing the pair. At best, they were low-level muscle. Still, it would pay to have some low level, inexpensive employees for the jobs that would require stints in jail. If he expected to expand his fledgling business empire, he would need some expendable, but loyal employees.

"I appreciate your coming to see me."

The thugs glanced at each other, struggling to hide their hopefulness of future employment.

"You took a chance coming here. That shows a bit of moxie, initiative. I'll keep that in mind. I might need your services in the future."

Grinning, the thugs could no longer contain their excitement.

"But let's get a couple of things straight right now. Cross me, and your frozen, mangled bodies will eventually be found in a waste disposal facility. Lie to me, and I'll kill you myself. Steal from me, or cheat me," the man paused for effect, "and it will be a slow, lingering death. Understand?"

Grins gone, the thugs nodded in unison.

"Now go. When I need you, I'll let you know. Don't let the door hit you on the way out."

Leaning forward in his chair, the man reached out and turned on the light on his desk, illuminating his bearded, scarred face. He rubbed his temples with the fingers of both hands, mussing his well-groomed hair.

"Getting a headache boss man," the henchman sitting in the corner respectfully asked. "Want me to get you something?"

"Yeah," the boss answered. "Go find out what you can about this troublesome priest."

◆◆◆

The single malt, from Earth no less, burned as it went down. Markeson stared at the painting on the wall of his apartment. Freshly showered, shaved and dressed for an evening out, he'd packed a bag. He wouldn't be staying at home until his locks and security system got the upgrade he'd just purchased.

So much for the two thousand credits.

His mind flittered back and forth between the alluring redhead and the obvious dangers to himself and his various business ventures if he threw his lot in with the Colonel. Dangerous in more ways than one.

But, Markeson smiled, what was life without a little excitement. The Colonel represented a challenge, and a challenge might be fun.

Sullivan though would be a problem. A frown replaced Markeson's smile. No woman was worth losing what he had worked so hard to accumulate in his life. Markeson had meant it when he'd told the Colonel he respected Sullivan as a detective. Personal animosity aside, if he needed a crime solved, especially murder, Sullivan was the Inspector he'd want on the case.

Setting the tumbler down, Markeson wondered if the redhead understood him when he said not to tangle with Sullivan. It had been close when Sullivan reversed the trap set for him and turned it around.

The cost had been high, maybe too high. His smuggling connection, Spencer Deveraux had been caught in Sullivan's trap. Deveraux's silence had been guaranteed that night when he received help hanging himself in his holding cell. It had been necessary to sacrifice Sergeant Bland, a useful man in many ways. Markeson felt remorse about Bland's death, but it couldn't be helped. He handled it himself to make sure Bland died instantly and didn't suffer. It was the least he could do for his former friend and business associate.

Sullivan had killed the Cowboy himself, solving the biggest problem of all. Long, the fool, had cracked. It would take a year to two to find and corrupt another official with the skill of Long and access to government funds.

Standing to leave for the evening, Markeson decided to maintain his timetable, he had to consider the Colonel's venture. It would be fun he told himself. It had been awhile since he'd done any actual detective work and the challenge of putting the sultry redhead under thumb would be fun, making it even sweeter when he took her into his bed and then kicked her to the curb once their partnership no longer served his goals.

Shutting the door behind him, Markeson secured it and walked to his prized Hovertron. He had some time to kill before dinner. Might as well check out a few things about Deveraux's old smuggling ring.

Within minutes he was comfortably cruising at 200 kph on the hoverway in his luxury Hovertron. His comm buzzed. A quick glance told him he didn't recognize the number, but he had a good idea who it was. Completing the link, he listened to the voice on the other end.

"I've been expecting your call."

CHAPTER FOURTEEN

I woke up with a pounding headache. It didn't happen often these days, especially since I gave up the booze two years ago. A drummer was beating a blistering rhythm on my temples. After about two minutes I gave up, fell out of bed and stumbled into my kitchen. A glass of water and two painkillers later, my drummer began to lose some of his intensity.

I read the label on the bottle of painkillers. It promised to eliminate any and all headaches in five minutes or less.

The miracles of modern medicine.

The thought of modern medicine made me open the refrigerator. Nothing was gone. I wasn't surprised, but still, I'd hoped Sarah had visited during the night, if for no other reason to warm up for a few minutes.

Fifteen minutes and a lot of hot water later, I felt almost human. I skipped shaving, used my ultrasonic brush to clean my teeth and gums and got dressed. After a quick glance around to make sure I didn't forget anything, I headed out for work for the day, securing my place when I left.

Passing through the lobby, I waved at Molly, the grumpy landlord who managed the building. I'd been wearing her down, waving and smiling at her each time I saw the old grump. Not because I'm a warm, friendly kind of guy. I figured she was grumpy and ill-tempered because she was lonely. Besides, in my kind of work, it pays for the landlord to keep an eye out for me.

Nearly thirty minutes later I arrived at Joe's. Sometimes a walk in the cold air would help clear my head, let me think better. No such luck this morning.

I sat down in my booth and nodded at Joe who was manning the checkout, taking payment from a customer. Alice came out of the kitchen a minute or so later, carrying two plates of food, wisps of white steam rising from the food before vanishing. She sat my food down and disappeared just as quickly as she had appeared.

Still not fully alert, I just stared at my food, scrambled eggs, bacon, fried something or other, a substitute for potatoes grown on Beta Prime, and a plate of pancakes. As I sat and stared, a coke, syrup and butter substitute appeared. Two more plates with the same fare also arrived.

I looked up to see the good Father. He prayed over our meal, not asking my permission as was his custom, and picked up the fork Alice had left with his food.

"One of these days I'm going to object Father."

"And on that day I will ask for your forgiveness. Until then, you are going to just have to tolerate my praying for God's blessing of our meals, our friendship, and your safety. Which, by the way, includes young Detective Josephson and the lovely Sarah."

We ate in silence, which was typical of both of us in the morning. I'm not a morning person, and the good Father tends to be reflective early in the day. I guess he does a lot of praying he would just as soon not have me take notice of.

I finished my pancakes and decided I didn't need to eat the native food portion of my breakfast. Father Nathan was chewing a mouthful and looking out the window, watching the people walk past. I couldn't help but notice the scrapes on the knuckles of his right hand. Mindful of my conversation with Ralph, I decided not to let it pass.

"Hit someone?"

"As a matter of fact, I did," he said sternly, his gaze snapping around to meet mine with an intensity I had not seen before from my religious friend.

"I take it he looks worse than you do?"

"They look worse. Two muggers thought I was an easy mark. They found out otherwise."

His attitude worried me a little bit.

"That's not like you Father. You tend to be more of a diplomat in these situations."

He frowned at me before looking back out the window. After a minute or so he took his right index finger and stuck it down inside his collar and ran it back and forth a few times, stretching the stiff collar as far as it would go. He looked back at me, still frowning.

"You're busy with a homicide. I understand. But I'm not making headway with my kids. This Boss Man of theirs has a psychological hold over them I can't break. So I'm going to find the creep and break him."

He was angry, and I couldn't blame him. My job was to find guys like this and toss them in prison. His job was to take the place of this creep and steer the kids in the right direction. He couldn't do his job till I did mine.

"Look, Father, the case I'm on is not just a homicide. It involves the military and some sensitive stuff. It's got Sarah spooked, and the pup almost got shot again yesterday. There's going to be more bodies, soon, if I don't figure this thing out. When it's done, you can come with me, and we'll find this guy together."

"Sully, I said I understood. You're trying to catch a murderer. I'm trying to help my street kids..."

I interrupted him by holding my hand up. "Look, Father, you're the most sincere religious person I've met in my life. You actually do the things your religion says God expects people to do. But something tells me you weren't always this way. Don't do something stupid. You do that, then who will the kids have?"

His face turned red at my words, and he did the thing with his collar again.

39

"My past is not the point! The future of those kids is!"

"Father," I said, trying to stay calm, "I agree with you. They don't need you in jail because you did something stupid and I don't want to identify your dead body," I snarled back.

"Then help me find this piece of garbage!"

Arguing with Father Nathan wasn't going to change anything in his state of mind. He was going to look for this "Boss Man" until the guy was behind bars or dead. I didn't want him to wind up in jail, or worse yet, dead. Nobody in our part of town looked out for those kids or the homeless for that matter. Father Nathan did a lot of good and didn't get much help outside of Ralph and Alice. Sometimes Joe. His parish dorm the street kids stayed in was Sarah's other refuge from the cold.

I looked at the fury in his eyes. The good Father had a past, and it tormented him. That much I was certain of. He talked about being forgiven and receiving grace from God all the time. He also liked to point out faith without works was empty.

I wasn't entirely sure what he meant, but I knew he believed it.

His faith was the driving motivation for everything he did. That, and I'm pretty sure, a need to feel like he's earned his redemption somehow, even though the good Father says it doesn't work that way.

He'd been there for me, just like he was there for those kids.

"Father, I can ask around at the precinct. Somebody will have something on this guy. I'll even talk to Chief O'Brian and see what can be done."

"I would hope the Chief would take action," he spat out bitterly. "This quadrant of town, our neighborhood, in particular, doesn't get enough police protection. Eliminate this scum, and I can stop a lot of the petty crime. Tell him that. It would be a sound investment of limited police resources," his words carrying a strong whiff of angry defiance.

"Just promise me, you won't go looking for this guy by yourself. Not until I've had a chance to check some things out and see what I can do on my end."

He glared back out the window and then closed his eyes. After a minute or so the angry red tone in his cheeks began to fade. I figured he was praying again. Fine by me if it calmed my friend down.

"I won't go looking for him. But if he comes looking for me, I'm not going to run away."

It was the best I was going to get out of him.

"Fair enough."

We both sensed a presence standing next to our booth. I looked up to find Josephson standing there, a grim expression on his countenance.

"There's been another death. An accident at the main rail terminal at the spaceport."

"We're on this SP case. Tell the Chief or Markeson to assign someone else."

"Sully," he said with more confidence than I thought he had in him, "this is connected. I'm sure of it. The dead guy was the conductor on my train back to Capital City."

I looked at Father Nathan. He just nodded, telling me he had heard me. I was proud of the pup, but I wasn't going to let him know that just yet.

This wasn't a coincidence.

◆ ◆ ◆

He scattered the old data disks of files around in the drawer, tossed in a pair of old tablets with dead batteries and shut the drawer of the filing cabinet and locked it. Bones turned the light off to the storage room and secured the door, changing the code to unlock it.

It took him just minutes to file the false autopsy report for John Brown, the dead SP. He sent a copy to Major Kilgore and Inspector Sullivan. When he'd finished, he opened the bottom left drawer of his desk and pulled out an unopened bottle of Baltarian wine.

Bones didn't plan on getting drunk. He just needed a good pull to calm his nerves, maybe two or three good swigs from the bottle.

Then he was going home and locking himself in his apartment to do something he hadn't done since his days in the military. He was going to sleep in his chair with his phase pistol.

Sullivan knew where he lived. Bones knew Sullivan wouldn't believe a word in the autopsy report. Bones just hoped he lived long enough to tell Sullivan what he'd found.

◆ ◆ ◆

Nothing Chief O'Brian did rarely bothered Markeson. To his surprise, the Chief's new desk chair, identical to his own, bothered him. O'Brian might be his boss, but Markeson believed himself to be the better cop, never mind he was bent, and O'Brian was mostly honest. His chair was a symbol to Markeson that he was better than O'Brian. It was a way to flaunt his superior status without the Chief being aware of it. Now the symbol of status no longer held its meaning for Markeson.

And he didn't like it one bit.

His mind turned back to the morning. Waking up in a strange hotel room was not an unusual occurrence for Markeson. Waking up to a stunning beauty like the redheaded Colonel, well, even for him that was a bit strange. He smiled at the thought. O'Brian was married and not prone to letting his eyes wander.

The Colonel excited him in ways he hadn't felt in a long time. She was dangerous, and they both knew it. The instant he was no longer of any use to her, his life would be in jeopardy.

His plan was fairly simple in principle, even if the details had not been worked out. Markeson would betray the Colonel the first chance he got, just as soon as she'd paid him enough money and he'd learned enough about her operation. He smiled as leaned back in his chair and put his feet up on his desk.

He would kill her himself. It would be worth the risk just to see the look on her face before she died.

◆◆◆

Shivering from the cold, Sarah slipped into the mudroom of the parish dormitory. There was never any mud on Beta Prime, which made her wonder why the room bore the name. Carefully she stomped all the snow and ice off her boots. After removing her knives and hiding them in her boots and clothes, Sarah hung up her greatcoat. She stood still, running her petite fingers over the material of the right sleeve.

It was the warmest item of clothing she'd ever had. Her search for Ellie, combined with the need to flee the hunters, had forced Sarah to travel from one world after another. Beta Prime was the first "ice planet" she'd lived on. It was not the first planet in her travels to have extreme cold.

Sarah loved the coat. Not just because it was stylish and warm, though she did like the figure she cut in it when she looked at her reflection in shop windows. It was the only material thing of any value ever given to her. It was hers.

Confusion mixed with a touch of fear passed through her mind, causing Sarah to drop the sleeve and step back.

The idea she liked the great coat because Sullivan had given it to her was upsetting.

Sully had told her it was an advance on her pay when he hired her. Now she wasn't so sure what to think. Sarah didn't know if she liked the idea or not.

It had been over twenty-four hours since her last meal. Father Nathan let her eat whatever she could find in the parish kitchen so long as she cleaned up. Sarah decided she would eat, clean up and sleep in her hiding spot in the dormitory. Sully could do without her for the next twenty-four hours.

Just to let him know she was mad at him, mad about the dead clone, the coat, everything. Then she would wait for him at Joe's. Alice would let her have something hot to drink, and if she were hungry she'd eat something with Sully and Father Nathan.

It would be okay to go back to work then. Sully would know she had been mad at him. The next time she told him one of her horrible secrets, he would believe her.

If she told him another one.

CHAPTER FIFTEEN

I checked my comm as I sat down for lunch at some classless dive near the precinct. No character to the place, not like Joe's.

Bones had sent me the autopsy report. I fished my tablet out of its pocket inside my greatcoat and transferred the file to it from my comm. It only took a few seconds to realize the report was a fraud.

I tried to send a link to Bones. The crusty old coroner didn't answer. That confirmed what I suspected. I'd find him later and get the exact details of what he'd found.

Staring at the keypad on my comm wasn't the same as sending a link. I just didn't want to talk to Major Kilgore. Not because of what I had to tell him. I just didn't want to talk to my old CO. I was still angry with him.

Angry about the dead SP's. Angry about my face, my eye, even my left hand. I was even more angry about the cover up and how I was drummed out of the Space Marines with a medical and he got his Captain's bars.

It couldn't be avoided, so I pressed the contact list and hit send. I heard the link connect and the sound of Kilgore doing something.

"Major, got a second?"

"Inspector, yeah, I got a second."

"Just got the official autopsy report."

"So did I. Just haven't had a chance to read it."

"Don't believe a word in it," I said softly.

Silence filled the link while Kilgore read the report.

"Sounds about right," he said a little too loud. "Cause of death, kinetic round wounds to the chest and one to the head. Death occurred almost instantly."

"Someone in your office," I asked in an even softer voice.

"Yeah, I agree. I'm starting to think my SP was in the wrong place at the wrong time, Inspector. We arrested two black marketers this morning who were in possession of Marine property."

"I see," I replied in my normal voice. "Can you hold them for me till I can get there tomorrow?"

"You can't come today?" Kilgore asked firmly. We needed to talk face to face, but it was going to have to wait.

"Got another murder. Might be related, or at least my Sergeant Detective thinks so."

"Another one," Kilgore barked.

"Yeah, I'm about to head up to the spaceport. There was an accident in the rail yard, and a conductor was killed. That same conductor was in charge of the train that had three container cars hijacked yesterday. The one you sent my Sergeant Detective back on."

"Really, tragic," Kilgore said in a non-committal tone.

"Yeah. The kid shot one of the perps. No sign of the body or the three cars when we got people on the scene. This accident smells. So we're going to take a look."

"That's strange," Kilgore told me, using the same voice. "Are you sure your guy is sure about that?"

"I'll contact you later," I replied, hoping he caught my drift. We couldn't talk with someone in his office. He broke the link. I pocketed my comm and tablet and tossed some hard credits on the table, enough to cover the lousy food and a tip for the even worse service.

Stepping out in the cold, I checked my chronometer. I had sufficient time to stop by Bones apartment and still get to the accident site to meet Josephson at the time we'd agreed on.

It was a short walk to the underground station. I was glad to feel the warmth as I descended the steps downwards to catch my train. I had a feeling it would be the first of many trips before I got home.

◆ ◆ ◆

Kilgore looked across his desk at the Colonel. Despite his best efforts, the officer had resented him from the minute he'd arrived. She'd gotten along well with his predecessor, so he didn't think it was an interservice rivalry issue.

"May I ask who that was?"

"A civilian police Inspector. He is investigating the death of one of my Shore Patrol officers that took place off base."

"Isn't that a bit unusual, Major Kilgore?"

"Yes, Colonel, it is. But I have my reasons."

"Does it possibly have anything to do with the pair of black marketers you mentioned?

"Colonel, I cannot comment on an open investigation."

"Of course, Major."

The officer stood, and Kilgore stood as well, quickly covering the two strides it took to reach his door and open it for her.

"I will expect your report by the end of the week, Major," the officer reminded him, her tone cold, hard and unfriendly.

"You'll have it no later than 0500 at the end of the week."

He watched the woman walk away, strolling in a most unmilitary fashion as she moved down the corridor. Kilgore shivered in disgust with himself for watching appreciatively.

Of all the officers at the base, the redheaded colonel was the only one he despised.

◆ ◆ ◆

Markeson shook the seldom-used comm. The link finally went through. He'd have to replace it. Within a few seconds, the tiny screen displayed two faces on a split-screen image.

"Governor. Mayor. Sorry to interrupt your busy schedules."

He watched as Rankin smiled his polished, practiced politician smile and said nothing. Mayor Xue, a nervous little Earth Asian, didn't smile, quietly nodding in acknowledgment.

"Gentlemen," Markeson continued, "I believe we need to meet. An opportunity has presented itself that is too good to pass up."

"We agreed to lie low," Xue whined. "Until we were certain it was safe. I still have anxiety attacks after the fiasco with Long."

Rankin leaned forward, his expression indicating interest.

"Xue, stop sniveling. You knew there would be risks. Captain Markeson dealt with the various issues quickly. If the Captain says this is an opportunity we must consider, then we will consider it."

Xue made a face but said nothing in response.

"We need to meet soon. Tonight. We have to move quickly if this is going to happen," Markeson informed the pair of corrupt politicians.

"Agreed," Rankin said, smiling. "The usual place. 1900 hours." Markeson could see the Governor counting his share of the credits in his mind as he broke the link. Xue made another face and broke the link, ending their session.

❖❖❖

The Colonel sat at her desk fuming. She should have listened to her old Sergeant. He'd offered to take care of the situation with the conductor, and she'd declined. The fools had botched the job. Somehow Sullivan had made the connection to the heist.

She thought back to her first meeting with Markeson. He'd told her Sullivan was good. She'd taken his statement too lightly. A mistake that would not happen again. Markeson was proving to be cagier than she thought.

A smile crossed her face as the Colonel recalled their passionate tryst in her suite in Capital City. It would be a shame to finish Markeson when the job was done, but the operation had to be cleaned up when completed.

Her comm buzzed, drawing her attention. A quick glance indicated it was a brief message from none other than the Captain. He would have word for her late that night.

The Colonel deleted the message. Time was of the essence. The product had to be moved off planet soon.

❖❖❖

Nobody noticed him, which of course was exactly what the man wanted. He was proud of his ability to move unnoticed in a street full of people and to avoid the CCTV cameras that were always watching, recording.

Ahead the tall man in the black clothes walked slowly, stopping occasionally to talk with someone. He even crossed the street once to help an elderly couple cross to the side the man had been walking on.

The watcher shook his head. The boss man was right. This guy was going to be a problem. He slipped into a small store and looked around for a few minutes before stepping back into the cold.

It took him less than a minute to find the troublesome priest. This time the man was helping a delivery man carry some boxes into another of the small retail stores. Supper-time couldn't come soon enough. Surely the priest would be hungry and go home.

After a day of being a do-gooder, the priest had to be hungry and tired the man thought. He was worn out just from watching the man. He noticed the priest had stopped and was looking about.

In all probability searching for more people in need of help.

As the priest's gaze continued to take in the area, the watcher stood still, facing the display window for a women's clothing store. In the window's reflection, the watcher could see Father Nathan clearly. He saw the priest's gaze stop and stare directly into the store's window.

The watcher simply walked away, not looking back. If the priest followed him, he would contact the boss man by comm and see how the situation was to be handled. If the priest didn't follow, he'd be back soon enough. Either way, he'd learned a lot that day about the priest's habits.

After several blocks walk, the watcher stopped and glanced back. The priest was nowhere in sight. He smiled at his skill, how he could slip away and vanish from sight. The watcher didn't spot Father Nathan standing inside a sandwich shop across the street, watching the invisible man slip away.

◆ ◆ ◆

I watched Josephson as he stood still and slowly turned around in a complete circle. He'd done it twice already, just looking. I nodded my approval when he glanced at me. The pup was getting a little better at "seeing a crime scene" and taking in as much information as possible.

The Railroad Police, that strange breed of policeman, had already marked off the accident scene, photographed everything and talked with the government's safety inspector while Josephson observed things.

The Railroad Police didn't care. They'd done the critical work. If they played their cards right, they could fill up the entire duty shift and not have to do anything else.

I'd done a quick survey of the scene and was waiting for Josephson to finish. Then it would be time to see what the Railroad Police and the government guy thought about the accident. I disliked the problems that came from one policing agency taking over a case from another force that believed their jurisdiction was being poached.

Josephson finally stood still, thinking. I watched him carefully pick his way through the various numbered markers on the ground and make his way over to me.

"Well?"

"I think the conductor slipped and fell under the locomotive switching the cars."

"That would be the obvious cause of death," I said simply.

"The railroad workers all wear boots designed to grip the ladder rungs or steps, even with ice. The gloves they wear will grip the grab irons in any weather. Their union is very big on work safety rules, and so is the management of the railroad."

"Is this one of your hobbies," I asked, fighting back a grin

I watched his face flush red as he looked down at his feet. "Yes, sir."

"Don't be embarrassed," I ordered. "A good detective tries to be as knowledgeable as possible about a wide range of things."

The pup looked up at me, still embarrassed, and nodded.

"Go ahead," I ordered.

"Conductors have to pass a series of tests and have seniority before they rate for that job. The union insists on it and management is picky about it. It's a job that requires railroading skills and thorough knowledge of operating rules and management procedures. The conductor is responsible for the operation of the train, seeing to it the freight gets delivered where it's supposed to go, empty cars get picked up, and all the paperwork is kept straight for billing."

"Your point?"

"See the blue piece of steel hanging on the freight car he fell off?"

"I noticed it."

"Inspector, that's an indicator railroad workers use to show that freight car is under repair. The locomotive should never have tried to couple onto it."

"He didn't slip and fall then?"

"I would think not sir. More like pushed in front of a moving locomotive."

"You have a problem there, Josephson."

I watched as the pup turned and pointed again, this time at a large metal device with green and red indicator signs. It was evident the device was meant to operate the switch to the track the damaged freight car was stored on.

"See the gray box on the side of the switch stand?"

"Yes," I answered, focusing with my cybernetic eye and snapping a still image.

"If you have the right codes, you could hack that. The switch can be thrown manually or automatically."

"There's hope for you Josephson. Spell it out for me."

"Someone hacked the controls, threw the switch while someone else shoved the conductor in front of the locomotive. Murder by a 100-ton locomotive. Now the switch crew has to deal with this. What do you think, sir?"

"Same as you. Just didn't know some of the details like

the blue men at work sign or how the switch stand could be hacked."

I strolled over to the waiting Railroad Police and the government rat. I didn't smile. They didn't smile back.

"Murder," I announced.

The Railroad Police nodded silently in agreement. The government rat began to protest, citing the weather conditions and the fact the engineer operating the switch engine was undergoing training when the accident happened.

"Murder," I repeated. "Do I need to call the Governor?"

The mention of the chief rat silenced the inspector but didn't stop him from making strange faces and turning a variety of shades of red.

"There is no need to duplicate good police work," I announced. "I'll need everything, images, your reports, the interviews of the crews, everything. The coroner will do an autopsy. If I need anything else, either my Sergeant Detective or I will be in touch."

Surprised at not having their case taken over, the two Railroad Policemen graciously offered to take Josephson and me for coffee. I declined for both of us and gave them the numbers to send the reports to with a reminder to keep the evidence under lock and key and make sure the chain of custody paperwork was done properly.

Josephson and I made our way back toward the hovercar the pup had arrived in. The government lackey followed, protesting the heavy-handed manner in which I had overstepped my authority.

I ignored him.

As Josephson drove off, I glanced back at the government man. He was on his comm reporting to whoever held   his   leash.

CHAPTER SIXTEEN

Northwest Capital City was nice, much nicer than the southern half of the city. Better even than the northeastern quadrant, hindered as it was with the spaceport, rail yard and other industrial buildings. It was Markeson's favorite part of town.

Sitting in the traffic with other high-end hover cars, Markeson noted the street crews had done their job well. Each morning, city workers cleaned all the snow and ice from the streets in the northeast quadrant of Capital City. Except for the pedestrians dressed in their heavy coats and boots, on a sunny day, it was possible to imagine Beta Prime possessed a pleasant climate.

Today was one of those days. Markeson looked forward to lunch. Good steak, a couple of drinks and a cute waitress. The company could be better, but Rankin and Xue were his partners in crime, and as such, he needed to meet with them from time to time.

This was one of those times.

For their part of the smuggling operation to succeed, he would need documents from the two men clearing the path for the illegal goods, whatever it was the Colonel was smuggling off planet, through Security and Customs. Xue would handle Security and Rankin would keep the notoriously corrupt Customs officials at bay.

Today was the first time Markeson missed Devereaux since the billionaire's "suicide" after Sullivan's botched hearing. Normally the arrogant businessman's shipping empire handled these things. It was enough for Markeson and the two politicians to simply find the customers.

He pulled into the circular hoverway of the Argentina, the best steakhouse on Beta Prime. Real beef, not tank grown protein slabs, a place where men could be men, smoke cigars, tell off-color jokes and flirt with cute waitresses. It was also swept for listening devices twice a day, making it a good place to conduct business of every kind, legal, illegal or political.

Handing his keys to the valet, Markeson adjusted his tie, ran his hand through his slicked back hair and smiled at the doorman, an old-fashioned custom dating back centuries, and entered the restaurant. The maître de greeted him with a smile; he better smile Markeson thought, given how much I pay the man, and led the detective back to his preferred table.

"Miss Jasmine will be serving you today, Captain Markeson," the maître de informed him with his too perfect smile, bowing slightly as Markeson seated himself in the booth. The man vanished, leaving Markeson alone.

Within seconds the chocolate skinned Jasmine appeared, one of the exotic beauties that worked as waitresses at the Argentina. She smiled, displaying her dazzling white teeth, expensive perfection and set a tumbler of whiskey before him. Markeson leered back at the Earth African beauty.

"Will you be expecting guests today," Jasmine asked politely with her silky smooth voice.

"Yes, I'm afraid I will," Markeson groused.

"Some of your esteemed friends?"

He tossed another leer in her direction. "They think they're important."

She smiled again and left, vanishing from his sight to await the arrival of his guests. The radiant smile disappeared from her face the instant Jasmine turned her back to the lecherous detective. As Jasmine passed the maître de's station, she gave him a look that could kill only to receive a shrug in return.

"He tips well, Jasmine."

"He doesn't try to put his hands all over you," she snarled back.

◆ ◆ ◆

He looked at the comm in his hand, feeling the blood pressure spike in his temples as his cheeks began to feel flush.

"If this job didn't pay so well, I'd just walk away," the mercenary said, just loud enough for the others in the room to hear.

One of the mercenaries sitting at the table, cleaning his weapons, frowned and asked the leader, "bad news, Captain?"

"That so-called Sergeant of hers, just reamed me out for how we handled the conductor. Seems he got a tip the cops have decided it was murder and not a work accident."

"Why didn't he handle the job himself then," the other merc asked. "We were good enough to hit the train, and that cost Buck his life. Can't get paid if you're dead."

The Captain shook his head in frustration. "We're not hit men. We're soldiers. Taking on the train, reasonable job. Taking out someone with a sniper. No problem. Next contract, I'm going to spell things out in more detail what we will do and what we won't."

His men nodded in agreement. Killing for hire in combat situations or pulling off a job was one thing. Murder for hire was another. They might be mercenaries, but they had standards.

◆ ◆ ◆

I needed to think. Josephson's driving still hadn't improved, so I told him to find a dive for us to stop and think. No reason for me to be the only one thinking about things. The pup was getting a little better at his job. Another death on my conscience was not something I wanted or needed. Better for him to learn this way when I could goose him in the right direction than for him to do something stupid and get killed.

We found a nice dive, parked the squad car and went inside. Nobody greeted us, so we sat ourselves. After a minute or so, a gruff looking waitress made her way over to take our orders. She looked worse for the wear, with her makeup caked on thick. Her teeth were yellow and stained. The lines around her eyes and the specks of gray in her hair told the story of the hard times she'd seen.

I ordered a coke, and the pup ordered black coffee. He was learning. When first assigned as partners upon my arrival, he drank this stuff that was more chemical additives and foam than it was coffee. If you're going to be a cop, you have to drink coffee like a cop. I told him he wouldn't see me drinking any of that diet coke stuff. If I was going to drink something bad for me, it was going to have real sugar in it.

"Think they're in a hurry to get whatever was on the train off planet?"

"Without a doubt," I answered. "The question is where is the shipment going?"

"What do you think was in those container cars?"

It was a good question, one that would impact a lot of factors.

"We know whatever it is, it's valuable. It's also perishable, that means they have to get it off-world in a hurry."

Josephson considered this for a moment. "Why not get it off-world quick regardless?"

"If it weren't perishable, I'd just store it someplace nice and safe. Sit on the goods until the heat dies down. Take my time finding a buyer who will pay top credit for the merchandise."

Josephson nodded in agreement.

"So, my question to you Sergeant, where would you ship the merchandise if it was perishable and needed special storage facilities? Where could you ship it and let it sit until the heat was off and a buyer ready to pay?"

My partner's eyes glazed a bit, which they were prone to do when he was deep in thought. His expression became focused as he stared at his cup of coffee.

"One of the moons, Serenity or Persephone. They have mining operations and military bases but no atmosphere. Everything is in a controlled environment. From what I've heard, they have lots of storage facilities up there. You can store just about anything until you need it."

"Good thinking," I told him. He was right. "So we need to focus on every flight from Beta Prime to the moons, starting with immediately after the train heist."

"Yes, sir," he responded, looking up, his eyes returning to normal. "You want me to check all the shipping manifests?"

"Yeah, but focus on craft owned by Devereaux's company. I doubt we came anywhere close to cleaning out all the smugglers in that outfit. I'm going to talk to a few people, see if I can't find out who might arrange transportation for a piece of the pie. If I can't get a handle on that, I'm going to look into who might be willing to stick their neck out storing hot goods for a cut."

We sat in silence, finishing our drinks.

It was going to be a long day. As we drove off, I worried about Sarah. Hiring her had been an exercise in babysitting. I figured I wouldn't have to worry about her if I could see her. Now I had placed her in more danger than before.

She was right about the dead clone. Whoever killed our dead SP probably knew he was a clone. Based on what I knew, more like what Sarah knew, bounty hunters were looking for any other clone on the planet. That meant they were looking for Sarah.

She was mad at me. I'd figured out that much. If I had taken all her talk about being a clone serious in the first place, or at least acted like I did, Sarah would be sitting in the back of our squad car, looking out the window and thinking about whatever it is she thinks about. But she would be safe, as safe as she could be that is.

Now Sarah was doing what she did when not on duty with me. She was wandering the streets.

No matter what Sarah said, I had the blood of her sister Maria on my hands. If something happened to my mysterious girl, I don't think my mind could handle the guilt of two dead sisters.

Both of them dead because I didn't do my job.

Josephson took a turn too hard, and I bumped my head against the plexiglass window. I had a stress headache coming on, and his driving wasn't helping.

◆ ◆ ◆

"Where's Markeson," Chief O'Brian shouted from the entrance to the detective's bullpen.

"Haven't seen 'em all day, Chief," called one of the detectives from the far back.

O'Brian didn't respond but rather turned and went back to his office. After the fiasco with Devereaux and the Internal Affairs hearing, O'Brian had started to wonder if his Chief of Detectives was corrupt. Not petty corruption common to most of the cops on Beta Prime.

In league with the Big Boys.

O'Brian returned to his office and sat down in his new chair to reflect. Reflect on the fact that he'd lost his way on his climb to the top of the police structure on Beta Prime. Cut too many corners. Made too many deals with politicians and their supporters.

It wasn't so much that he'd taken money or material goods. It was the promotion here for looking the other way. The promise of a good word there, if a piece of evidence went missing.

Now he was a divorced father of three. His ex-wife had sole custody of the kids, and she'd moved them to Delphi III. Half his income was spent on alimony and child support before it even hit his bank account. His kids hated him, thanks to his ex-wife poisoning them against him.

He got the flat in the divorce, mainly because his ex-wife couldn't take it with her. Evenings were spent alone. With the divorce, he'd learned the hard way their friends were really his wife's friends.

At first, O'Brian hated the man his ex-wife had the affair with. Hated how she threw in his face this Oscar of hers was all the things he wasn't. How Oscar made her happy. In the end, she'd left O'Brian and taken everything that mattered to him.

Of course, Oscar had never proposed, O'Brian thought bitterly. If they got married, he'd be off the hook for the alimony, and the loss of cash flow would cut into their lifestyle. Better to live in sin and have him pay for a big chunk of it than do the honorable thing by his Julia.

All he had left now was his job.

For the first time in a few years, O'Brian thought about doing his job. Doing it the way it should be done. At least he would have that.

Maybe it was time to start keeping a closer eye on Markeson.

CHAPTER SEVENTEEN

He watched the nervous Xue enter the Argentina and look about as his eyes adjusted to the interior lighting. A second later, the taller, more confident Ranking stepped through the door. Without a word, the maître de led the two politicians to Markeson's table, smiled his too perfect smile and departed in silence.

The three men sat watching each other in silence as Jasmine appeared, replacing Markeson's whiskey with a fresh one. Two glasses of red wine were set before the politicians. All three men watched Jasmine perform her job with appreciation. Not for the manner in which she did her job, but rather the figure she cut while doing the job.

Like the maître de, she smiled her perfect smile, displaying the dazzling white teeth set perfectly in her mouth, and without a word, she disappeared.

"I took the liberty of ordering for us," Markeson announced, taking control of the meeting.

Rankin frowned at the news. As Governor of Beta Prime, he was of the opinion it was he who should be in control. The fact Markeson was the real brains behind their operation never occurred to him. The Mayor was a worrier and happy to let Rankin and Markeson be in charge. So long as he got his cut, he was happy.

"We have an unexpected opportunity, and we need to act fast," Markeson informed the pair in a low voice.

"What kind of an opportunity," Rankin snapped back.

"Somebody I've come in contact with has several freight containers of goods that need to be somewhere else fast. They would like to avoid any problems that might crop up with Security and Customs."

A moment of silence passed while the three sat and looked at each other, each man counting credits, both in expenses and profits for this possible venture. Risk was factored into the expense column in the process.

"I will handle finding the lift vessel. Devereaux's wife is running the shipping company now. It shouldn't be a problem finding a tug to take the containers up as part of a load to the space station's port. What she doesn't know won't hurt her," Markeson informed the others.

"Is this a one-time consultation fee we're talking about," Xue interjected in his nervous voice, his hands moving busily on the table. "Or will there be repeat business?"

"I would imagine if we provide good service with this initial consultation, there is great potential for future contracts," Markeson answered, smiling in an effort to relax the nervous little man.

"Where do these goods need to be delivered," Rankin inquired.

"The customer believes they have warehouse space available on Serenity," Markeson explained. "Either way, they'll have to pass the containers through the docking station, so they'll need advice on how to clear Security and Customs here before the lift into orbit. Then they'll need advice on how the shuttle process to Serenity works.

The Governor nodded, satisfied with Markeson's explanation. "Simple enough arrangement. I can handle the consult for Customs, though there will be some expenses that need factoring into the consulting contract."

"No problem. I explained we would do this first contract for a flat fee for consulting plus our expenses. The client seemed amenable to the idea."

"Security clearance won't be a problem at either port of call," the Mayor informed Markeson, more confident now that the Governor had agreed to the deal so quickly.

"There will be expenses incurred. It is just the way things are."

"Good. I will let the client know," Markeson answered, smiling at the sight of Jasmine returning with a large circular tray perfectly balanced above her shoulder on one hand. The men fell silent as the waitress gracefully distributed their food. She asked if they needed anything else and then slipped away, leaving them to their own devices.

"I will let you know the specifics as soon as I have them. Regular fees and expenses for this job. This is a quick turnaround. If we show we can deliver on our end, we can raise our rates."

"That, my dear Captain," the Governor spit out in his commanding tone, "is the one thing about this job I don't like. It's too quick. You just met this client, did you not?"

"Be sensible," Markeson growled in protest. "We've all taken a hit in our cash flow. For each of us that presents different problems. Without Devereaux, we have to handle things more directly until we can establish a new network."

Worried suddenly by the Governor's protest, Xue weighed in with his own concerns, "I agree with the Governor. This is very sudden."

"Look," Markeson growled, irritated by the vacillation of the two politicians, "elections are in nine months. That means money to grease palms is going to be needed. You can't possibly tell me neither of you couldn't use a nice campaign contribution?"

He looked at the two men squarely in the eyes, first the Governor and then the Mayor. "Let's not forget those nice little apartments where you keep certain friends, and the expense accounts those friends have."

Rankin's face indicated he'd made a decision. Markeson struggled to keep from smiling. Rankin's greed was his weakness. Greed for money, power, women, whatever it was he wanted at the time. Xue was easy to manipulate. If

Rankin went for the scheme, Xue always signed on.

"You have a point. Just make sure this is all handled cleanly and the consulting fees find their way into the appropriate accounts."

Markeson raised his glass in a silent toast to his partners, relieved they'd agreed so easily.

◆ ◆ ◆

He watched the priest take the wallet and watch from the young boy and grab him by the arm. None too gently he dragged the boy across the street and approached an elderly man standing with his wife, looking through the window of a bakery.

In less than a minute the stolen property was returned, the youth had apologized, and the priest once again helped the recalcitrant male cross the street. As they grew nearer, he could hear the two talking.

"Father, I won't have enough to pay off the Boss Man at the end of this week. Please, don't make me give back any more of my take!"

"Paulo, stealing is a sin! You don't need to steal. I give you shelter and food. You should be in school during the day instead of roaming the streets stealing."

The boy pulled away from the priest and took several quick steps to put some space between the big man and himself.

"Father, it's not that simple. The Boss Man will beat me and the others if we do not bring him enough. We can't quit. We don't have a choice. Please," the boy pleaded, "don't be angry Father. We appreciate everything you are trying to do for us."

"You know, Paulo, this is new for me," the priest replied. "It's been a long time since anybody has been more scared of someone else than me."

Paulo lowered his head, more in frustration with his situation than anything else. If it were just him, he would do as the priest wanted and take his chances with the Boss Man. But now that Toby and Anna were gone, it had fallen on him to take care of the other kids. A burden Paulo would gladly give to Father Nathan if he knew how.

"Go on Paulo. It will be dark soon, and it's going to be a cold one tonight. See to it as many of the kids make it to the church as possible."

Relieved, Paulo vanished into the throngs of workers making their way to and from work during the evening shift change. The priest turned and headed the other way, crossing the street and walking toward Joe's.

Reaching into his pocket, the man pulled out his comm and opened a link.

"Boss, this guy is trouble. He's trying to get the kids off the street. Get this, he wants them to go to school."

The man listened intently, nodding his head in agreement.

"Will do Boss. Tomorrow night good enough?"

Again he listened.

"In front of the kids, Boss?"

He smiled at the answer. "I'll be happy to."

Closing the link, the man watched Father Nathan enter Joe's. "Better enjoy your meal preacher man. Say your prayers too. You won't be doin' much of either after tomorrow night."

◆ ◆ ◆

"Are you sure Private Johansson?"

"Yes, Major. Three container flats. Each has a sealed container. The locomotive arrived an hour ago with three empty container flats. The containers were loaded on to the container flats and secured. As soon as the loading process was complete, the train departed."

39

"No signals? No sign of crew?"

"No, Major. The containers were sitting on the loading dock. The only other personnel I was able to identify was the crane operator and a civilian who ordered him to load the containers."

"A civilian?"

"Yes, Major. Tall, dark headed man. Acted like a Sergeant the way he gave orders to our crane operator. Army guy though, you can always tell, you know how it is Major."

"Private, this is a classified matter. Do you understand?"

"Yes, Major. I have no desire to be transferred to the base on the South Pole. I will never speak of this matter again unless authorized by you, and you alone, Major."

Kilgore struggled to refrain from smiling at the young private's eagerness to obey.

"That is all Private Johansson. Dismissed.

Kilgore waited for the Marine to shut the door behind him. Quickly, he opened the middle drawer in his desk and removed his secure comm. He pressed the necessary contact and waited for the link to form.

"Sullivan, Kilgore."

He listened to Sullivan for a moment before continuing.

"Another of those mystery trains has left the base. Three containers just like the train we saw."

Sullivan answered.

"I agree. Probably be part of tomorrow's mixed train. I doubt they'll do it the same way this time. Too many things they couldn't control. Get back with me once you decide how you want to handle this."

Kilgore broke the link and put the comm in the inner pocket of his tunic. He hated waiting, but there was nothing he could do at the moment. Not until Sullivan contacted him.

◆◆◆

Somebody slipped into the seat next to me in my booth. I didn't look up from my tablet as I continued to scan for information on warehousing on Persephone and Serenity, Beta Prime's two moons. After a bit, a petite, slender hand moved into my field of vision.

I guess Sarah was ready to talk.

I looked up and glanced at her. A neutral expression occupied her face. Only her eyes conveyed any emotion, a combination of irritation and fearfulness.

"Are you ready to go back to work?"

"Are you ready to acknowledge I'm a clone and everything I told you was true?"

This was getting us nowhere.

"I'm willing to stipulate to the facts, whatever they may be."

"Don't talk all legal to me," Sarah chirped back. "Sarah's a clone. Say it."

I sighed. Sarah wasn't going to let this go. I thought for a moment. I believed Sarah was a clone. I believed everything she'd told me. I just couldn't bring myself to say it out loud.

The other part of me wanted to put Sarah across my knee and paddle her like the five-year old she was in so many ways.

"Sarah's a clone. Until the facts prove otherwise, I will stipulate to the fact Sarah is a clone."

She wrinkled her nose up and tilted her head to the side, deciding whether or not that was good enough.

"Okay. I'm not mad at you anymore."

"Good, now, I've got a bone to pick with Miss Sarah."

Sarah frowned at me, pushing her lips together in a pout.

"I was mad at you. You wouldn't listen, Sully. If you

want me to be your assistant, you have to listen to me when I know something. I know a lot more about clones than you do. I know a lot more about what happens to clones, and I definitely know more about the people who hunt us."

"I pay you to work."

"You pay me to work, AND so you can keep an eye on me," she replied without batting an eye.

Josephson couldn't stop the snicker that her response triggered. I gave the pup my evil eye, the cybernetic one no less. That stopped the snicker and removed the grin from his face.

"Besides, I kept an eye on Father Nathan for you."

"Who said I wanted somebody to keep an eye on Father Nathan?"

Sarah responded by reaching for a fresh roll sitting on my plate and taking a bite out of it. She chewed it quickly and swallowed.

"You want to know what I saw or not?"

Needing to finish the word games with Sarah and settle her down so Josephson and I could finish our respective searches, I decided to play along.

"What did you see?"

"A watcher was following him. Pretty good too. Not as good as me, but he gave Father Nathan the slip the one time he spotted the watcher."

"Are you sure?"

"Yes, I'm sure," Sarah replied in exasperation as she buttered her bread. "Sully, you seem to forget I've managed to avoid capture while traveling from planet to planet." She gave me a good eye roll while she chewed.

"I listened in too."

"Listened to who?"

"The watcher. He called the "Boss Man" whoever that is. I think they're going to try to hurt Father Nathan, so you need to do something about it."

CHAPTER EIGHTEEN

I didn't need more stress. Sarah deciding to be cooperative was a positive. The news Father Nathan might have a hit on him was not. Josephson, sensing an explosion was impending, did the only thing he could think to do.

He went and got Alice.

She took one look at me and promptly announced Sarah needed to be fed and led the child-woman off to the kitchen to see to feeding her.

"Get Joe or Ralph. I don't care which," I ordered Josephson.

The pup headed off in search of Ralph, Alice's cab driver husband, and Joe, the owner of the fine establishment.

"Priorities," I whispered aloud to myself.

As important as dealing with the murder of the dead SP was, clone or not, I wasn't going to let someone else who mattered to me get hurt.

Father Nathan was not going to be cooperative. Of that much I was certain. He was determined to find this Boss Man and remove him as an influence on his kids' lives. As far as the good priest was concerned, the sooner the two met, the sooner the issue would be resolved.

Truth be told, I had to admit to myself if the fight was fair, just the Father and the Boss Man, whoever he was, I wasn't worried about Father Nathan.

It wasn't going to be a fair fight.

"I couldn't find Ralph."

I looked up to see Josephson standing there with Joe.

"Joe, we've got a little bit of a problem.

74

◆ ◆ ◆

A warm front was coming through, bringing above freezing temperatures with it. At least that was what the weather report claimed, such that these things can be trusted.

It would make things easier. Having lost one man already, the mercenary Captain had changed the plans for the second raid. Two men would be hidden on the container flats as the mixed freight left Brownstown.

The train would not be stopped a second time. His men would simply uncouple the container flat coupled to the last passenger coach, allowing the train to simply pull away, leaving the three container flats with the "packages" to roll along to the siding.

His men would use the hand brakes to keep the automatic brakes from setting when the brake line separated. If the weather cooperated, the ice so often found in the points of the switches would be melted for once, allowing the cars to roll on the siding under their own momentum. Then the hand brakes would be used to stop the cars.

Fifteen minutes later, the hovercraft would arrive, and nobody would ever be the wiser the theft had taken place.

It was a good plan. Better than the one the Colonel had ordered.

◆ ◆ ◆

Things were going to have to change. In fact, if things were going to change, Markeson decided, they might as well change a lot. His timetable called for him to push O'Brian into retirement gradually, or arrange for a scandal and force the man out.

Fuming at the hour's worth of questions from O'Brian, many of which he hadn't had an answer, was making him rethink things. For some reason, the Chief of Police had decided to actually take an interest in doing his job like an efficient, honest cop.

Efficient was one thing. Honest was another thing altogether. An honest boss would make his life miserable, not to mention the negative impact it would have on his income and plans for the future.

Then there was the timing of it all. Police work, especiaully administrative police work, was not what he needed to be doing at the moment. Investigating the scam the Colonel and her henchman were running was his priority. Markeson sensed a highly lucrative opportunity was at his fingertips. If only he could determine what the game was and take advantage of the situation, he might make enough money and collect enough political currency to get off Beta Prime and get himself appointed Chief of Police on a decent planet.

One with lots of opportunities for wealth and political gain.

◆◆◆

Kilgore adjusted his scope. Just as he expected, the local switch engine had made up the train for the morning mixed freight back to Capital City. The night train had just departed, a long drag of loaded ore cars. The evening passenger train had left just minutes before.

Sitting on a siding next to the waiting mixed train consist were three container flats with loaded and sealed containers sitting. Whatever those containers carried would be safe for the night. The Railroad Police hated insurance claims. Once in possession of a customer's cargo, they did an excellent job of making sure thieves kept away from loaded cars in the freight yard to prevent vandalism or theft.

Kilgore decided to return in the morning to watch the

mixed train depart for its run to Capital City. He was confident between now and the train's departure, those three cars would be coupled onto the train.

◆◆◆

"Colonel, the cargo is in the freight yard. The Railroad Police have it under both human and CCTV surveillance."

"Good. Things are moving forward nicely," the redhead replied. "I believe if you act quickly, you will catch the next hovercraft back to Capital City without any problem Sergeant."

"Yes, Colonel."

An empty pause filled the link.

"I believe it is time you made your visit to our friends on Savannah II to finalize the arrangements."

"Do you feel confident the detective will be able to fulfill his end of the agreement?"

The redhead smiled a particularly wicked smile. "He will be duly motivated. I promise you Sergeant. Make sure you are properly motivated."

Closing the link, the Colonel thought of her pleasant tryst with Markeson. "Yes, Sergeant, Detective Markeson will be adequately motivated. By money as well as other things."

On the other end of the broken link, the loyal NCO seethed. He'd ended his career in the military to serve the woman he loved. A forbidden love, not because of her beauty, but because he was a lowly non-com and she was an officer.

She had threatened him! After all he had done for her, his Colonel had threatened him! At the same time implying she planned to take the corrupt detective into her bed. He could overlook her occasional dalliances with men. They meant nothing. But this loathsome detective had caught her fancy.

Despite his loyalty, his love for the beautiful creature who inspired him, the Sergeant's greatest loyalty was to the cause they had both pledged their lives to serve. As he hurried to his hover car to go to the air terminal, worry crept into the Sergeant's mind. Mixed with the anger he felt, doubt began to worm its insidious way into his mind.

Could his Colonel have lost sight of their goal? Could her weakness for men and the luxuries of life have caused her to stray from the mission?

This he would not allow. If necessary, he would terminate the detective himself once the man no longer served a purpose. As to the Colonel's needs in the boudoir, he decided it was time to eliminate the barrier between them. If necessary, he would even use force. It wouldn't be the first time.

◆◆◆

Father Nathan looked less than happy surrounded as he was by Joe, Ralph, Josephson, Sarah and me.

"It's my business. Nobody else needs to be involved."

"Wrong," I told him. "It's my business and the business of Josephson here. We're the cops. You're a priest. Besides, I promised you I would find this guy."

He glared at me with a rage I had seen before in men, but not the good Father. It was the kind of rage that could lead a man to kill.

"Those kids are more afraid of this "Boss Man" than the Lord or me. He has some kind of evil hold over them. Do you understand me?"

"I read you loud and clear, Father. You need to calm down."

"I'm not going to calm down, Inspector. I no longer hold you to your promise. I am perfectly capable of dealing with this on my own."

"Which do you want me to do Father," I snarled, matching his anger with my own. "Identify your dead body in the morgue, or would you rather I arrest you for murder? Which is it, because the way you're acting, that's how things are going to end!"

"What do you care? You certainly don't care about these kids! You care about your dead victims! You want to know why? Because you don't have to feel Sullivan! The dead don't cause you any grief! The living? The living terrify you! You might have to care!"

I stood up from our booth shaking in rage.

"You don't have a single clue what you're talking about. You have no idea what I've been through in my life."

I didn't say another word. I just left. I had plenty to do. Things that would keep other people from winding up dead.

◆ ◆ ◆

Bones flipped through his security systems visual image data. It was Sullivan. He deactivated his alarm system and entered the codes to release the locks to the entrance. Phase pistol in hand, he waited just inside his living room, giving himself a line of fire without being seen by whoever entered the room.

Sullivan stepped in and shut the door behind him.

Bones motioned in silence for the Inspector to follow him. He reactivated the alarm system and secured the locks again before holstering his phase pistol. Only then did he lead Sullivan to his secure room where the real autopsy results were waiting.

◆ ◆ ◆

Joe looked at the group of concerned faces at the booth.

He didn't like getting involved. It would lead to trouble, and he knew it. But two of his friends, not to mention good customers, were about to get themselves into a dangerous situation. Besides, Alice would be furious if he didn't act and Joe had seen the tongue-lashings Alice gave Ralph when he screwed up on occasion.

It was a matter of which situation would be the most trouble. Joe decided intervening in the mess Sullivan and Father Nathan had caused would be the lesser of the two evils.

"Ralph says Father Nathan made it safely back to the vicarage. My guess is they'll snatch the Father sometime tomorrow, probably during shift change when the streets are crowded. We just need to keep an eye on him. Once they grab him, we follow them to this Boss Man. Josephson, you and Sully arrest the guy and put him away. Problem solved."

"For now," Alice said.

"What do you mean," Ralph asked. "Father Nathan will be happy. The kids won't have a reason not to move into the dorm and go to school. Sullivan won't have to worry about Father Nathan and one more criminal will be in prison."

"Until the next time this crops up," Alice pointed out.

"Alice is right," Joe said, sighing. "These two see the world differently. They both see the evil in people, but Father Nathan sees those who want to be redeemed. Sully just sees the evil. They'll clash again."

The group sat in silence, knowing Joe and Alice were right.

"Sully does too see the good in people," a tiny voice whispered. "He's just been hurt by too many things, too many people. So he just made a choice not to get hurt more."

Everyone looked at Sarah who had not spoken once other than to describe the watcher.

"Sully tried to save my sister. He saved me," she said softly before nodding at Josephson. "He worries about you, feels responsible for you. It eats him up that you got hurt in that raid. Sully worries about all of you, even you Joe."

Josephson's face flushed red with embarrassment at the surprise of learning his boss liked him. "How would you know," he snapped at Sarah. "You're never around most of the time. You don't talk to anyone. So, like I said, how would you know?"

"I listen," Sarah hissed back, snapping her body forward like a snake striking. "Everybody talks because they want to be heard, but they never listen to anyone else. I listen. People say the most without using words. Sully is easy to listen to. All you have to do is just watch and listen. You can read him like a book!"

◆◆◆

Sometimes it's nice to know I'm not the only paranoid person on this planet. What Bones had learned from the autopsy on the dead SP had scared him plenty. There was no doubt the man was a clone.

A genetically enhanced clone.

Based on what Bones could determine from a dead example of the geneticists work, the dead clone could withstand extremes in temperatures, go for extended periods of time without food or water, simple wounds would heal faster than normal, and the man possessed better than normal sensory ability.

He was a male version of the mysterious Sarah. I didn't mention her ability to present herself as an adult female in a range of ages from her twenties to her late thirties. I certainly wasn't going to tell him about Sarah's ability to hide in plain sight. If it weren't for my enhanced vision due to my cybernetic right eye, I would probably never spot Sarah when she was of a mind to not be seen.

I asked Bones if he could make any determination about the mental capacity of the dead clone or his state of psychological development. His comment about not having all the dead clone's brains being a problem was pretty snide, but then I guess I had it coming.

I told Bones to secure the evidence, which he assured me had been taken care of. I loaned him my .38 caliber revolver and some rounds. He appreciated having a kinetic energy weapon to go with his phase pistol. Bones understood the value of a large exit wound instead of just burning some flesh off.

◆◆◆

Kilgore lay on his bunk, trying to decide the best course of action. Sullivan had sent a secure message confirming the dead SP, one John Brown, was indeed a clone, military grade and highly illegal.

He thought again of the research facility on the base. Nobody knew what went on inside, making it a constant topic and source of speculation at mealtime or during the dead time all military bases have. Kilgore wasn't worried about what went on in the facility.

He worried about who else knew.

◆◆◆

I looked at my comm. Josephson had messaged me about the situation with Father Nathan. I messaged back we'd meet in the morning at Joe's. In the meantime I wanted him researching the shipping manifests for the freight shuttles lifting cargo containers up the space sport where the big freights docked and the barges carried cargo to Beta Prime's two moons.

A front was coming through. I figured a walk would do me some good to clear my cluttered mind. I was furious with Father Nathan.

I had a dead body on my hands. The answer to who the dead SP really was, who killed him and how he got to Beta Prime might cause, or prevent, an interplanetary war.

It might also get Sarah killed.

I could not let that happen. My mistake had cost Sarah one sister.

Father Nathan was a good man. I didn't believe all the things he believed. But the priest was a good man. How he couldn't see that his actions placed his friends in jeopardy was beyond me.

Helping the widows in our neighborhood was great. Working with troubled youth, that was great too. But risking his neck over kids who were already criminals? No. That's where I drew the line.

I found myself standing outside the parish church's grounds. I had no idea how I wound up there, but there I was. A warm breeze blew, carrying with it a damp smell, like standing water on a planet where it was wet and humid.

The wind howled as the front blew in quickly, bringing with it an ominous fog.

CHAPTER NINETEEN

It doesn't happen often, but on occasion, Beta Prime's weather changes for the better. A warm snap will come through. Temperatures get above freezing. It's nice for all of about thirty minutes. Then the snow and ice start melting, and water is running everywhere. When a warm spell hits, the next cold front is not far away. And that front never starts out as snow.

It rains.

This morning was one of those days.

I walked the streets, looking for Father Nathan. I was wet and cold.

As I looked for the good Father, I had to wonder why he was so determined to help the people of this planet, this city. To look at them, it was hard for me to understand why.

Most of them don't deserve help.

In fact, I was having a hard time understanding why I worked so hard as a cop. I believed in the idea of law and order, of justice. But those things aren't people. They are idealistic concepts, pure and beautiful.

People are corrupt, evil creatures. Every day I see what man is capable of doing to his fellow man, most of it not good.

Watching the people of Capital City made me wonder why I was still a cop. I watched my fellow man slog around in the bitter cold as the rain came down. Everyone looked miserable, alone, just wanting to get through the day and go home just to get up and do it all again.

Walking among the throngs were those who looked to

victimize as many people as possible. My job was to catch them and lock them up so the average Joe was safe.

I was starting to wonder what was the point.

No matter how many of the scum I shot, arrested or beat up, there was another thug to take the first scum's place. I was wasting my time. Dealing with the victims sometimes was worse than dealing with the criminals. It got to where sometimes I couldn't tell who was the victim and who was the criminal.

I stopped under an awning for a local shoe store and looked around, watching the swarm of humanity trudging past in the freezing rain. Soon it would turn into sleet, laying down a layer of ice as the temperature fell. Then the snow would come and cover the slippery substance with a deceptive layer of beautiful powdery white crystals.

The weather was like most people, one thing on the inside, another, deceptive thing on the outside.

The irony of it gave me a good laugh.

Yet, here I was. Out in this terrible weather. Looking for a man I call my friend, a man who agreed with my view of humanity except for one small point. He believed people could be redeemed. It was what drove Father Nathan to invest so much of himself in trying to help others. Many of whom society would be much better served if I just went ahead and locked them up for good.

Standing there, I realized how cynical I've become. I have only a few friends on Beta Prime and those I do have I haven't tried to cultivate. Guilt and remorse will do that to a man. If you don't have friends, you can't hurt them, and they can't hurt you.

Having a friend means you have responsibility. Responsibility means you can let that friend down. More guilt. More need for forgiveness that will never be granted.

Once this Boss Man was found and dealt with, Father

Nathan and I were going to have a talk about things.

His vendetta had forced Sarah out on the streets to look for him and the watcher as she called him, placing her in danger. She'd laughed it off, saying she was always in danger. It was my fault her sister Maria was dead. I can't, I won't let the same thing happen to Sarah.

The pup was out wandering around too. I didn't ask for a partner, but Markeson stuck me with one. I was responsible for Josephson, and as much as I hated to admit it, the idealistic rookie detective had grown on me. Kind of like a dog person given a kitten learns to like cats. Well, one cat.

Father Nathan was going to have to understand, I was okay with him trying to save the unfortunate and the downtrodden, even some of the petty criminals. It was his choice. But him forcing my hand and placing the few friends I let myself have in danger, that, that was not acceptable.

◆◆◆

Ralph spotted the two thugs before anyone else. It wasn't until Sarah pointed out the watcher that everyone else saw him. Josephson reminded everyone to stay out of sight. If things looked like they were going to get rough, he was the one with the gun.

Sarah's response was to get out of Ralph's cab and vanish into the morning rush of people as the night shift went home and the morning shift came on. Joe eased out of the cab and looked carefully before crossing the street to the other side of the parish complex. Alice kissed Ralph, gave him a knowing glance reminding him not to get in trouble with the law, and like the others, exited the once crowded cab.

It hurt Ralph to watch the crowds of people hurrying about in the cold rain and not have his light on, indicating he was available to pick up a fare. He sat and watched the entrance to the vicarage where the two thugs were doing their best to make their presence known.

The door opened and Father Nathan stepped out and greeted the pair of hoodlums with a smile, locking the door behind him. The two looked surprised the priest was expecting them.

After talking for a minute or so, the pair cautiously led Father Nathan away from the vicarage, one on each side, just out of arm's reach of the big man. Ralph chuckled. They might be dumb thugs, but they understood pain and violence. Neither intended to let the priest get a clean shot at either of them.

◆ ◆ ◆

I got a comm message from Josephson and headed down Canal Street, the other main boulevard in the southwest quadrant of Capital City. Father Nathan had simply gone with the thugs this Boss Man had sent to grab him. The watcher was nearby, but he'd lost visual contact. My blood boiled when he messaged Sarah was following and would keep an eye on the watcher.

Half an hour passed while we followed at a distance, spread out so if the trio suddenly took a turn down a side street someone could spot them again quickly. It was evident we were close because the neighborhood was getting rougher and rougher, which was saying a lot in this part of Capital City.

I turned a corner and made the trio as they entered an industrial building that also had a warehouse. I stepped back around the corner and watched the street. Several minutes passed before the man Sarah designated as the watcher casually appeared and strolled up to the entrance of the warehouse and walked in like he worked there.

I waited a bit before I rounded the corner and ran

across the street. Upon testing, the door was unlocked and didn't make a sound as I eased it open just enough to slip in. Standing completely still, I could hear voices talking. I drew my .50 cal and cocked it as I adjusted the sight in my right eye for the dim lighting and pulled up my targeting software.

If there had to be shooting, I wasn't planning on missing.

Moving further into the building, I discovered it was largely empty except for a couple of dozen dirty, ratty mattresses scattered about on the floor with blankets laying on them. Instantly I knew it was all the good Father could do to not explode in a rage. The conditions his kids were kept in before he arrived were appalling.

A cold draft brushed against me, alerting me to a presence behind me. I looked back to see Josephson, his phase pistol drawn and ready. His face was pale, and a sheen of nervous sweat covered his brow. I couldn't blame him. The last time he'd entered a warehouse he'd lost a hip, a lot of skin and muscle and killed a man.

The pup had more guts than common sense.

Shouting from deeper in the warehouse got my attention. I started walking quickly, no longer trying not to make noise. If tempers had flared enough to start shouting, I doubted anyone would hear footsteps.

"You stuck your nose where it didn't belong," one voice screamed, on the verge of sounding hysterical.

I recognized the second voice. "You don't have a right to treat these children like property. Slavery was banned seven hundred years ago." If Father Nathan wanted to provoke the Boss Man, he was doing a good job.

"Slavery? These kids work for me," the voice answered.

"No, they don't. They steal for you, which is something entirely different. If you had them peddling trinkets, I would feel differently. Let's be honest. You're nothing more than a human trafficker. What do you do with the girls when they get old enough? Sell them into prostitution?"

"None of your business, preacher man."

"It is my business. These are my kids," Father Nathan growled back.

"Your kids? Now they're your kids?" The Boss Man laughed. "Who said they were your kids?"

I flinched at the words. I'd said the same thing once and gotten a theological lecture in return. The good Father's response surprised me.

"You're right. They aren't mine. They belong to the Lord."

Laughter from the Boss Man, who I could now just make out, and the two thugs echoed throughout the warehouse.

"That's a good one preacher man! Do you see God here," the Boss Man said, drawing a phase pistol from inside his coat. "No, I don't think you do," he said grimly, answering his own question.

Father Nate looked at the gun and back at the Boss Man. "The Lord gave me the responsibility of looking out for those kids, getting them off the streets."

Tired of the verbal sparring, the Boss Man raised his phase pistol and took aim. "I hope you're all prayed up preacher man because I'm done dealing with you."

I couldn't stand by and watch. I couldn't. My training kicked in, and I bellowed, "Drop your weapon! Freeze! Police!"

The Boss Man jerked his head to look at me. It was all Father Nathan needed. He stepped forward with purpose, swinging downwards and across his body with his right arm with enough force to cause the Boss Man to drop his phase pistol. Stepping across with his right leg and driving his hip into the Boss Man's abdomen to get leverage, Father Nathan grabbed the Boss Man's right arm and threw the thug over his shoulder, slamming the Boss Man flat on his back.

A shot rang out from behind me. I saw an explosion of blood and tissue come from the good Father's left shoulder. I turned to see Sarah's watcher lining up his sights on my head. I squeezed my trigger and watched the man's head explode like a melon, covering the wall behind him with bone, blood and brain matter. His decapitated body stood still for what seemed like minutes before it collapsed to the floor, lying with its limbs bent at unnatural angles.

Turning back, I saw the Boss Man scramble to his feet and aim a kick at my friend's abdomen as he tried to regain his feet. Father Nathan grabbed the foot and twisted, producing a scream as the Boss Man's leg rotated further than it should, tearing tissue in the ankle. Father Nathan was on him in a flash, raining blows down on the helpless man's face.

The first blow shattered the nose, crushing the bone and tearing the cartilage. Blood exploded from the damaged nose, covering the Boss Man's mouth and shirt. A second blow knocked out all of the scum's front teeth, sending broken teeth flying like bits of broken glass. Blows rained down, splitting the Boss Man's cheeks open as Father Nathan's right fist fell like a hammer.

I'd seen fury like that before. Holstering my pistol, I dove into the side of my friend, driving him off the unconscious and helpless criminal. I put Father Nathan in a restraining hold that he promptly reversed, springing to his feet, landing in a fighting stance, his right hand at the ready while he struggled to lift his left arm.

Panting, he cried out, "Why did you stop me?"

"You were going to beat him to death!"

"Some people just need killing," he snarled back. His words shocked me.

"Not by you, they don't," I snapped back in anger, the

cop in me getting angry.

"Are you going to arrest me," he challenged.

I paused to think about it. One dead criminal, probably a hit man, and a small time crime boss who ran a gang of pickpockets, probably trafficked in young girls and prostitution, who was going to do a very long stint in prison. Throw in the fact the guy was going to kill Father Nathan, and I could make a good case for self-defense.

Josephson looked like he was about to puke. To his credit, despite the fact the gun was wobbling due to his shaking so badly, he had it trained on the two wannabe thugs who'd brought Father Nathan to the Boss Man's lair.

"It was self-defense," I said firmly, looking directly at the pair. "Do you two understand? Because if you don't, you're going down for kidnapping the Father. In case you didn't know, that is an Interplanetary offense. You'll do your time on a prison asteroid."

The taller of the two was clearly the smarter. He elbowed the short one and nodded. "It was self-defense, no doubt about it. The Father had no choice. Yeah, self-defense, I'll swear to it in court."

Feeling the need to get his two credits worth in, the smaller thug chimed in, "Yeah, self-defense."

Father Nathan walked off to a corner and leaned over, his hands on his knees. I left him alone.

"Sergeant, call a meat wagon for the dead perp. Have them send a bus for this one," I said, pointing down at the bleeding Boss Man. He took a sudden gasp, swallowing blood and spittle in the process. His eyes fixed on the ceiling. And then he was gone, his last breath rattling as his body expelled it.

"Josephson, never mind. Just get a meat wagon."

"What do you want to do with these two?"

"Take their statements and get a known address. Then cut them loose."

He motioned for the two to follow him. I stood alone, looking at the bloody mess that just minutes ago had been a small time hood. I looked at the Father in the corner. His body was shaking violently.

He was coming down off the adrenaline rush of combat. It was evident to me the good Father had been a highly trained soldier in his life before the priesthood.

CHAPTER TWENTY

Watching from his vantage point, the mercenary leader adjusted his binoculars for a better view as the train slowed its pace slightly for the large curve it was approaching. It would pass a short stub siding used to set out Maintenance of Way cars. One of his men was hiding in the snow by the siding, ready to throw the switch points when the train passed.

As the lead locomotive eased into the curve, he turned his gaze to the rear of the train. The first of the three container flats coupled onto the last passenger coach suddenly separated. He could hear the squeal of steel wheels going through a curve. Nobody would hear the sound of the hand brakes being applied on the three container flats.

The last passenger coach passed over the switch, clearing the siding. His man emerged from his hiding place and threw the switch. Still rolling at a good speed, the three container flats rolled onto the siding as the two mercenaries who'd hidden on the cars frantically tried to stop the cars with just handbrakes. As the three flats rolled by, the mercenary manning the switch set it back for the main line and put the company lock back on the switch stand, locking it.

Slowing rapidly, the three container flats and their cargoes simply had too much inertia for just the handbrakes to bleed the speed off and bring the cars to a stop. To make matters worse, the cars hit a patch of ice on the rails, in effect negating the braking action. The huge snowdrift at the end of the short siding brought the runaway cars to a complete stop.

Pressing the send button on his encrypted comm, the leader held it up to his mouth. "Snow Rabbit calling Little Bird. Snow Rabbit calling Little Bird."

"Copy Snow Rabbit. This is Little Bird."

"Come and get the Worm."

"Roger, Wilco."

In less than two minutes the converted military landing craft, now configured to appear as if it was for simple civilian use, hovered over the three stationary container flats. The craft's bottom doors opened, revealing its large cargo bay. It's internally mounted crane lowered down cables to the waiting mercenaries on the ground. In less than sixty seconds the first of the three flats and its container had vanished into the gaping maw of the converted military craft.

Another two minutes passed before the stolen railcars had vanished along with the mercenaries into the hovercraft. It would only take half an hour, and the wind would cover any sign of the theft with a thin layer of snow and ice.

◆◆◆

Josephson had finished taking the two wannabee's statements and let them go. Happy to not be headed for the clink, they'd vanished quickly. Sarah and Ralph were waiting outside, and I was glad for it.

They didn't need to see the bloody mess inside. It was one thing for me to put down a career criminal. I didn't want them to see the good Father's handiwork.

Joe had wandered in and was standing by the Boss Man's lifeless body, lost in thought. He motioned for me to come over without looking up from the blood mess lying on the floor.

"Yeah, Joe?"

"Inspector, I recognize this man. Don't ask me how okay?"

He looked up at me, his eyes pleading with me to not violate his trust. Joe knew things. Things an honest businessman shouldn't. Sometimes he shared what he knew with me. This was going to be one of those times.

I nodded that I understood.

"He's a bent detective. Too corrupt even for the cops here, no offense."

"None taken. What was his name?"

"Detective Winston Vitter. Worked out of your precinct."

I understood why Joe needed me to be discreet. The Boss Man may have worked for Captain Markeson.

I would have to be careful how I handled this.

Thinking about the various ramifications of this bit of information, I let out a low whistle.

"Yeah," Joe said, nodding in agreement.

◆◆◆

Markeson logged out of the bank account. The transfer of funds complete. Governor Ranking and Mayor Xue had handled their respective ends of the process quickly and efficiently. Like nothing had ever changed.

He noted the exact amounts of the "expenses" involved for the bill he would present to the Colonel. Markeson looked forward to the meeting when he did so. It promised to be a revealing moment. One he needed to handle with great finesse.

Pulling his comm from his pocket, he called up the number he'd been told to use when finished with his portion of the job. Markeson sent a link and waited.

"Yes," the deep male voice of the man Markeson had learned through his sources was known in Brownstown as "the Sergeant."

"Everything is done on our end. I'm going to transmit the codes you'll need when we're done here."

"Very good," the Sergeant replied stiffly. "Have you arranged for appropriate transport out of the system?"

"I have several possibilities waiting. Until I know the final destination, I cannot finalize that aspect of our consultation."

"How soon do you need to know?"

"No later than thirty-six hours. The first of the space freighters will be departing then. This is just a small part of their complete cargo, so they won't wait."

Irritated, the Sergeant snapped at Markeson through the comm link. "You couldn't arrange for a dedicated vessel to move the product?"

Markeson growled right back. "It's a good thing you hired me as a consultant. That sort of thing draws attention. Better to have your containers mixed in as one of many smaller shipments for transport to another world. More paperwork to confuse things if necessary and it provides plausible deniability for the smuggler."

"You should have explained this up front," the Sergeant said firmly.

"Why? Then we don't get paid. You pay us for what we know and who we know."

"I see your point."

Markeson shook his head in disbelief. It was possible he was dealing with incompetent idiots. He would have to tread even more carefully if that was the case.

"I need to know the destination and when the cargo will be ready for uplift to the space port. Once you provide me with that information, I'll tell you which ship and docking bay."

"You did not include this in the information provided," the now irritated, deep voice said.

Markeson rolled his eyes and glared at his comm before

answering. "You have the information you need to clear Security and Customs. That's all you get until I get paid. I have expenses, obviously. You pay me and tell me the next bit of information, and we move on to the next phase."

"Must this be so complicated?"

"Yes," Markeson sighed. "It must. It provides verifiable accountability for both parties. Trust is always an issue in matters of this nature. Doing it this way addresses the trust issue. Things go wrong. Doing things piecemeal allows both parties to walk away with plausible deniability. The only loss is the cargo, which can be replaced in most instances, and the money invested. I shouldn't have to point out that smuggling carries heavy prison sentences. Certain items carry even harsher prison sentences."

"Forgive my ignorance," the Sergeant replied. "My skill set is of a very different nature. As you have pointed out, we are paying you for your knowledge and who you know."

"I'm glad you understand that," Markeson answered through clenched teeth.

"I will pass on the information. Message me the exact amount we owe for this stage of the contract. Include valid expenses. I will see to it you are compensated no later than 1700 hours today."

The link went dead, causing Markeson to stare at his comm in anger. He decided the Colonel's right-hand man was going to vanish as well if he eliminated the red headed siren.

◆◆◆

Moving past the checkpoint, Kilgore pulled his collar tighter and hunched his shoulders in a vain effort to reduce the amount of his body exposed to the wet, cold wind.

Despite his posture, Kilgore marched with purpose as he made his way around the perimeter of the mysterious research facility. As the commander of the Space Marine detachment, it was his prerogative to inspect the Shore Patrol as they stood their duty posts.

As discretely as possible, he glanced at the facility. From the outside, it appeared to be a large, nondescript building. Typical of most buildings found on military bases, it was square, had little architectural detail and was painted a bland uniform off white. The building had one entrance, but no guards were posted. Kilgore had no doubt the entrance was under constant electronic surveillance, had guards inside and required multiple clearances, biometric scans, and knowledge of the entry code. In the entire time, he'd been posted at the Brownstown facility he'd never seen anyone enter or leave the facility.

"It's because the real entrance is underground," he whispered aloud. Kilgore finished his circuit of the building and made his way toward the base administration building. It was possible the information he needed could be uncovered there.

◆◆◆

"He's growing suspicious," the Sergeant stated a second time.

"I heard you, but there is nothing we can truly do about it," the Colonel snapped back.

"Have you heard from the others off-world?"

"Yes. Our plan has been approved."

"Good. I don't like dealing with this Markeson. Once we have the necessary contacts, he must be eliminated. The only reason I haven't terminated him now is he believes we are incompetent."

"Now, now," the red head answered. "You're feelings

are just hurt because I needed to have a little fun. You know you're my Sergeant," she purred soothingly, massaging the man's wounded ego. "Until we've finished our missions, I can't mix my pleasure with business. You know how important you are to what we're trying to accomplish."

Silence filled the link.

"Yes, Colonel. Of course. But I insist this Markeson be terminated upon completion of the mission. He must not be allowed to compromise you."

It was subtle, but it was there, and the red head heard it. The only underling she trusted was angry with her. Angry because it was not him she shared her bed with, which was a shame. He was so good at his job, and loyalty like his could not be purchased. Nor could his skilled, ruthless approach to his job. Her Sergeant was totally devoted to her, more so even than the cause.

"When this is all over. When we have finished our last mission, things will be different. The business will complete, and it will be time for pleasure. Pleasure that should be shared together." She listened to see if the promise of what he desired most would mollify him.

"Yes, Colonel. As you say, things will be better when all of this is over."

"Don't forget that Sergeant," she told him. "Things will be better."

The link broke. Brushing a lock of her fiery red hair out of her face, the Colonel considered the man's tone in his last words. He seemed to have believed her. She shrugged. It wouldn't matter really. She'd kill him too if it were necessary.

◆◆◆

For once it didn't bother me that Josephson's driving skills were substandard. Every time he took a turn too fast,

Father Nathan would groan in pain. We made it to St. Christus hospital without the good Father dying on us. In the process, we passed two other hospitals, but the stubborn man insisted on going to St. Christus.

His wound wasn't life threatening but required treatment. As mad as I was at him I was okay with the idea of him being in pain.

"So when did you plan on telling me that in a past life you were a soldier?"

"None of anyone's business," he replied. "That was a long time ago." The Father shot me a look telling me that was all he was going to say about the matter. It was okay. Cops have ways of finding out what we want to know.

"You happy now?"

"Yes, I'm happy that my kids will be free of that man's horrible influence. Am I happy that I beat a man to death with my bare hands? Hardly."

I couldn't resist the urge to needle the good Father like he needled me at times.

"You said he needed killing," I reminded him.

"I was wrong to have said that. Wrong to have even thought it," he sighed. "Thinking that is the same as killing the person the thought is about."

"No, it's not. That makes no sense. It's one thing to think it. It's another to do it."

He shook his head. "Murder in the heart is the exact same sin as actually killing the person."

"I don't understand you." I was getting tired of his constant word games. "I saw the look in your eyes when you talked about this man. You had no problem with him winding up dead."

"You're right Inspector. And I'm telling you, it was wrong of me to have thought that, to have felt the hate that led me to do what I did."

"But your kids are safer now."

"They would have been just as safe if he was sitting in your jail."

"What makes you believe just thinking you wanted to kill the guy is a sin?"

Father Nathan just looked at me with that look he'd give me.

"I see. It's something Jesus said in your Bible."

He proceeded to ignore me. I wasn't having any of it.

"It doesn't seem to bother you that I killed a man to-day."

"It was in self-defense. You were protecting not only yourself but young Josephson as well, possibly myself. I beat a defenseless man to death. There is a big difference."

"I saw you afterward. You had the shakes like you get after combat. I've had 'em myself and seen lots of soldiers get 'em."

Father Nathan looked at his right hand. I noticed slight tremors still.

"I get them every time."

"So you admit it. You were a soldier."

He looked up at me, his expression somber and con-trite. "I was. Then I dishonored my military service. I became a mercenary."

I let it go. That one fact explained why Father Nathan never talked about his past. Probably explained why he tried to help people, especially kids.

"You talk all the time about guilt Inspector. About peo-ple being worthless. You've seen and done things that would make any sane person feel that way. But I've done far worse."

I started to feel uncomfortable. "I'm not judging you, Father."

"Didn't say you were. But you judge yourself. I judge myself. It's a horrible trap, Inspector. Neither of us can forgive ourselves for what we've done, maybe for what we haven't done. But man is redeemable Inspector. We just can't redeem ourselves."

"Maybe it's because we're unredeemable? Have you considered that Father?"

"Of course it's because man is unredeemable," he laughed, irony filling his laughter.

"It's not funny," I snapped. "I don't much like having friends. Friends get killed, sometimes it's your fault, and some times it's not. Friends can betray your trust, cause you pain."

He just looked at me, looked through me with an expression I couldn't read.

"I came to this planet with enough guilt and pain to last ten men a lifetime. I also came without friends. I was fine with that. I was sent here to do a job, and I do it. But despite what I want, I find myself with friends. Do you understand me," I shouted.

Father Nathan flinched at my shout.

"Yes, I do. I caused you to put your friends at risk in your mind. Even worse, I put them at risk."

"So, you can understand why I'm so mad at you," I said with a sarcastic smile etched on my face.

"Absolutely, but know this Inspector, life has risk. It is filled with pain. God doesn't promise to spare us pain. Pain shapes us. So you have a choice, my friend. You can feel the pain of broken trust and lost friendship because you first trusted another enough to be their friend. Or you can feel the pain and misery of bitter loneliness because you chose not to have a friend. I prefer to take a chance and have friends, friends I place my trust in. I have lived with the other choice, and I won't live that way again."

Silence filled the squad car. I realized Josephson had parked the hovercar at the hospital emergency entrance and was sitting in silence, listening to the Father and I bicker.

The door opened, and hands reached in to pull Father

Nathan out. In seconds he was gone, rushed inside to be cared for. Somebody shut the door. I didn't know what to think or even say.

"Inspector, let me take you home. I can take care of the paperwork. Why don't you get some rest, okay?"

I know I didn't answer the pup, but he took me home anyhow. I woke up on my couch. I wasn't drunk or hung over, but I had no recall of how I got there.

CHAPTER TWENTY-ONE

I finished my breakfast at Joe's and left. Father Nathan had done fine in surgery and was in a private room. Everyone had gone to see him, and I was fine with that. Gave me a chance to eat alone and not answer questions or be guilted about anything. Like the huge argument, the good Father and I had in front of Josephson.

My first stop was to drag Bones out of his apartment fortress. I needed autopsies done on the two dead stiffs in his morgue, courtesy of Father Nathan and myself. I wanted to put the entire episode behind me and move on.

Internal Affairs could wait on their investigation. I wasn't handing over my .50 cal until I finished up the mystery of who put my dead SP on ice. I wasn't worried about putting those buzzards off. The last time IA tangled with me, several of them found themselves transferred to remote mining or farming villages far from Capital City.

Once I got Bones to work, I planned to spend most of the day going through the shipping manifests and seeing if any of the other detectives had snitches on the space station where starliners and space freighters docked. Passengers or cargo would then be brought down by barge or shuttle to the Capital City spaceport.

I promised myself I would go to see Father Nathan before my evening meal. The longer I put it off, the harder it would be. Just better to do it and be done with it, our friendship would survive or it wouldn't.

◆ ◆ ◆

"Everything is actually as it should be," the deep voice said from inside the last container. Stepping out from inside the container was the dark headed man who had hired the mercenaries. The leader of the mercs knew the man was simply an intermediary for their real employer.

"You sound surprised," was the Captain's gruff response.

"Perhaps I am being a bit judgmental," the Sergeant replied in his arrogant tone, the condescension unhidden in his attitude. "The accident you arranged was amateurish. So please forgive me if I am pleasantly surprised the cargo is all in acceptable condition, delivered on time, and has been properly maintained."

Tired of his employer's elitist arrogance, the Captain deliberately abandoned his respectful attitude, adopting an ominous tone to his speech. "We aren't murderers for hire," the Captain informed the man.

"You're paid killers," was the Sergeant's sneering response.

"Sure, we're killers. We kill people in combat. You want a heist pulled that requires gunplay. We can do that. But we're not hitmen. You want a hit done, talk to a local crime lord in the future."

Noticing the other mercenaries in the unit had all moved over by the six containers and were observing the conversation with great interest, the Sergeant made the wise decision to be gracious. As the Captain said, they were killers, and he was alone.

"Point taken Captain. Accept my apology. For what it is worth, I told my superior the same thing. Combat troops do not have the skill set for that sort of wet work."

The Captain laughed in disbelief. "What makes you think I believe that?"

"I see." First raising his hands so his palms faced out, the Sergeant next slowly removed his thick outer coat and set it on the warehouse floor, followed by his immaculately tailored suit coat. He removed a platinum cufflink and slipped it into his pocket. Slowly he rolled up the sleeve of his shirt, revealing a tattoo on his left forearm.

He expected a different reaction from the mercenary's leader. More respect.

"So you served in the Army's Special Forces black ops. We're all Marine shock troops, the best of the best. You want to force a landing on a heavily defended planet? You send us."

"If that were the case, why are you and your men all mercenaries now?"

The Captain and all of his men took one menacing step forward in unison. "Because some politician back on Earth made the case the Space Marines had grown too large. Typical lefty who wants to curry votes by cutting defense spending. So we all got riffed. What's your story?"

"My commanding officer left the service. Like you, I found myself with a particular skill set and with the Expansion Wars long over the Army felt I was redundant. My C.O. offered me employment, and so here I am."

Taking another look at the tattoo of a dagger piercing a sniper's scope at a right angle in red and black ink, the former Marine took a step back.

"Look, neither of us is doing what we were trained to do. Just be respectful to my men and me, and I'll see to it the same respect is shown to you. Call it professional courtesy."

"Agreed. I apologize. And know this, I will see to it in the future that any wet work is not assigned to you and your men."

The Sergeant slowly dressed. The Captain escorted him to the exit of the warehouse where he paused, extending an open hand. The two soldiers shook, each testing the other's resolve.

"I promise I will make sure my superior is aware you

have fulfilled the original obligations of your contract in an exemplary manner, as would be expected of Marines."

Upon exiting, the Sergeant walked slowly and deliberately, not giving the sniper on the roof of the warehouse any reason to take the shot.

He had meant what he'd told the Captain. He was impressed by the work they had done, showing initiative and discipline. If the situation in the near future required it, he had the funds in his personal account to hire them for one very specific job. One that would be well suited to their skill set.

◆ ◆ ◆

I sat in Bones office. His computer network could use a bit of updating. Data searches without warrants are tedious affairs to begin with. A slower than normal network makes the job seem like having my teeth filed.

Without warning Bones entered, closed the door behind him and locked it. He didn't say a word; he just vanished into his storage closet and shut the door behind him. Seconds later he emerged with a state of the art sweeper to check for electronic surveillance. Three passes around the room later, Bones seemed satisfied we could talk.

"Are you trying to get me killed," he hissed in a low voice.

"Not at all. I just have to clear this up so I can move ahead on the, ah, other matter without having Internal Affairs giving me grief."

"Well, you have a funny way of demonstrating your concern for me," the paranoid coroner shouted in a whisper, which is not an easy thing to do.

I considered his paranoid response for a moment.

"Which one of them?"

"One of 'em I can handle. Your source was right. The DNA matched right up with what we had on file in employment records. It's Winston Vitter. Bent Detective who got careless. You have to act at least like you're not on the take. Five years ago he was cashiered and sent to the medium security facility on Persephone for six months."

"The other one?"

"Related to your friend."

"My SP friend?"

"No. The pretty one."

I grabbed the sweeping device and did a fourth sweep of the room as my paranoia raged. I was as spooked as Bones was now.

"She called him a watcher. None of us ever spotted him unless she was with us and pointed him out."

"Hide in plain sight."

I hated to ask Bones to do what I was about to ask. Not because we would both be guilty of tampering with evidence, but because it wasn't fair to the deceased.

"Have you got a John Doe you haven't autopsied yet?"

"Way ahead of you Inspector. This little talk never happened."

"I may need a real report in the future."

"Just give me enough advance warning, and I will produce it and the actual evidence. But promise me this Inspector, don't ask for it unless you can actually put somebody away."

"Don't worry, Bones," I promised. "I'm not going to let anyone hurt my pretty friend. I'll take this to my grave if I have to."

◆ ◆ ◆

"I was quite pleased," the Sergeant reported. "Our packages are in immaculate condition. The labor force changed the procurement method, showing initiative. In doing so, they left absolutely no traces of their work and no witnesses."

"That's a different song you're singing now," the red head groused, rubbing her aching temples. The painkillers weren't working fast enough to relieve the relentless pounding of her stress headache.

"I told you," the Sergeant snapped, letting his irritation show, "specificity of labor is required. Our labor force has excellent skills for the original task we contracted them for. Work of a wet nature should be left to me."

"Fine," the red head snapped, not noticing the change in her Sergeant's attitude toward her. "If we have need of such skilled labor in the future, you will be assigned the task."

He nodded, only slightly mollified his Colonel had accepted his appraisal of the mercenary's performance and his demand she allow him to handle the special, solo tasks their mission might require in the future. Like making a certain Chief of Detectives vanish from existence.

◆ ◆ ◆

Chief O'Brian looked as surprised to see me walk into his office as I was to be there. I shut the door quietly, pulled out my own sweeping device and checked his office. He didn't object.

"So, Inspector, may I ask why I have the pleasure of a visit from you today?"

I didn't say a word. I reached into my greatcoat and pulled out a tablet and laid it on his desk. He picked it up, pressed his thumb on the biometric scanner and began reading. I let him.

Three minutes later he laid the tablet down and rubbed the bridge of his nose.

"Winston Vitter. That's a name I had hoped never to

hear again."

"Tell me what's not in that file Chief."

"Why do you need to know Inspector?"

"I can't go into it right now, but this Vitter was running a gang of pickpockets in the neighborhoods around where I live."

"Go on."

"He had in his employ an individual who may, or may not, be involved in the murder case the military requested me to take on. That's all I can tell you."

"The murder in Brownstown. Dead SP."

I nodded.

"Sensitive matter. What do you need to know? I'll tell you what I can."

"I don't believe in coincidences, Chief."

"Of course not. They don't exist. Every decent cop knows that."

"So tell me Chief, who was Vitter close too? There is no record of a partner. I've picked up he got careless, and that's how he got busted."

I watched Chief O'Brian rub the bridge of his nose again. He didn't want to relive this, but I had no choice. I had to know if what I suspected was true.

"It was right after my wife left me for another man. Took the kids and filed for divorce."

I didn't say anything. What can you say to that?

"Sully, all I have left is my job." He looked at the pictures on his Wall of Fame. "I haven't done my job the past years like I need to and that's part of why you're here. To clean up a mess, I should have handled."

He paused to collect himself.

"The Vitter case almost got me relieved of my duties as Chief of Police for Beta Prime. Markeson stepped in and, how shall I say it, handled some of the backroom political deals I am terrible at. I was a good cop, Sully, a good administrator too. I got sent here to clean things up. Made a good start, but then my wife left me. I just lost it for awhile, and all the ground I'd gained was lost and then some."

I had to get him back on track. "Vitter, sir, if you don't mind."

Still staring at the images in his Wall of Fame, he spoke softly. "Vitter was Markeson's partner before he was promoted by my predecessor to Captain and made Chief of Detectives. Do I really need to say more?"

It was pretty obvious. Markeson made the Vitter situation go away, saving O'Brian's job. O'Brian looked the other way afterward, giving Markeson a pass to do whatever he wanted so long as it was discrete. Markeson got Vitter to keep his mouth shut and do the time. Six months in any jail was a long time for a cop. Markeson had to have promised Vitter something for when he got out.

Police corruption usually meant five to seven if the cop was lucky. A six-month hitch in a medium security facility close to his home planet was more than Vitter could have expected. A sentence that sweet meant politicians had to be involved. Politicians Markeson either had in his pocket or was in bed with.

I thought back to my hearing. Just to make sure, I pulled up the video of the hearing right before it started. My memory was correct. Governor Rankin and Mayor Xue had both attended. I was starting to see the bigger picture.

I picked up the tablet and turned to leave.

"Inspector, a moment, please?"

I turned and looked back at the Chief.

"I want my dignity back. The only way I can get it back is to do my job the way I should have done it the last five years. I plan to do that. Please, I ask you to be patient with me and to believe me when I tell you I was a good cop."

I didn't say anything. This sort of thing makes me uncomfortable.

"I need to find a way to make amends. I can't live with myself otherwise."

I hated even to think it, but the Chief would probably benefit from a talk with the good Father.

CHAPTER TWENTY-TWO

I wasn't expecting a visitor. I certainly wasn't expecting a visit from a man I wasn't fond of. So when the Desk Sergeant paged me, I was curious what would bring Kilgore to Capital City. He could have just sent me a comlink.

We didn't speak in the lobby. I showed him to an interrogation room and made sure all the recording equipment was turned off. I sat down across the table from the Major.

"Why are you here?"

"This couldn't be done any way other than face-to-face."

I nodded I understood.

"I think the source of the clone is the research facility on my base."

I didn't say anything while I thought about this.

"Are you sure," I finally asked. "What led you to this conclusion?"

"In all the time I've been stationed there, I've never seen anybody enter or leave the facility."

"That doesn't mean their cloning humans."

"It doesn't rule it out either," he said adamantly. "The entrance has to be underground. That would allow people to come and go as they please. They could get the clones out that way too."

"Makes good sense," I told him. "But any entrance, underground or not, would have to be carefully controlled so nobody gets wise to what's going on."

Kilgore nodded in agreement. "Let me rephrase this then. There are multiple approaches to the entrance. I pulled up all the plans for the base since it was built two decades ago. Lots of modifications and some of them are classified. But when you sit down and start piecing everything together, there have to be three tunnels to the entrance. Sully, there's even a secondary tunnel that leads to our freight house where the rail spur is serviced."

I nodded again. Then I sprang a surprise on the Major.

"One of the clones is lying in our morgue. You can't tell anyone."

"How do you know," Kilgore asked, the concern growing on his face by the second.

"I blew it away myself. It was drawing down on me so I didn't have any other choice."

"So you shot a guy Sullivan, that doesn't answer my question."

"Two ways. Remember Sarah?" He nodded. "Let's just say in the course of a police matter our surveillance never uncovered this guy until Sarah spotted him. He had the same ability she does to hide in plain sight, just vanish in a crowd."

The Major shrugged. "You know as well as I do most Marines and Army Special Forces are trained to develop that skill."

"I understand. But think about it. What if some of these clones, like the dead guy and Sarah, were genetically engineered to have this ability? How much more effective would they be?"

"Why would this guy be loose in society?"

"No idea. Maybe there was something wrong with him, or he just went off the grid on his own accord. Sarah certainly has ideas about not being property."

"Still doesn't mean he's a clone."

"My coroner says he's a clone."

Kilgore sat in silence, thinking. I let him.

"This is above my pay grade," he finally said. "The problem is, if I kick it upstairs, I might be kicking it right

52

to the person running the illegal program."

"Raid the place. Act like you didn't suspect cloning. Say you had evidence black marketers were getting into the facility; selling off secrets or technology they stole. Beg for forgiveness later."

He sighed. This was weighing heavily on the man.

"That's what I thought, but Sullivan, you know as well as I do, people get killed in raids."

I didn't feel too sorry for him, considering our past.

"That's why the Corps pays you the big credits."

"It's also why you get paid big credits," he responded, reaching into his pocket. Kilgore pulled out two military comms and sat them on the table.

"Secure, one channel only, encrypted burst transmissions. Nobody can intercept anything between these two comms."

He pushed one across the table to me.

"The raid is going down at 2100 hours. Bring Sarah. I need someone who can spot clones visually. Don't worry. We won't bring her in until the facility is secure."

I pocketed the comm. "I can't promise Sarah will be there. She's pretty spooked, and given what I know of her past, I can't blame her. I'm not going to force her to go on the raid. I'll ask, but that's all."

"Fair enough. I'll have one of my Marines meet you at the building where the dead SP was found."

Kilgore stood up, indicating the meeting was over. I stood and opened the door for him. He didn't say a word, just walked out and left the building.

I had a lot to do today if I was going to make it to the rendezvous on time.

◆ ◆ ◆

Markeson let himself in O'Brian's office and took a seat. "You wanted to see me Chief?"

O'Brian placed his tablet down and rubbed the bridge of his nose again, the headache that had started earlier in the day was still pounding away.

"I have some news for you. Figured you'd rather hear it from me than through the rumor mill."

Markeson tilted his head in concern. Something was up.

"There's no good way to put this so I'll just tell you. In a police matter, your ex-partner was killed. Vitter's body is in the morgue."

O'Brian watched Markeson's face carefully for any tell. The Chief of Detectives handled the surprise news well. The only reaction his countenance betrayed was a hint of sadness and disappointment.

"I'm sorry to hear that, but I haven't seen Vitter since he got sent away. It's not wise to be seen with ex-cons who are cops."

"Still, he was your partner. Evidently, Vitter didn't learn his lesson. His is not the only body in the morgue. We believe the other stiff is a hit man in Vitter's employ."

Markeson nodded. "Who was the officer who put him down?"

"Sullivan."

◆◆◆

I had to find Sarah. For a bunch of reasons, I thought she had a right to know about the raid. So I headed for St. Christus Hospital. I figured she was comfortable enough now to sit with the Father for a spell and might be there. So I decided to kill two birds with one stone.

I took my leave of the precinct, letting Josephson know where I was going. I also told him we would be leaving for Brownstown again right after dinner. The evil in me prevented me from telling the pup we were flying. I didn't want to give him a chance to bail on me.

Ralph picked me up in his cab and hustled me over to the hospital. I told him to leave the meter running, I'd be back quick.

Just like I thought, I found Sarah with Father Nathan. Her nervous pacing when I entered the room told me Sarah was about at the end of her rope. She could only be confined for so long, even when it was her choice.

"Sarah, we have work to do. Are you up to leaving with me?"

She nodded, relieved to have a reason to cut the visit short.

"Father, how are you feeling?"

"I've felt better," he grumbled. "Physically and spiritually."

"Sorry to cut and run, but something has come up. Turns out the dead perps might have something to do with my dead SP. That's all I can tell you."

Father Nathan brightened at the news. "I told you the Boss Man was no good."

I smiled. Despite our disagreement, it made me feel better to see the good Father still had some spunk left.

"Yeah, maybe more than you realized."

I extended my hand to him. "Are we going to be okay Father?"

He nearly crushed my hand. "Of course we are, in time. I can forgive most things."

"I'm glad," I told him and slipped my hand out of the vise.

Sarah was standing at the door, ready to escape. She gave Father Nathan a quick smile and slipped out.

I stopped at the door and looked back. My friend gave me a hard look. "We're going to talk later. Take care of yourself and keep an eye on Sarah."

I just nodded and followed Sarah, letting the door shut behind me.

◆ ◆ ◆

Sitting in his office, Markeson didn't notice the buzzing of his comm until it stopped. He picked it up and looked at the number and tossed it back on his desk. Nothing important.

Sullivan was getting to be a real problem. His share of the take from the operation Vitter ran was not huge, but as far as Markeson was concerned, every credit counted. Despite his well-deserved reputation as a lady's man who liked to have a good time, Markeson had plans for the future.

Those plans required large amounts of capital. To make sure that capital was available to him with no strings attached, the detective had long ago set up hidden accounts where the income from various enterprises as he liked to call them was deposited and never touched.

Vitter's operation was one of those streams of income.

Unable to do anything about the situation, Markeson decided the current scheme with the Colonel was now paramount. He trusted her about as far as he could throw her and he trusted her henchman even less.

"Time to dust off your investigative skills Markeson," he told himself. "Find out where the money's coming from, where the product is coming from and become the sole supplier."

In the process, perhaps he could find a way to rid himself of Sullivan.

He picked his comm back up and sent a link. A leer spread across his face at the sound of the familiar voice on the other end. "We need to meet. Now. I'll come to you."

◆ ◆ ◆

Without warning the door to his office opened causing Bones to jump in his chair.

"Sorry, didn't mean to surprise you," Chief O'Brian told the nervous coroner.

"It's okay, Chief. Sometimes it gets a little creepy down here, that's all."

"I suppose it would at that," O'Brian said, looking around the office.

"Anything you can tell me about the two dead perps Sullivan brought in?"

"Uh, yeah, Chief. I haven't finished the final reports yet, but I can tell you this much. Cause of death for Vitter, the ex-cop, was repeated blows to the head. The other dead perp, gunshot wound to the head. No ID on him. Ran the DNA and didn't get anything. I'm thinking he's from off-planet, new gun for hire."

"What's Sullivan thinking?"

"Same thing. I believe Sullivan thinks Vitter was looking into moving teenage girls in the sex trafficking trade. You'd need some hired muscle to move into that racket."

"Makes sense," the Chief replied, nodding in agreement.

"Anything else?"

"Yeah, when you see Sullivan next, tell him I want to be kept up to date on this one."

O'Brian left and shut the door behind him, leaving Bones to try and stop his hands from shaking.

"Sullivan, you owe me," he whispered to himself. "You really owe me."

◆ ◆ ◆

O'Brian walked to the elevator pressed the button and waited. The doors opened, and he stepped in, touching the number for his floor. In seconds the elevator was speeding him on his way.

He stopped for coffee on his way back to his office, watching the police officers that worked under his supervision going about their jobs. Most of them that is, some were slacking off, just waiting until the end of their shift to leave.

Determined to change things, O'Brian entered his office and sat down, taking a sip from the hot, bitter liquid. He looked over at his Wall of Fame and stared at the photo of Governor Rankin swearing him in as Chief of Police of Beta Prime.

"What game are you playing Sullivan," he said softly. "What game are you playing?"

◆◆◆

Sarah nudged me, breaking my concentration. I looked up from the tablet with all the scheduled arrivals and departures at Beta Prime's space station. Josephson had done a good job assembling all the data in such short time.

"I'm not apologizing for making him fly with us," I told her for the fifth or sixth time. "Josephson has to get over this fear of his if he wants to make Inspector."

She frowned in response and cut her eyes towards of the concourse. I took a quick glance and saw what had gotten her attention. Sarah stood up and hurried off in the direction of the little girl's room. I can't say that I blame her.

"Inspector Sullivan," Markeson declared. "Heading back to the scene of the crime?"

"Yes, need to follow up on some things."

"Taking your team with you?"

I nodded. "You going to Brownstown as well?"

He laughed in response, running his hand through his hair, making sure every strand was in its place.

"Don't worry, I'm not going to be looking over your

shoulder. It's a routine administrative visit. I do have to make those from time-to-time."

Josephson stumbled over, looking pale as a ghost, and saved me from what could have been an awkward situation. He sat down and gave me the evil eye. Markeson laughed at the young detective.

"Don't like flying, Sergeant Josephson?"

"No, Captain."

"He doesn't know," I spit out, annoyed by the entire situation. "He's never flown before."

"Take some air sickness meds. They help until you get used to it," Markeson offered as advice.

"Yes, sir. I have already," the pup replied, his answer lacking any hint of confidence the meds would indeed be of any help.

The terminal's AI announced it was time for the hovercraft to depart for Brownstown. We all stood. Josephson and I gathered the few things we were bringing, and Sarah returned from her trip to the restroom. She didn't speak but did slip behind me, placing me between her and the Captain.

I could sense the anxiety coming off her in waves. Sarah had an instinctive ability to read most people. Markeson's presence on our flight was troubling her and probably for reasons I couldn't understand.

The fact he was making a routine inspection trip bothered me. With a raid looming in hours, it was odd timing on his part.

And I don't believe in coincidences.

CHAPTER TWENTY-THREE

Kilgore checked his chronometer. Sullivan's flight should have landed. He stood up and peered out the window in his office. It was a bleak day. The irony of it made him laugh a humorless laugh.

The last time he'd been in command of a potentially dangerous action, he'd made a mistake. He hadn't listened to his sergeant. That mistake had cost nine men their lives and seriously injured the best sergeant he'd ever served with. The blast ended the sergeant's career in the Space Marines and nearly ended his own.

Today could go just as badly.

To make matters worse, the same sergeant would be involved in the raid. Kilgore questioned his motivation to take such a risk. Men could die. His men. The Interplanetary Alliance wasn't at war. He didn't have to take the risk.

The Major wondered if his motivation was to remove the black mark on his career. To remove the shadow that had hung over him for so many years. Or was he doing the right thing for the right reasons? As much as Kilgore believed he had no choice, part of him wondered if his decision was motivated to try somehow to make amends for that horrible day.

Looking out the window at the dreary landscape, Kilgore replayed the argument with his sergeant again. Orders were orders he'd insisted, and the battalion commander wanted the checkpoint set up by the town square, close to the market.

Sergeant Thomas Sullivan had argued with him, pointing out suspected insurgents had been spotted in that part of town. Setting up the blockades exactly as ordered would allow a suicide bomber to take out the blockades and kill civilians in the busy market.

Sullivan wanted to back the checkpoints away from the entrance to the town square, creating a buffer zone between the blockades and the market. It also created a kill zone to take out any insurgents who attacked.

Still a wet-behind-the-ears Second Lieutenant, Kilgore's pride and arrogance had gotten the better of him. To prove who was the boss, he'd refused to move the checkpoint. Sullivan had argued the Colonel who'd given the order would agree with the changes. The commander on the scene always had the latitude to adjust orders to conditions in the field.

Less than twenty-four hours later a suicide bomber drove a hover car into the blockades and detonated it. Nine of Kilgore's Shore Patrol officers died in the blast or succumbed to their wounds. Eighty-nine civilians died as a result of the bomb. Sullivan lost his left hand, right eye and his career in the Space Marines.

If it had not been for his parents, Kilgore would have been drummed out of the Space Marines. As it was, there had been many a day where he believed that should have been the outcome. He should be a civilian and Sullivan should still be in the Shore Patrol.

When assigned to the base on Beta Prime, Kilgore had vowed if he had a chance, he would make amends with Sullivan. He couldn't change what had happened, but maybe he could make up for his mistake. Prove to Sullivan he'd learned the humility a good officer needs. Prove the deaths of the men who died that day had not been completely without meaning.

Kilgore shook his head, breaking his reverie.

The match to the comm he'd given Sullivan buzzed. He read the message. His old sergeant was at the tunnel entrance. He'd brought his Sergeant Detective with forensic equipment. Sullivan had also managed to convince the clone, Sarah, to come.

Running through his roster of Marines and SPs in his mind one final time, Kilgore told himself to stop. The plan was good. He paused and said a quick prayer, asking if any Marine had to die that day, for God to let it be him and not one of his men.

◆ ◆ ◆

Markeson spotted the Colonel as she entered the restaurant they'd met in. She looked stunning, drawing the attention of every male in the establishment and she knew it. The Colonel's minion, the Sergeant, had not accompanied her.

A seductive smile on her lips, the red head strolled over to meet Markeson, exaggerating the roll of her hips as she moved for his benefit. He stood up and took her hand, kissing it before giving her a modest hug.

"Captain Markeson, such a warm welcome," she purred, stroking his cheek with the back of her left hand.

The detective seated her opposite his own seat and sat down. The pair of predators eyed each other, sizing the other up for the struggle each knew was about to begin.

"I wish we could meet under more pleasant conditions," Markeson said politely.

"Oh, but I think it's wonderful you came to visit me and had the foresight to make reservations at the very establishment we first met in." She smiled at him seductively, looking for a weakness to exploit. "It's romantic, don't you think."

He motioned for the waiter who approached with a bottle of wine. Markeson went through the motions of approving the wine. The waiter filled their glasses, placed the wine in the chiller and left.

Markeson raised his glass as did the Colonel. "To success," he said with a smile.

"To success."

"I hope you don't mind, but I ordered for us."

"Of course I don't mind. This wine is excellent!"

"It should be. It's from some place on Earth called France, Bordeaux, I think. It costs enough."

"Well, you certainly have good taste, Captain. Now, please tell me, what can I do for you today? Will it be business, pleasure or both?"

The smile vanished from Markeson's face as he sat down his wine glass.

"All business today, my good Colonel. I need the departure times, destinations, everything. There's a lot of risk for me in this little arrangement of ours. I want to finalize everything as soon as possible."

"My, aren't you in a hurry," she replied, forcing a smile to remain on her face.

"You pay me for information. Not just the shipping arrangements. There have been developments you don't know about."

The smile vanished from her face.

"Explain."

"When we first met, you brought up one of my Inspectors."

"Inspector Sullivan."

"He killed a clone in Capital City."

She was unable to keep the surprise from her face. Markeson was a better card player. His stone faced expression revealed nothing.

"I find that hard to believe."

"Well believe it." Markeson's pulse quickened. He'd been right. Her interest in the death of the SP and her feigned disinterest in the dead clone hit man connected the dots for him. The long persistent rumors of a secret clone program at the base were true.

"How many clones are you selling?"

"Who said I'm selling any clones Captain?"

"Let's not kid ourselves Colonel. You seem to forget, I'm a detective. Information is like money. Good cops save information for a rainy day just like good investors save money."

Irritation caused the red head's porcelain cheeks to flush red through her delicately applied rouge.

"The consulting fee just tripled."

"Tripled! How dare you!"

"Easy, I can arrest you right here," he whispered. "Now, don't make a scene because you have real problems. You need my help if you want to get off this planet."

The Colonel's face twisted, turning her beautiful features into a hideous, rage filled mask. "What makes you think I need your help?"

"Sullivan is here, in Brownstown with his team. Just what do you think he is looking for?"

She smiled, her face returning to its regular appearance. "Why should I worry?"

"Because he's good, very good. Sullivan's got the scent, and he won't let go until he figures this out. The closer Sullivan gets, the quicker he puts it all together. You don't have much time."

The Colonel exhaled in frustration. She sat in silence and thought. She needed time, something it would appear she didn't have much of at the moment. The waiter arrived with their food, giving her time she needed to alter her plans. She was too close to success; to getting her revenge to let a mere civilian Inspector and a corrupt Chief of Detectives stand in her way.

◆ ◆ ◆

Things were going smoothly. The Sergeant looked

39

about his quarters. It would be the last time he visited them. All of his possessions had been packed and shipped ahead to Capital City. One final inspection allowed him to feel confident he'd left behind nothing capable of incriminating him or revealing any information of value to a competent investigator.

If all went as planned, the troublesome Markeson would be dead soon. The clones would be en route as planned and it would be time. Time to settle things between him and the woman he loved.

She would accept his declaration of love and vow her faithfulness to him, and him alone or her life would come to an end. It would hurt, but he would heal. A broken heart was simply another wound for the veteran soldier.

He took one final look in the mirror, brushing off an imaginary speck of lint. The movement made him chuckle. Markeson had nothing on him when it came to vanity about one's appearance.

Securing the door, he walked down the corridor in his measured military stride. If he couldn't have her, nobody would. The cause was more important than a mere woman, even if it was the love of his life.

◆◆◆

Wiping his mouth with the linen napkin, Markeson decided to ask a few seemingly irrelevant questions. The answers of which might give him the edge in the dangerous game the two were playing. Watching the red head eat had given him no additional clues about the game she was playing.

"Why?"

"Excuse me," the Colonel answered, looking up from the slice of triple chocolate cake Markeson had ordered for their dessert.

"Why are you doing this? I checked this morning. You're still in the military. Your title, Colonel, is your actual rank. You're going to desert when you get the merchandise off Beta Prime. Nobody throws away a career like that just for money."

The seductive smile made its appearance on command, but the raw hatred in her eyes answered his question. It was one of the oldest motives in the history of humanity.

"You seem to be full of surprises this evening Captain Markeson. It would appear I underestimated your skill as a detective."

He pressed his advantage. "Answer the question, or I'll arrest you."

She laughed, a deep full laugh that drew the attention of diners near their table. "You would be placing yourself in a great deal of danger."

"Hardly. My tracks are completely covered. I have a dead SP I can pin on you. The investigation, by my star Inspector no less, will tie all kinds of things, illegal things, to that one dead body. My fingerprints won't be on a single thing. It will be your word against mine, and might I add, the word and reputation of Inspector Sullivan."

Seeing no way around the issue, the Colonel decided to answer Markeson's question. It hardly mattered. He would be dead soon enough.

"I was unjustly passed over for promotion. The General in command of the base, I'm sure you've researched the fair Brigadier Janice Savier, slept her way to the promotion that was mine."

His poker face in place, Markeson nudged her one more time.

"So is it jealousy or revenge?"

The Colonel looked away, the muscles in her face straining as she fought to control the emotions raging inside.

"A bit of both I would suppose. But there's more." Her

emotions tucked away again, she looked at Markeson and smiled, continuing in her bedroom voice, "More than that, I cannot tell you. You, of course, are aware I'm in Military Intelligence. There are limits."

"Fair enough," he answered, smiling his most charming smile. "I have one more question I insist you answer."

"Please, ask and get this inquisition over with Captain."

"Is there a suitable hotel nearby where we could get a room?"

◆ ◆ ◆

He would be glad to get off Beta Prime. The Captain watched the snow and ice covered buildings flash past as the convoy traveled slowly toward the spaceport's ground terminal.

The documents and details had arrived electronically earlier in the day. It had taken less than an hour for his disciplined men to pack up their gear, clean the warehouse until it was ready for a Drill Instructor's inspection and supervise the civilian trucker's loading of the containers.

Each truck had a mercenary riding in the cab, all with credentials as hired security for the cargo. The Captain's remaining men traveled in a hired transport, their weapons, and equipment close at hand.

Losing a man on a job was never good. Buck had only been with them for two contracts, but his loss had been preventable. Their employer had a sense of the dramatic that was unnecessary. A good leader controlled what was controllable and planned proactively for every foreseeable disaster and built in appropriate responses. All plans fall apart upon contact with the enemy. The trick was to know where the enemy was.

Buck had died because the employer had not done an adequate job of recon. Insisting on using the plan as devised had been foolish. The Captain blamed himself for not walking away since he had not been allowed to plan the raid.

It was the first contract with this employer and eager to make a good impression, he'd made a military decision based on business reasons. Something he disliked doing. It got men killed. They might be mercenaries, but they were still his men.

Once again, the limited amount of information concerned him. With the cargo in transit, it was not inconceivable he and his men were heading right into an ambush.

CHAPTER TWENTY-FOUR

Kilgore marched into General Savier's office with four SP's in formation behind him. He ignored the protests of the Staff Sergeant as he brushed past the reception desk and burst unannounced into the General's office.

"Excuse me," an irate Savier, blurted out, startled by Kilgore's sudden entrance.

"General Savier, I'm afraid matters of security are going to require I ask you not to use any electronic devices until otherwise notified. Nor are you to access any databases, computer files or communication devices of any kind."

"Have you lost your mind, Major Kilgore?"

"No, General I have not," Kilgore replied tersely. "I will be leaving four of my Shore Patrol officers to make sure you comply with my instructions and that you do not leave your office."

Savier stood up and leaned over, placing her hands on the desk as she did so. "A good officer's career can withstand one black mark on his record. Some say the best commanders all have a black mark on their record. But no officer, and I mean no officer, no matter how well connected, can survive two black marks. Do I make myself clear, Major?"

Kilgore looked the brunette square in her hazel eyes, noting the resolve behind the threat.

"General, threats only work if the party being threatened cares."

Kilgore turned and looked at the Sergeant he'd brought with him.

"If General Savier fails to comply with any of my directives, place her under arrest and detain her. If the General resists, use whatever means is necessary to subdue her."

"Yes, Major.

Kilgore turned to face the still standing general. "Don't think for one instant I'm bluffing General. What's more, you're Army. Don't forget SPs are part of the Corps. They'd love nothing better than to rough up an Army officer."

Savier glanced at the expressions of Kilgore's four SPs. There was no doubt in her mind where their loyalty lay. Nor did Savier doubt they hoped she would give them a reason, any reason, to settle a score between the Army and the Space Marines.

◆◆◆

It always amused Markeson that women snored. He stretched and got out of bed. As he dressed, Markeson kept an eye on the sleeping red head. For a Colonel in Military Intelligence, she was a loose cannon. It was far too easy to get information out of her. He hadn't even had to get her drunk.

He checked himself in the mirror, straightened his tie and combed his hair. Having restored himself to an immaculate appearance, Markeson slipped out of the room. Minutes later he was traveling in a cab to catch a hovercraft flight back to Capital City.

Leaving Brownstown without the identity of the actual clients didn't concern Markeson. The Colonel had told him enough. Besides he mused, it would be fun using his detective skills in one of his side ventures, particularly one as potentially lucrative as this one.

Now that he knew where and when the double cross would take place, Markeson needed to act. There were tracks to cover and scores settled.

The red head had been a pleasant diversion.

Perhaps he could actually team up with Sullivan on this. Build a little plausible deniability with the Inspector.

The thought of being one of the good guys for a change amused him.

◆◆◆

I looked at my chronometer. It was almost time. I'd tucked Josephson and Sarah away in a storage room and told them to stay put until I sent for them. Josephson was happy to comply and had done his best to calm Sarah down. I felt bad about caging her up like that, but when the bullets and phase pulses started flying, I wanted her safe.

Exactly at 1700, the Marines breached all three entrances to the research facility. Power was cut. Before the emergency generators could kick in, flash bangs went off through out the facility, stunning any personnel near the breach sites.

In less than a minute, the few armed soldiers inside were dead. The gun battle had been intense. Civilians have no idea how loud combat is and the effect it has on the combatants. I followed the SPs as they moved in to secure personnel and evidence.

I wore my badge on my jacket, having left my great coat with Sarah and Josephson. Despite the earplugs I wore, my ears were ringing. I moved quickly through the facility, avoiding the bodies lying on the floor and the pools of blood forming beneath them.

My nose itched. I made the mistake of scratching it, dislodging one of the filters I had inserted. It had been awhile since I'd experienced the smell of combat. Cordite from kinetic energy projectile weapons filled the air with smoke and its peculiar smell. Adding to the odor was the smell of burned metal and plastisteel from errant phase weapon fire. The worse smell of all was the odor of burned flesh and ruptured intestines.

I gave up on trying to get the filter back in place and just pulled the other one out and pocketed them both. I had to communicate so I pulled out the earplugs as well. The moans of the wounded made me regret my decision.

I saw Kilgore approaching. He looked relieved and upset at the same time. I waved over an SP and sent him to fetch Josephson and Sarah. We needed to collect evidence as quickly as possible.

"Casualties," I asked.

"No SPs. A ricochet hit one of my Marines, but his body armor stopped it. Couple of broken ribs, nothing serious."

"What about the Army guys?"

He shook his head sadly.

"One hundred percent, dead or wounded."

I watched with the Major as the Navy Corpsmen attached to his Marine unit worked on the wounded. The most serious had already been moved out of the facility. The dead covered with the body bag that would be used to move them when time permitted.

"Collateral damage?"

"Two, but I don't feel too bad about them. Come with me Sullivan. I think we've found where the proof we need is."

◆◆◆

Ralph eased his cab up to the door of the vicarage and got out. He hustled around to the other side and opened the door for Father Nathan, helping the priest ease out.

"Is it my imagination Ralph or is it colder than usual today?"

"Father, it's five degrees colder than normal. Forecast calls for dreary weather for the next few days. Fog, snow, the regular when it's overcast, just colder than usual."

The priest forced himself to stand up straight. He adjusted the sling holding his left arm causing his black greatcoat to slip off.

"Here, let me help you, Father," Ralph said, scurrying to pick up the priest's great coat and drape it back over his shoulders.

"It's all right Ralph, I can manage."

"Father, you do enough for others. Let us help you for once."

Too tired to argue, he smiled at the cabbie and turned to enter his home.

"Let me get the door Father," Ralph insisted, hurrying to beat the priest to his front door.

Holding his hand up to stop Father Nathan, Ralph fiddled with the door lock, knocking loudly on the door twice in the process.

"Hold on one second Father while I get this open."

Seconds passed before Ralph finally opened the door and held it for Father Nathan. The priest removed his Fedora hat and stepped inside where he commanded the vicarage's AI to turn on the lights.

"Surprise!"

It was all Ralph could do to keep the much taller and thicker priest from stumbling and falling. The vicarage was full of people from the neighborhood. Homeless, elderly parishioners and other's who had become part of the parish congregation. Squeezed into the small remaining space in front was a dozen or so of his kids.

"Welcome home Father," a smiling Alice announced, stepping around one of the street urchins. "You look tired, let's get you to bed. We just wanted to let you know how happy everyone is you're going to be okay and that you're back at the parish."

As if on command, Joe began shooing everyone out. In less than a minute the vicarage was empty of people except for Alice and Father Nathan. She helped him lie down on the couch and then covered him with a blanket, taking his hat from him and placing it on his coat rack.

"This really isn't necessary Alice."

"Yes, it is," Alice said in her assertive waitress voice. "You do so much for people around here. You can let us take care of you for a day or two. Ralph and I will take care of the kids tonight and see to it they're settled in for good in the dorm."

Alice moved a small table close to the couch and set a tray of food on it.

"Joe sent over your evening meal. You send a link if you need anything."

Alice slipped out before Father Nathan could say a word.

He looked at the plate of food and lifted the cover. Wisps of steam rose slowly, caring the aroma of the hot food with it. Father Nathan set the cover down and leaned back, resting his head on the pillow Alice had fluffed up for him.

Tears ran from his eyes as he spoke softly. "God, I don't deserve this. But it means a great deal to me. I thank you, and I will be sure to thank my friends and parishioners."

◆ ◆ ◆

I watched two Marines fixing charges to a heavy steel door. Sarah fidgeted next to me while Josephson roamed around the facility, taking photographs of everything.

All of the wounded had been moved to the base clinic for care. The civilian workers were huddled in a corner under guard by three heavily armed SPs. The remaining SPs were busy marking everything for cataloging as evidence. Kilgore had declared the entire facility a crime scene.

I hoped for both of our sakes we found evidence of crime.

The Marines finished setting the charges, and we all took cover. I don't know what it is about blowing things up, but the two of them started bickering over who would get to set the charges off. Kilgore grinned at me and winked before settling the argument by holding out his hand for the detonator. It was all I could do not to challenge him for it.

Disappointed, the Marine handed the device over and then settled down behind some heavy machinery with his buddy and plugged his ears.

"Fire in the hole," Kilgore shouted and pressed the detonator switch.

A loud bang went off with a bright flash of orange light as the charges both melted through the steel in a microsecond and blew the door out of its frame. An even louder boom sounded when the solid steel door slammed into the floor. Weapons at the ready, the two Marines vanished into the room while the smoke cleared.

Sarah curled her nose up at the smell of the burned steel and the thermite charge. She looked cute, so I laughed at her.

She wasn't amused.

"My ears hurt," she complained. I nodded my understanding. My ears were ringing too, and I didn't have her sense of hearing. Looking about the place, I was more certain than before Sarah was telling me the truth about her enhanced abilities.

A tense voice carried through the opening. "Major Kilgore?"

Smoke from the melted steel obscured the view inside the door. I followed Kilgore as he cautiously stepped through.

I turned to stop Sarah from following only to find I was too late.

◆◆◆

"I don't care if it upsets your precious schedule Governor. We're about to be double crossed," Markeson declared.

"Don't even think of blaming this on me," he shouted into his comm in response to Rankin. "Every deal we make could be the one that ruins us, and you know it! I might also point out that of all our enterprises, the most lucrative are the ones I bring to the table!"

His temples throbbing from his burst of fury, Markeson waited for a response. Silence was his answer.

"Bring Xue with you. Be on time. Same place as last time."

He broke the comm link and pocketed the device. Thought better of it and pulled it back out, pulling up his contacts. A minute later, the reservation made, the comm was returned to its place.

He had time for a shower, shave and a change of clothes. Feeling stressed, he thought of the lovely Jasmine, the waitress he'd requested. As yet, she'd yet to succumb to his advances. She would be a nice distraction for an evening.

Stepping into the stream of hot water, the detective tried to relax as the steam floated around his face, warming him. Not tonight, he decided. Jasmine would have to wait. There was too much to do, starting with getting Sullivan on board for the end game.

He would save the lovely Jasmine for another time.

I hated having to do it, but I had to manhandle Sarah out of the secure room and get one of the Navy Corpsmen to sedate her. Josephson started to protest until he saw the two Marines puking their guts up just outside the door to the lab we had entered.

I watched his expression turn from one of anger towards me to concern for Sarah. "I know Inspector. You can't unsee some things once you see them. I'll keep an eye on her."

"Sorry, not this time. You're going to have to go in with the SPs and help document everything. This is a mess, and we've got to keep a lid on it."

"A lid sir? Cloning is illegal. We need to be making arrests, don't we?"

The pup hadn't even started to put it all together. If we didn't get a lid on this, a war would start.

I checked Sarah one more time as she lay unconscious one more time and admonished, well threatened actually, the female SP tending to her. I was pretty certain she got the message to make sure nothing happened to Sarah until I returned.

Josephson went through the door before me carrying his camera and satchel of evidence bags. I steeled myself for the smell and the sights I would never unsee and followed behind.

Josephson was doubled up retching what little was in his stomach onto the floor. I didn't say a word and nor would I.

We were standing alone in a charnel house.

A dozen steel mortuary tables were perfectly aligned along the right wall. Behind each was a door similar to what one would expect to see in a morgue. I was certain that was the set-up we were looking at.

Lying on each of the tables was the remains of a human body. Each was hooked up to monitors and what had to be some sort of life-support system.

Each body had been surgically cut open with most of the internal organs missing. The smell was horrible.

Josephson stood up slowly and turned to face me, his eyes wide with horror.

"It's a human chop shop. They're selling organs. They have to be."

I didn't say a word. I was more worried about the fact Josephson had drawn his weapon and had turned to face the two dozen terrified technicians a pair of Marines were guarding.

"You animals," he screamed at them, aiming his weapon. The Marines looked at me, unsure of how to react.

"You butchered them!"

One of the technicians turned red in the face with rage. Before I could react, the fool spouted off the last words he would ever speak.

"They are clones, you ignorant cop! Clones! They are nothing more than property! Tissue for experiments! You have interrupted..."

I'd have to talk to Josephson later, and a black mark would go in his file. I was all right with that, and I'd keep Internal Affairs off his back. Usually, you can't just go and shoot a material witness like that.

But this time I think it was justifiable. The Marine guards certainly did.

◆ ◆ ◆

The Colonel settled comfortably in the first class seat of the hovercraft. The flight to Capital City would be short. Her Sergeant had changed the accommodations she would be staying in to avoid contact with Markeson. At 1100 hours she would be off world and heading to her next plum assignment.

It saddened her for a moment. Never again would she be Sandra O'Donnell. Colonel Sandra O'Donnell. But, her rank would soon change in the new organization. The thought of her first star put a smile on her face. Brigadier General Molly O'Toole. Despite her Sergeant's advice, she had insisted on her new identity reflecting her Earth Irish ancestry.

Wealth, power, and recognition would be hers now. Finally, Sandra, no, make that Molly O'Toole would have what she had worked so hard for. General Savier would suffer for stealing what had been meant for Molly O'Toole's friend, Colonel Sandra O'Donnell.

◆◆◆

"Sir, she woke up. There was nothing I could do. The sedative I gave her should have kept her under for hours. No way am I giving her another dose."

I raised my hand to calm the nervous Corpsman. "It's all right. I need Sarah to be awake anyhow."

Trembling, Sarah stood up and threw her arms around me, sobbing. I didn't know what to do, what to say, so I just stood there and let her cry.

Josephson stepped into view. The pup looked terrible. It was understandable. He cut his eyes back toward the slaughterhouse.

We had to get this over with.

"Sarah, I need your help for just a few minutes. I don't want to ask..."

She stepped away from me and looked up, wiping her

eyes.

"I know. Nobody else can tell you what you need to know. I need to look myself."

It suddenly hit me why Sarah needed to look, her sister Ellie.

I walked back over to the door with Sarah and Josephson following. I looked back at Sarah before I stepped through. I hated having to ask her to do this, but we had to sort a bunch of things out quickly. Sarah could do in seconds what would take us days.

Tears started leaking from her eyes again. It was all I could do not to draw my weapon and finish what Josephson had begun. Sarah took my hand, surprising me with the strength of her grip.

Brushing her long brown hair from in front of her face, Sarah stepped through the door first, and I followed quickly.

"Cover your eyes," I ordered. "Keep them covered until I tell you to open them."

"No, Sully," she whispered. "I have to know if Ellie is here. If she's one of them."

Sarah's sister meant nothing to me. But I was responsible for the death of her sister Maria. Responsible because I hesitated before taking the shot that killed the serial killer who had taken Maria's life. She had to know. I just didn't want her to have to look.

"Sarah, no."

I had to spare her. She didn't need to see the butchered clones. Sarah just needed to know if Ellie was one of the victims.

"Sully..."

"She's a clone. Even if Ellie dyed her hair or has it cut short, she's your twin. I'll look."

Sarah nodded, the tears flowing freely now. She let go of my hand and covered her eyes.

I looked at Josephson. He understood and gently put his hand on Sarah's back, whispering for her to let him guide her to where we needed her to help us. I waited until my team was past the butchered bodies.

From where I stood, it was easy to see seven of the twelve bodies were male. I only had to check five faces. The first was the hardest. The young woman had long brown hair like Sarah. The last had brown hair cut short. Like the first four, she looked nothing like Sarah.

All of the victims were still alive. None of them would live without the machines they were attached to. I know a fair bit of human anatomy. They were all missing their kidneys, liver, and pancreas. The women were missing their ovaries and uterus. All of the victims were missing at least one lung, most both. Two still had their hearts.

I drew my .50 cal. and walked over to the prisoners. I picked the most arrogant looking of the bunch and placed the barrel against her temple.

"Where are the organs?"

She smiled. "Killing me won't change anything."

"Yes, it will," I answered. "You'll be just as dead as your friend lying there."

Her smile slipped a little bit.

"Plus, the next person I ask the same question will have the benefit of knowing I'll pull the trigger."

"You have no idea what you've done."

"Don't really care. What I see here are humans who have been chopped up. Alive. Vivisection. Which happens to be a capital crime. Clones. No matter what space you live in, that's illegal. So, I have to ask you, do you have any idea what you've done?"

"Changed the course of humanity," she sneered.

I cocked my revolver.

Her smile vanished.

"You've probably started a war. Do you have any idea how many people will die?"

I have to hand it to her. She spoke with conviction.

"It will be worth the price."

I hit her hard with the barrel of my revolver. I watched her eyes roll up into her head as she collapsed to the floor, blood trickling from the laceration I'd opened up on her scalp.

I moved the barrel to the scientist standing next to her, another arrogant looking woman, a bottle blonde.

"Same question."

I gave her a second to look down at her unconscious colleague.

"They were shipped out yesterday."

"Where?"

"I have no idea," she replied, looking back up at me. "We were about to finish with these specimens. Harvesting muscles and skin tissue does not take nearly as long. The only difficult task that requires any skill to be performed today was the eyes."

She joined her more arrogant partner on the floor. The laceration on her scalp was much larger.

"We don't know where the organs go. We just do the technical work."

I looked at the speaker, a short, nervous looking man. He was bald and possessed a hook nose.

"What happens to the victims when you're done?"

He glanced about nervously hoping someone else would answer.

"We terminate them. There is no reason to keep the remains alive after the harvesting of the requested organs and tissue is complete.

"So that's it."

He looked at me, unsure of what to say.

"I don't know what you want from me," he whined.

"To show a little respect for the humans you just murdered, because that is what each one of you is going to be charged with. First-degree murder, plus accessory to murder, murder for hire, kidnapping, illegal sale of human organs, violation of the Anti-Cloning Treaty are just what I can think of at the moment. You're going to get the death sentence."

I stepped close enough to smell the man's body odor, a vile mix of his cologne and fear.

"Before they put the needle in your arm, you're going to spend the rest of your days in an Alliance Supermax on some hell hole of an asteroid."

He just fainted.

I couldn't resist. I kicked him.

◆◆◆

"Are you sure that is the wisest course of action?"

"It's the only course of action Governor. We have to get ahead of this. All of our financial tracks are covered."

"I say we just let them double cross us on payment and consider it an investment gone bad," Xue offered.

"You don't seem to realize," Markeson snarled. "They've seen my face. Don't think this is just my problem. If I go down, we all go down."

Markeson let the truth of his threat hang in the air.

"Do you really think involving this Inspector Sullivan is the best course of action?"

"He's like a pit bull from Earth. The military called him in on a murder of an SP that took place off base grounds in Brownstown. The dead SP was a clone."

"How do you know?"

Sarcasm and irritation were written on Markeson's face as he answered. "I am a detective."

Markeson watched as the two corrupt politicians looked at each other, communicating silently. The Governor made a decision, and the Mayor concurred.

"Make sure Sullivan never connects any of this to us."

"Don't worry. I plan to make sure Sullivan catches the people who started the operation and the parties we dealt with either escape or," he paused ominously, to ensure his partner's understood his drift, "they never have a chance to rat us out."

◆◆◆

Sarah stood in a corner, looking at the floor. Josephson stood in front of her, making sure she didn't look around.

"Ellie wasn't one of them."

She burst into tears yet again and clung to me. Josephson looked away, embarrassed at the normally reserved Sarah's emotional display. Typically, Sarah usually only exhibited glimpses of childlike amusement or anxiety and fear at being hunted or trapped, unable to escape at a second's notice.

After a few minutes, Sarah collected herself and let go of me. She wiped her face and pulled her hair back, letting it fall down her back.

"What do you need for me to do?"

I motioned for her to follow me. I stopped in front of another steel door. This one was not secured with security locks, having only a simple latch.

Sarah looked at me and opened the door, stepping inside. I followed quickly, determined to not let her face what was inside alone.

She looked up at me, her face filled with rage.

"They're all clones. They haven't been birthed yet."

I nodded. I figured Sarah knew what she was looking at.

"Let's get you out of here. Major Kilgore has a place you can rest. It has a window and exterior exit. Two SPs will be posted on guard. Is that okay?"

Sarah nodded and took my hand, pulling me back toward the entrance to the medical house of horrors. She made it past the butchered bodies but made the mistake of glancing at the monsters responsible.

She launched herself at the soulless monsters, pummeling the first one she came to with both fists. I let her get it out of her system. Josephson and the two Marines stood next to me and watched as she moved on to another hapless monster. This time the nervous little man with the hook nose.

I figured enough was enough and pulled her off him. His nose looked better broken.

CHAPTER TWENTY-SIX

Cargo handlers took over once the containers cleared Customs. The Captain felt a sense of relief at how easy it had been to pass through Security and Customs. Whoever their employer had paid to grease palms knew what they were doing. He glanced at the man who served as the intermediary between his outfit and their employer. The man didn't say a word, instead merely glancing in his direction and nodding.

The Captain turned away and headed over to his waiting men. "I'll be glad when this job is over," he told his sergeant who just grunted his agreement. "As soon as the freighters disembark from the station, the contract is finished."

"Sir, I know it's not my place," the sergeant said, speaking in a respectful, but firm voice, "but the men would just as soon not work for this employer again. It's not about losing Buck. Heck, the work wasn't that dangerous. There's just something not right about this entire job."

"I know what you mean," the mercenary officer replied. "This job has cluster written all over it. I just want to get it done, get paid and go home."

◆ ◆ ◆

Kilgore had deposited General Savier in the base's lone interrogation room. I stood watching the woman via the monitor. If Savier was concerned about the events of the past few hours, she didn't show it outwardly.

I decided never to play cards with the woman.

Josephson was busy organizing all the digital evidence he'd collected, and while keeping one eye on Sarah in the room Kilgore had provided. She'd stretched out on the floor and gone right to sleep. I guess this was all too much for her and sleep was a good way to not deal with it.

The door opened behind me, and Kilgore entered. We stood and watched the woman for a few minutes in silence.

"How do you want to handle this?"

"The General ought to have to urinate by now," I said. "That won't be a distraction for her. She impresses me as a tough bird mentally."

Kilgore nodded. He'd never handled many interrogations so we'd play this anyway I wanted.

"Has she been arrested formally yet?"

"No. I suppose I need to read the General her rights under the Military Code of Justice," Kilgore mumbled. "Not that she deserves it after what I saw in that lab."

"Don't," I told him. "Just sit and watch if you don't mind Major. Look angry and mean like any good Marine would."

We entered the room and sat down across from the table. As per standard procedure, the General was handcuffed to the table. Her legs bound to a steel chair efastened to the floor and designed to be uncomfortable.

I didn't say a word. Just sat and stared at the officer who'd supervised this abomination of a program. Most people can't handle extended periods of silence in situations like this. Often they'll start talking just to fill the void. Savier didn't have a problem just sitting there.

"I have a few questions," I told her.

She smiled. "I haven't been read my rights, as is required by military law. So I won't be answering any questions until I have counsel and I have my rights read to me."

"You aren't getting either," I told her.

To the General's credit, her smile didn't slip at all.

"If you leave this facility, it's straight to a particular black site on a rock in the asteroid belt on the edge of this system. If you think Beta Prime's cold, this place makes our lovely planet look like a tropical paradise."

"This is getting old," Savier said. "You have no idea who you're tangling with. Release me."

I leaned back in my chair, putting my boots up on the table. I stared at the general for a few minutes.

"Then again, depending on my mood, you could be arrested and made to stand trial for murder and a wide range of other crimes right here in Alliance Court. It would make great media. The networks in Capital City would make a small fortune broadcasting the trial."

That got her attention.

"You don't want to do that."

"Actually, I do." I gave her my best nasty look. "The military screwed me over years ago. I'd love nothing better than to screw the military back."

"I had nothing to do with whatever happened to you," Savier protested.

"You're dead either way General. Cloning is a capital offense. You didn't just clone people. You butchered them. The Confederation and the Caliphate both will see this as the Alliance military trying to build up its forces in secret. If we don't hang you out to dry, it will probably mean war."

"You have no idea what is going on Inspector," the General snarled. I was getting on her nerves.

"Explain it to me then. Make it nice and clear, so simpleton's like the Major and I can understand."

Savier looked away. I could see the wheels turning as she worked through every scenario she could think of to escape the situation she found herself in. I sat and didn't say anything. If she needed time to decide to talk, I'd give it to her.

"What do you want to know? If I tell you something of value, I want the needle off the table."

I ignored her last request.

"Who's behind this? The Army? The Navy?"

"I can't tell you that."

"Well, what can you tell me?"

"Ask something else."

I thought for a bit. Savier didn't say anything, giving me time to think.

"How many planets have facilities like this one?"

"All I'll say is this is the only facility on Beta Prime."

"So, there's more than one of these nightmare shops."

The General didn't react one way or another.

"In what we believe is an unrelated matter, during a police investigation, it was necessary to use deadly force on some hired muscle, a hit man we believe."

The woman just shrugged. The information meant nothing to her.

"The individual was a clone."

Her face didn't move. It was the eyes that gave her away.

"This is not the first clone wandering around Beta Prime, particularly Capital City, that I've come across in my duties. Anything you can tell us that would shed a little light on how military grade clones can be found wandering around in the general civilian population? Oh, and then there is the small matter of the dead SP here at your base, which I am certain you knew was a clone."

"I have nothing to say."

"Okay, last question then. Since my investigation of the dead SP started, six standard freight containers have left this facility by rail transport. I know for a fact three of those were hijacked and I'm pretty certain all six were. Is there anything you have to say about that?"

Torture probably wouldn't have broken General Savier. That simple statement did.

"You can't let those containers get off Beta Prime. If they fall into the wrong hands, it will mean war. War like nobody has ever seen before."

"Who has them?"

She shook her head in fear. Her olive skin had turned pale, making her jet-black hair look even darker.

"I don't know their name. All I know is it's a group of elitists who believe they are better than anyone else. It's like a cult."

"I'm not following you."

"They're not part of the Alliance. They're not Confeds or fanatics from the Caliphate. They operate in all three."

I laughed at Savier. "A shadow government in all three Intergalactic Empires? You think I'm going to buy that? This interview is over."

Kilgore and I both stood up to leave.

"This group is why we started up the cloning operation again."

I stopped. Seemed like the General wanted to talk now.

"Why the chop shop?"

"It's an expensive program to run. So we fund it off the books."

"Why now? Why risk war developing banned technology?"

"Because we'll need cannon fodder for the next war," she said in a whisper. "You have no idea what Military Intelligence has found out about this group."

"For the last time, why have I found clones in my city?"

"We let them go sometimes. We have to evaluate them. How the genetic modifications work. Do the clones adapt to normal society effectively? It's all research."

I felt sick to my stomach. My government was using its citizens as guinea pigs without their knowledge or consent. Clones who had no control over their own life and civilians who were ignorant of the potential danger they were in.

I motioned to Kilgore to step outside.

"I need a break," I told him. "She's tough. Whoever this group is, Savier is more scared of them than me taking a hammer to her bones. This is going to take awhile."

He rubbed his temples. It had been a long day for him.

"You did good today Major. That was a good op you planned. All of your personnel came through, and only bad guys died."

Major Kilgore smiled at me. He knew those words weren't easy for me to say.

"Let's get something to eat. I have to keep a lid on this until I can figure out which brass can be trusted with this."

We had just about made it to the end of the corridor when a shot rang out. I pulled my .50 cal. as we sprinted back to the interrogation room. A second shot rang out.

I yanked on the handle to the door of the interrogation room. It was locked. I clenched my left fist and slammed it repeatedly into the door. On the sixth blow, the plastisteel cracked from the force of my hardened steel fist. I leaned back and kicked the door in.

The Major pushed past me, and I followed. We both entered with weapons ready.

Lying dead on the floor was an SP. She'd put the barrel of her service weapon in her mouth and taken her own life. Lying face down on the table in a pool of blood was General Savier. Her head was mostly gone as a result of the impact of the projectile at such close range.

I looked at Kilgore in disgust. It wasn't his fault. The real SP had probably been dead for some time, weeks or months. That's the trouble with clones. They look like and can pass for the person they're a copy of. This SP had fooled all the biometric security checks for some time.

"You had no way of knowing," I told him. I reached for

my comm. I told Bones to be on the next flight to Brownstown.

◆◆◆

One of the advantages of being the Chief of Detectives
was being able to find out what his Inspectors and Ser-
geants were up to. Or at least what they were supposed to
be up to without arousing any suspicion as to why he
wanted to know.

"Brownstown? Again? Inspector Sullivan better be
close to finishing that case with all the taxpayer's money
he's spending traveling," Markeson complained. Not that
he ever worried about taxpayer money himself. He just
couldn't let the other detectives spend what was in the
budget.

It left less for him.

He thought for a moment. Might as well get this started
he decided.

"Tell Chief O'Brian I'm headed to Brownstown. We're
going to get this dead SP matter resolved."

The gray headed desk Sergeant nodded. She had no use
for the pretty boy Chief of Detectives. As far as she was
concerned, he could set up shop and run the planet's detectives from Brownstown.

Markeson pulled out his comm and checked the flight
schedule. If he hurried, he could catch the last scheduled
flight to the mining town. Without a word, he left the precinct.

He didn't hear the desk Sergeant mumble as he left.

"Don't let the door hit you on the butt on the way out
Captain Markeson."

◆◆◆

He felt less tense with the containers stored in Customs. The Colonel had arrived safely in Capital City and would be at the terminal soon. Once she and the cargo were lifted up to the space station and loaded on the smuggler's ships, he would feel better. He'd feel even better when all the ships had departed for their destinations.

The Colonel had been promised a promotion along with a new identity. The Sergeant wished it hadn't had to happen this way, but he didn't know how else things could have played out.

He loved his Colonel, almost as much as he loved the ideas behind the cause. General Savier's promotion had been most unfortunate. If the Colonel had been promoted, as she so justly deserved, the operation would have been so much easier. He could have stayed in the Alliance Army and controlled things from the base in Brownstown.

The Sergeant shook his head. For all of her strengths, the Colonel simply was not capable of planning an operation like this one. Securing information from humans was her gift. If she survived the next few months, he would make sure he did all the planning in the future. He loved his Sandra, but the cause came first.

If he could protect his Sandra, no, he smiled for a second, his Molly, from herself, they might have a future together. But Molly had to be faithful. To him and most of all to the cause.

He watched the mercenary Captain approach. The man had done a good job. The glitches had not been the fault of the mercenaries, but of the Colonel's sloppy planning. He had the authority to pay a significant bonus.

Dead mercenaries don't get paid. Poor planning by the employer made mercenaries unhappy, understandably so. The loss of a single man did not bother the Sergeant. He also knew, in time, the mercenaries would close ranks and move on. Death was an occupational hazard.

Employers who planned poorly, on the other hand,

were to be avoided as often as possible. The mercenaries had probably already complained to their leader about their current contract. The bonus would be large.

"Sir, my men are in place. The first containers are due to be lifted by barge in about an hour."

"Excellent," the Sergeant replied, allowing a hint of cheerfulness to creep into his voice. "If you check your account, you will notice an additional payment has been made. You will receive final payment as soon as the last freighter leaves the space station."

The Captain didn't say a word; he just turned to return from where he'd come.

"Captain."

The mercenary stopped and glanced back at the man he distrusted.

"If I were you, I would be very hesitant to contract with our employer again. Trust me when I say the planning for this contract could have been better. I think we can both agree on that much."

The mercenary still didn't speak.

"I have been authorized to award a significant bonus in light of your performance under the circumstances."

"How significant?"

"Each enlisted man will receive a twenty-five percent bonus. Your Sergeant a thirty-five percent bonus and you sir will receive a fifty percent bonus. I hope this will make up for any difficulty you experienced that you felt was due to poor planning on our employer's part."

He watched the mercenary think for a moment.

"Losing a man is tough. Buck was a good soldier. Include a bonus for him. His wife will need it. The life insurance is never enough. As to working for your employer again, I don't know. Something just smells wrong about this job. All I can say is if you need our services again, we'll talk. Beyond that, I won't promise anything."

The Sergeant nodded in understanding. "I will see to it

your request is honored."

He watched the mercenary vanish among the containers. The Sergeant recognized a professional when he saw one. It was a shame the politicians in the Alliance didn't respect the men and women who served.

The cause he now served would punish them for that lack of respect.

CHAPTER TWENTY-SEVEN

A knock on the door woke me up. I'd fallen asleep going through the files on every clone produced at the facility. Josephson was furiously working on organizing the overwhelming amount of evidence he'd collected since the raid had ended. Sarah was still asleep.

"Enter."

The door opened, and Bones peered inside.

"Did you really have to call me in for this?"

"Who else was I going to call?"

"I figured as much," he groused. "Where are the bodies?"

I didn't really want to go back to that place, but somebody had to show him where the work was.

"We won't be able to remove the bodies," I told him. "All of the remains will be cremated and disposed of here."

I shot him a look to let Bones know not to complain. He'd understand soon enough.

We finally arrived at the lab. The two Marine guards nodded and let us through. Bones took one look at the carnage and stepped back outside the lab. A few minutes later he returned, his face pale.

"I know those are clones," he whispered. "But to butcher someone like that, I've never seen anything like that before."

Bones walked over to the nearest body, applying gloves as he did so. He started a cursory examination that lasted all of two seconds before he was glaring at me.

"They're still alive!"

I shrugged. "I didn't know what to do."

To my surprise, Bones stepped away from the vivisected corpse and bowed his head. I could hear him praying. I hadn't figured Bones for a religious man.

"Forgive me, God," he whispered. Bones went down the row of steel examining tables and pulled the plug for the life support machines. The monitors of each victim immediately flat lined, indicating the remains were no longer alive.

"I don't know what to do with this either," he said looking at me with a weariness that seemed to age him ten years.

"Let me give you this before you go," he said suddenly. Reaching into his pocket, he produced a drive. "Official autopsy of the SP. Unique sized kinetic projectile did the job, a .42 cal." He looked at me and then glanced to see if the two Marines had heard him.

"That's a unique caliber," I whispered.

He nodded. "Army Special Forces or Military Intelligence. My guess is we have a trained assassin wandering around on our planet."

I left to find Kilgore. This case just kept getting worse and worse.

◆◆◆

Markeson was less than happy with the reception he received at the base entrance. Having never served in the military, he had no idea of just how impossible what he wanted was.

"Sir, I readily acknowledge your status as a civilian. If this base were not military, you would have already been admitted."

He frowned at the SP.

"Why again is it you won't admit me?"

"The base is on lockdown."

"Why is it on lockdown?"

"I don't know sir."

"Why don't you know?"

"I don't need to know. If my superiors wanted to me to know, they would have told me. They didn't, so I don't need to know."

"Is this normal?" Markeson barked at the SP in frustration.

"Sir, with all due respect," the SP answered politely. "It's obvious you've never served in any branch of the military."

"What makes you so sure," the detective snapped back.

"If the military, any branch of it sir, wants an enlisted man to have an opinion, they issue it to him."

Markeson had to laugh at the beleaguered SP's remark.

"Can you at least send a message to my Inspector? He's on the base, conducting an investigation of a dead SP, one of yours," Markeson added for emphasis.

Without speaking the SP nodded at the other guard to keep an eye on Markeson. Stepping into the guard booth, the SP contacted Major Kilgore. A few moments later the SP reappeared.

"Major Kilgore has granted clearance."

"Finally," Markeson grumbled. "Let me in."

"That's not possible, sir."

"You just said I was granted clearance!"

"Yes, sir."

"Then let me in!"

"You'll have to wait for an armed escort sir."

Markeson glared at the SP and then the other standing duty.

"I'm not going to get in until Kilgore is good and ready, am I?"

"No, sir."

A sudden gust of freezing wind hit the detective square

in his face, blowing his perfectly groomed hair about. The two SPs were standing at ease again, staring off into space. The conversation was over.

He would have to wait in the bitter, freezing cold until Sullivan was good and ready for him to enter the base.

◆◆◆

Two hours had passed since Markeson had shown up. The SPs on sentry duty had been rotated twice because of the cold. I decided I'd had my fun. I told Kilgore to have him escorted in. He was my boss.

I waited outside the underground entrance to the research facility. There was no hiding what we had found from him. To be honest, this was a mess that could spill over and bring down a lot of very influential people in the Alliance, not to mention, start a war. Markeson might be a weasel, but he was a smart weasel, and this was right up his alley.

Why not drop the mess in his lap?

When Markeson rounded the corner, I had to laugh. I'd never seen him with a less than perfect appearance. His hair looked like it had been through a storm of static electricity, each strand was standing straight out from his scalp. A crusted layer of snow and ice covered his expensive designer coat. His nose was bright red from the cold.

It had been a long day, and I didn't feel like listening to his guff, so I just entered the facility. I figured he would follow.

"Sullivan," he bellowed. "You have some explaining to do! I didn't authorize a raid on this base!"

He kept it up in that vein until we entered the butcher shop. That shut him up.

"Major Kilgore ordered the raid. I was invited because of the investigation of the SP and the fact his men needed help with the forensics. This is your problem now, Captain."

"My problem," he stammered.

"Yes, sir. Because you see sir, the dead SP was a clone. What we have uncovered is an illegal cloning operation. One that was run for profit I might add. Jurisdiction is ours because the initial murder took place off base. That and I doubt the military will be allowed to investigate its own illegal cloning operation."

I'd never seen the smug, arrogant, self-righteous narcissist be at a loss for words before.

I'll give him one thing. He thinks quick on his feet.

"We have to keep a lid on this. Word of this gets out, war could break out. You've seen the bodies. What were they thinking? Running a chop shop for human organs. That's got to be at least a dozen laws they violated per body. I see you brought Bones in, good thinking. Where are you on this?"

"Josephson has documented a lot of the crime scene digitally and is organizing the material now. He's pulled as many of the hard drives as he can. Our Forensic IT people will have to go through those."

"Any arrests? Please tell me you've made arrests."

The base commander is dead. Assassinated in the interrogation room in the brig by a clone who then committed suicide.

"So nobody convenient we can pin this on?"

"I'm afraid not, Captain. That's why you get paid the big credits. I'm just an Inspector."

"My hair's a mess. I can't think," Markeson announced to nobody in particular. "Any idea on who the initial shooter was? With the dead SP that is?"

"No, sir, but we do have evidence indicating it was a hit carried about by Army Special Forces."

"Oh, great. We're on an Army base. Like that is going to help any."

Markeson went and sat down on a box. He pulled a comb out and took nearly ten minutes repairing his hair. It was interesting to watch the man's CPU run at maximum while he tried to piece how he was going to get out of this one.

Josephson made an appearance and handed me a message.

"From forensics back at the precinct. It would appear the Boss Man wasn't really the boss. He was just a district manager so to speak. Our forensic accountants tracked the money to an off-planet account, and then it disappears."

At the mention of the dead Boss Man, Markeson came to life.

"Who is this dead Boss Mann?"

"Different case, Captain."

Markeson's expression had changed from panic to anger. Something wasn't right.

"But, it has a link to our situation here."

"How so?"

"This Boss Man used to be your old partner, a Detective Vitter."

I had to give Markeson credit. After his initial lapse in control, he did a good job with the news.

"Vitter. That's a shame. You probably know he did some time."

"Yeah, and his hired muscle was a clone."

"A clone! Like what's back there," he said, pointing back at the secure portion of the facility.

"Before she was killed, General Savier informed us they would cut loose a clone or two into the general civilian population to see how they assimilated. This one went bad evidently."

"Please tell me you have this General Savier's interview recorded," he moaned.

"Yes sir, along with the clone executing her. The General didn't even look surprised when the clone came in and aimed at her."

Markeson sat back down on his box and entered his own mental world. He looked up after a bit and waved Josephson and me over.

"I read the report on the train robbery. You think the cargo came from here?"

"It's obvious now, but yes. General Savier was less than happy about the fact," I informed him.

"It's a different case that I'm working on," Markeson told us, "but I think I know where whatever was taken is, or at least where it will be.

"Sir?"

"Smugglers. It would appear some of Devereaux's old crew is still trying to make a few credits on the side. We need to go."

I was suspicious. We had too much work to do still here at the base.

"Sir, we need to finish processing this crime scene," I insisted.

"No, we need to catch the people who are smuggling clones off this planet. We catch them in the act, we have leverage, and we can pull in the big wigs!"

Markeson was right. It made no sense to shut down one chop shop just for the others to stay in business. General Savier had alluded to the fact this was just one research facility.

"Major Kilgore," I asked, turning to my old C.O. "Can you keep this place locked down for another forty-eight hours?"

He frowned. For a base this size, communication was a constant, on going process. To simply black out for any duration of time would arouse suspicion, especially if those trying to communicate were the individuals responsible for the cloning operation.

"I will do my best. That's all I can promise."

Markeson looked at Major Kilgore in an odd manner. I should have recognized what he was thinking, but I didn't.

One more thing to feel guilty about.

"Major Kilgore, do you have anyone you could leave in charge, run things via a secure comm? These people might have some military personnel with them. It would be helpful to have you and a couple of SPs in tow."

He frowned at Markeson.

"Just where are you going?"

"The space station. If I'm right, they've lifted the cargo up, and the smugglers will be loading any time. We need to go now," he insisted.

Kilgore just nodded yes and left to issue orders.

I rounded Josephson and Sarah up. If Markeson was right, we didn't have a lot of time.

CHAPTER TWENTY-EIGHT

The shuttle approached the docking ring of the passenger terminal. To the Sergeant, it traveled at what seemed to be the slowest possible velocity any shuttle could maneuver at and maintain control. Finally, it docked, and the automatic airlock sequence started, securing the shuttle to the terminal and filling the vacuum in the lock with breathable atmosphere.

His patience wearing thinner by the minute, the Sergeant checked his chronometer while tapping the toe of his expensive, handmade, leather shoe on the steel deck of the waiting area.

After what seemed to him to have been several hours, but was less than two minutes, the first of the shuttle's passengers disembarked. The seventh was Molly, his beloved Colonel. She flashed a dazzling smile upon spotting the Sergeant and strolled toward him.

He smiled his best smile in return and offered his arm. The Colonel gracefully took his arm, and the pair sauntered toward the station's best restaurant.

"Have my bags arrived?" the Colonel purred.

"Yes, Molly. They have been checked aboard the *St. Gabriel*. You will be traveling in a first class cabin the first leg of your journey. The steward will provide you with the rest of your travel arrangements once the *St. Gabriel* is underway."

"You've thought of everything. What will I do without you?"

"Try to stay out of trouble I would hope," the Sergeant replied, his tone unpleasant and openly threatening.

"Excuse me?" The Colonel stopped and pulled her arm away. Her left eyebrow arched in anger. She glared at the man she viewed as beneath her.

"Do not make a scene," the Sergeant replied, smiling like nothing was wrong, He took the Colonel's arm and guided her toward the restaurant again. "I understand Anderson's is not bad for a back planet facility like this one. We might as well be on one of the Rim Worlds."

"How dare you threaten me," the Colonel whispered through clenched teeth.

"How dare you ignore me Molly. Your failures as an operational planner have not gone unnoticed. Those in the Society who are interested in these matters are well aware of your, how shall I put it, shortcomings, Molly."

"What are you talking about," the red head asked, stopping suddenly, a confused expression darkening her refined features.

"Things did not go smoothly in the acquisition of the cargo. As you are well aware, I was forced to terminate an SP off base. Forced because you let the SP follow you to the rail siding. Not to mention, that Inspector Sullivan nearly killed me while I was attempting to finish cleaning the crime scene and uncover just how badly you'd compromised the mission."

The maître de of Anderson's approached with a smile as the Colonel stood in silence. She stared at the Sergeant as if he were a complete stranger.

"A table for two? Would you prefer the bar?"

"We have time to dine," the Sergeant replied graciously. "Perhaps a private table for the two of us?"

"But of course, I know just the table. Wilhelm will be your waiter. I believe you will find his service to be exemplary."

Tightening his hold on the Colonel's elbow by clinching his forearm tighter, the Sergeant gave her a sharp tug.

"The mercenaries we hired did excellent work. Your poor planning for the first raid caused them to lose one of their number. It required a significant bonus to appease them."

"You were authorized to pay a bonus," she muttered, confused by her servant's attitude.

"Yes, I was. But you were not authorized to engage in activity that would produce no intelligence or secure the property and safely deliver it to our superiors."

The maître de seated the Colonel. Smiled and departed.

"You know when this is all over you'll be the only man I want," the Colonel told the Sergeant.

"I would much rather be the only man you take into your bed, starting now," he replied, his words, chilling the Colonel.

"You informed on me," she hissed in shocked anger.

"I wouldn't use that exact word. I simply filed a report with more truth to it than perhaps you would have liked."

His face clouded over. "From now on, you will be faithful to me and to the cause. There will be no more dalliances. Act like a general, Sandra, excuse me, Molly. Otherwise, the duration of time to enjoy your new rank will be short."

◆ ◆ ◆

It had been some time since I had planned an operation similar to the one we were about to mount. Markeson had explicit details regarding which freighters would be carrying the contraband. As luck would have it, they were all docked in pairs, but in three different locations on two different docking rings.

I dislike having to divide forces. It only leads to problems.

Even worse, we would have to rely on the police stationed on the space station. They were good at public relations and searching for wanted individuals trying to leave Beta Prime or sneak through Immigration and Customs to get down to the surface.

Providing tactical support of the type potentially needed was not their strong suit. It made me wonder what went through Chief O'Brian's head sometimes. Or rather, what Markeson talked the Chief into when it came to allocating resources.

I didn't ask Markeson how he came by his information. It could be legit. Every detective develops sources, snitches, whatever you want to call them. Or he could be trying to cover up his involvement in a smuggling scheme.

I figured it was about fifty-fifty one way or another.

Sarah sat quietly, watching Beta Prime rise up above us. Despite the horrors she'd experienced in her short life, Sarah still possessed such a childlike innocence at times. She smiled at the colors of the stars and the view of Beta Prime and its two moons. It did me good to watch Sarah let her guard down for a moment, to see her smile at the wonders of space travel.

Josephson, on the other hand, looked like he would rather be anywhere else but strapped into his seat. Markeson had managed to talk Kilgore into having a military shuttle fly us to the space station. Military pilots, as Josephson had just learned, love to hear the words "get there as fast as you can."

The result was a rougher than normal ride as the pilot used maximum thrust to lift the shuttle out of Beta Prime's gravity well and atmosphere. We were now bouncing along on the very edge of the planet's atmosphere, making for an incredibly rough ride.

"Get him to fly a little higher," I demanded. "My Sergeant here won't be able to function by the time we arrive at this rate."

Kilgore unstrapped and went forward. By the time he

K.C. Sivils

returned and strapped back in, the shuttle was cruising at maximum speed in the void of space. Kilgore made eye contact with me and shrugged.

Navy pilots were notorious for giving civilians a rough ride when the opportunity presented itself. This trip was no exception.

I looked back down at my plan and shook my head. I didn't see any other way to deal with the situation with the resources available.

"Okay," I announced. "In hopes of getting as few of us killed as possible, this is the best approach for this raid. Feel free to offer suggestions."

Markeson turned his chair to see the hologram I'd created. Josephson just turned his head far enough he could see the image through the one eye he'd forced open. Kilgore, who had no real jurisdiction, was along in an "advisory capacity." He was a badly needed gun in a situation I was certain would involve gunplay.

"Captain Markeson, Major Kilgore will be with you. You will take this route to approach..."

◆◆◆

Sullivan and Markeson were going to be the death of him yet O'Brian thought. Either that or the end of his career, one or the other, possibly even both. A panicked Station Chief had just gotten off the comm with him. Markeson had just demanded the use of nearly every officer on duty in the station for a raid.

O'Brian knew it was Sullivan's plan. Markeson would never launch a raid with this kind of risk. Too much could go wrong, and as the ranking officer, the Chief of Detectives would have to take the blame. Of course, if Sullivan's plan worked, Markeson would be more than happy to take the credit.

Whatever the cause was, the two had some explaining

to do when they returned. Even Sullivan was not prone to committing career suicide on such short notice. O'Brian looked at his chronometer. There was nothing he could do until the raid was over. He'd be plenty busy afterward. Either running cover for his detectives or trying to leverage the success of the raid into more resources.

Either way, it was going to be a long evening. O'Brian decided to take a break and eat somewhere besides his desk.

If the raid went badly enough, it might not be his desk much longer.

◆◆◆

Molly O'Toole fumed in silence. Her last day on Beta Prime ruined by the arrogance of the man Molly had believed was loyal to her. Not only that, she hadn't been able to enjoy the exquisite meal he had ordered for the two of them. As soon as she arrived at her destination, she planned to set things straight about the operation on Beta Prime.

Primarily, Molly O'Toole intended to point out the fact if she had been promoted and placed in command of the base at Brownstown, the stream of clones, body parts and technology would have been constant. None of this stealing and sneaking about to get the "packages" off world would have been necessary.

The dead SP was the Sergeant's fault too. The man had simply lost his mind and shot a perfectly good clone dead. That had led to the need to rush things. She could hardly be held responsible for that fool Savier agreeing to Kilgore's request to bring in this nuisance of an Inspector.

No, she decided. None of it was her fault. Her Sergeant had betrayed her. Molly O'Toole planned to make him pay for it. She had grown weary of his professions of love anyhow.

The man whose demise she was contemplating interrupted her pity party.

"We have a problem," he said in disgust, pocketing his comm device. "We need to get you on the *St. Gabriel.*"

She made a face indicating disgust before protesting snidely, "I'm not done with my dessert."

The Sergeant stood abruptly, throwing his linen napkin on the table. "You will go now. The Marines and the Planetary Police raided the facility. It's all over. Savier is dead. As second in command, the police will be looking for you."

"This is not possible," she protested, shaking as she stood up. The Sergeant took her by the arm, guiding her from the restaurant toward the concourse.

"It's not only possible, but it was also inevitable. You cannot draw attention to anything you do on operations of this nature."

"I told you we should have just killed that Inspector, what was his name? Sullivan? Then this would have never happened."

Despite the need to hurry, he stopped abruptly; grabbed the red head by both arms and gave her a hard shake. "My source informed me not only was Sullivan and Kilgore present, but your newest conquest, Captain Markeson. Just what did you tell him? What secrets did he pry from you during pillow talk?"

For the first time, it dawned on the Colonel the degree of danger she was in. "I didn't tell him anything!"

"No, but you bribed him. If we go down, he goes down. He'll do everything he can to make sure we don't get off this ball of ice alive."

"Why would he do that," she protested. "He was well compensated. There is nothing linking him to our operation."

"You make me sick with how simple minded you are."

Taking her by the arm again, he began dragging the Colonel toward the boarding area for the *St. Gabriel.* "Somebody will talk if they catch us. My money says it will be you."

♦♦♦

"Trouble Captain!"

Looking up from his tablet, the leader of the mercenaries frowned.

"What is it sergeant?"

"Police are prepping for a raid."

"The containers?"

"I think so sir," the NCO replied, slipping the headgear back on both ears. "I'm picking up orders for the police to slow boarding on the two starliners docked and for the rest of the officers to report to Rings Four and Six on the freight portals."

"Great," the Captain complained. "Just when this job is about to wind down and we're getting off this miserable planet."

He motioned to the Sergeant to come over to where he was sitting. The two quickly began planning the best method to deploy their soldiers to allow the freighters to escape.

Angry at the turn of events, the bad luck of it all, the Captain made a mental note to himself. If he survived, he was demanding bigger bonuses for the men and himself.

CHAPTER TWENTY-NINE

I watched as the pilot approached the space station above Capital City at a speed that would cost a civilian pilot his license and docking privileges for a year. I decided Markeson could add that to his list of things to clean up with the station administrators when this was over.

I had to say though, the pilot knew his business and had the shuttle docked in seconds. There was no impact of note, just a gentle hiss of the air pressures equalizing.

Everyone checked his weapons as we waited for the hatch to open. Sarah didn't carry any side arms, but I was certain she had bladed weapons hidden somewhere on her person. I made her promise me again, for the third time, she would stay out of harm's way.

Waiting for us were the assembled police officers that would participate in the raid. Their Station Commander had divided them into three groups and given them a rough briefing of the plan. Markeson would take one group to search the two docked starliners for the individuals he believed were in charge of the operation. Kilgore would accompany him. Immigration and Security had already taken steps to dramatically slow the boarding process, giving Markeson and his men time to arrive and start the search.

Josephson would command the second group. Going with him would be the Station Commander. The pup's team was going to try to take the two pairs of freighters on the outermost ring, Ring Six. I assigned him the bulk of the experienced officers and the Station Commander.

I took command of the last group. Our target was the

two freighters docked on Ring Four.

I addressed the assembled group who was drawing the attention of tourists, locals who worked on the space station and anyone who happened to be passing by.

"These people may or may not know what they are transporting. If they do know, they will be extremely dangerous. Shoot to kill if they open fire. If they do not know what the cargo is, in all likelihood, they will dump the containers and leave. If that happens, just let them and we'll retrieve the containers."

A hand went up.

I waited for the obvious question.

"What is in the containers Inspector?"

"It's classified. Trust me. You don't want to know. Any more questions?"

I looked at the scared faces staring back at me. I hoped they would all be going home at the end of their duty shift.

"If that's all, let's get this done."

◆◆◆

Markeson hurried along with his group, pushing his way through the growing crowds of irritated passengers wanting to board their starliner. The faster he pushed his way through the throngs of angry humanity, the greater the distance he put between himself and the officers assigned to him.

He'd provided vague descriptions of the Sergeant and the red head. Vague enough it could be any male traveler with a red headed female companion. It would slow the officer's search down considerably. He hoped it would give him time to find the pair and do what he had to do.

Stopping to catch his breath, Markeson spotted a tall, dark headed man with military bearing stepping into the concourse leading to the docking ring the St. Gabriel was berthed at. On the man's elbow was a tall, stunning red headed creature.

He'd found them.

◆◆◆

Josephson let the Station Commander lead the way to the service elevators that would allow the group to rush to the Sixth Ring. Everything moved in a blur for him. The fear of being in space meshed with the adrenaline rush of the impending raid had alternately sped things up and then slowed them down. He wished it was all over and he was back home, safe in his apartment in Capital City.

The door to the service elevator opened and the officers began to deploy. Before the entire group was able to exit the elevator, the first blasts from phase rifles tore through the officers, knocking several men down. To Josephson's horror, among the wounded was the Station Commander.

He had no choice. Shaking violently from sheer terror, Josephson froze. Seconds passed as the fire continued to rip through the ring. His comm device buzzed, the familiar sound pulling his mind together long enough to answer the link.

"What is going on up there," Sullivan bellowed. "I can see flashes from down here."

"Phase fire," Josephson managed to mumble. "Station Commander down."

"Get the men under cover, return fire and secure those ships," Sullivan bellowed through the static filled link.

He closed the link and pocketed the comm. A quick glance around the area showed the officers who'd not been hit had all taken cover. The rate of fire had slowed to a steady rhythm. No additional officers were hit, and despite lying exposed and in the open, none of the wounded officers had been targeted.

Looking back down the ring corridor behind them, Josephson realized they had walked into an ambush. The lack of attackers behind them puzzled him. In the strategic games he liked to play, double envelopment, surrounding an enemy and pinning them down in a crossfire was a tactic he used many times to win games.

The attackers were smart enough to establish the ambush but had not done so in a decisive manner. An officer tried to break across the open corridor to reach one of the wounded and was hit by a phase blast. The woman fell and rolled toward Josephson. He darted out and grabbed the screaming woman by the arms and pulled her behind the small freight container he'd taken cover behind.

"You're okay, I promise," he told the terrified officer, a female of Earth African descent. He examined the wound and discovered it was a severe burn. Nothing like the wound he received in the ill-fated warehouse raid he'd led.

"You're gonna be okay, I promise. Their weapons are set on stun. It's okay."

The woman looked at him as if she was seeing him for the first time. She stopped screaming and caught her breath.

"It hurts so bad."

"I know it does. But you're going to be okay, I promise."

He took another peek around the container. Whoever it was, they were not intent on killing any of the officers. A few well-placed grenades would be devastating. The phase weapons were set on stun, not kill. There was no crossfire.

Josephson pulled off his greatcoat and shirt, leaving on only his white undershirt. He tore it off and tied it to the end of a scrap of metal conduit lying along the ring wall. Slowly he extended the makeshift white flag into the view of the attackers.

"Cease fire."

Josephson peeked out and then jumped back.

"We won't shoot," a strong, commanding voice shouted. "Don't do anything stupid and you'll be okay."

◆◆◆

I watched flashes of hot orange light fill the windows of Ring Six. Josephson had walked right into an ambush. There was nothing I could do. It would be over by the time I reached the action.

A quick glance around proved the station officers had all taken cover. There was no sign of anyone ahead where the two freighters were docked.

There was a limit to how much of what went wrong on this raid I could, heck, was even willing, to hang around Markeson's neck.

I adjusted my right eye for optimum combat conditions. My targeting system was on as was my movement detector and infrared vision. If it moved or had a pulse, I'd see it.

Given my mood, I was going to shoot first, maybe ask questions later.

I drew my revolver and stepped out from behind the portable 3-D printer used to create one-of-a-kind parts for some of the old junkers that stopped at Beta Prime. Freighters so old spare parts weren't manufactured for them anymore.

Frightened station police stared at me as I slowly moved toward the two docking bays. I stopped and scanned the area. The two freighters were relatively new container carriers. Instead of an enclosed hold, a long keel ran the length of the ship. The bridge and crew quarters were all located in the bow. Engines and repair facilities were located aft with a long corridor connecting the two sections. Located in each of the primary habitable sections were escape pods. In between, on the exposed keep was a skeleton framework that allowed freight containers to be stacked, exposed to the open vacuum of space.

The design allowed for ease of unloading and loading. Sealed containers that had been searched by Customs sped up the process of clearing Security and Customs. A process I was not too thrilled about. It was too easy to bribe a Customs official to look the other way and seal a container loaded with contraband.

At Markeson's order, the Station Master had locked the docking rings on the six freighters we were after. At best, it might slow them down till we could breach the airlocks and board the ships.

Smugglers who know their business prepare for any emergency that might delay their escape.

I pulled out my comm and initiated a link.

◆◆◆

Markeson jumped the barrier and ran as hard as he could down the concourse to the boarding gate of the *St. Gabriel*. Carrying his badge high and away from his body with his left hand, Markeson held his phase pistol in his right.

"Stop! Police! Don't let them board!"

The Colonel spun around, the shock of seeing Markeson written on her face. The Sergeant moved away, reaching into his jacket, watching the two stalk each other. The *St. Gabriel's* greeting staff backed away, moving slowly back into the safety of the starliner's airlock.

"Captain, so nice of you to come and see me off."

"Save it. You blew your operation. Now I have to clean up the mess you've made for me."

Markeson moved slowly, his anger and frustration at being placed in a situation he couldn't completely control caused him to focus his vision on the source of his problems. The Sergeant recognized the blind rage of the detective and slowly moved further out of Markeson's range of vision, moving around and behind the out of control cop.

"You are under arrest," he roared, shoving the Colonel in the shoulder, spinning her around. He pocketed his badge and holstered his gun, pulling out a set of handcuffs. Taking the Colonel's left hand, he slapped the first cuff around her wrist and activated the electromagnetic seal.

He didn't sense the Colonel shifting her center of balance and initiating a spinning reverse turn, striking him square in his cheek with the back of her clenched right fist. The blow staggered him, causing him to stumble backward and fall over.

"You fool," the red head snarled, contorting her features, in the process revealing her true face. Stunned at the hideous expression of evil, Markeson crawled away from the monster facing him. She reached into her purse and pulled out a lady's kinetic energy weapon.

"This is a beautiful weapon," the Colonel informed Markeson. "Small caliber, but the projectiles do considerable damage." Her most sultry smile appeared, sickening Markeson. "They tumble. Go in small, come out big, lots of damage in between."

Slowly the Colonel raised the pistol, aiming it square at Markeson's heart. Her mouth opened, emitting a high-pitched laugh, chilling to any who heard the insanity it unleashed.

"Oh, relax Detective Markeson." She placed the strap of her purse back over her shoulder and put her left hand on her hip.

"I know you have a vest on."

With a slight shift, the Colonel adjusted her aim and squeezed off a shot. The .22 caliber round slammed into Markeson's left shoulder, passing under his clavicle before slamming into the scapula and shattering it.

Gasping in agony, Markeson clamped his right hand

over the wound. As he writhed in pain, the Colonel adjusted her aim a second time, firing directly into the prone detective's right shin. The round passed between the tibia and fibula and through his calf, tearing away muscle and tissue as it created an exit wound.

Another agonized scream filled the on ramp of the concourse. Sweat poured off Markeson's brow as he began to slip into shock from the pain.

The Colonel leaned over and smiled. She winked before she spoke, "You aren't much of a cop. You should have known I would be armed. Don't worry Detective. You won't last long. Shock and blood loss will end it soon."

Markeson mumbled, trying to tell the woman something. His mouth was full of blood, and his bottom lip split wide open from the blow to his face, preventing Markeson from speaking. The Colonel just laughed and turned to board the *St. Gabriel.*

She never saw the .45 caliber revolver the wounded detective pulled from his shoulder holster under his left arm. The roar of the discharge echoed down the tunnel into the terminal. Markeson could hear the screams of the terrified passengers waiting to board.

His vision began to blur as he dropped his weapon to the floor. Barely able to make out the body of the Colonel, he exerted the effort to bring her form into focus before he passed out.

"Nice small entrance wound. Nice big exit wound."

CHAPTER THIRTY

"Whoever you are, you aren't going to make it off this station," Josephson shouted.

"That is where you are mistaken officer. We're going to be leaving in just a few minutes. If you try to stop us, you'll regret it."

"You're outnumbered," Josephson shouted, unsure what else to say.

"You're outgunned. We didn't use deadly force. We didn't use anti-personal mines nor did we set up a crossfire. Instead of using projectile weapons, we used phase weapons set on stun. None of your officers are severely wounded. If we had wanted to, we could have annihilated you and your officers the second you stepped off the service elevator. If we'd really wanted to cause problems, we would have wired the elevator and blown you to bits."

"Okay, you've made your point," Josephson shouted back. "Know this, the cargo you are protecting is not worth it. I take it your mercenaries. You can't spend money if you're dead or in prison. What is in those containers will start wars. The Alliance will hunt you down."

"We'll take our chances," the voice called back. "Now, just make sure you and your fellow officers stay under cover and don't do anything stupid. We're changing over to projectile weapons now. No more games."

Josephson sighed. Sullivan would be furious. He shrugged and slowly backed up before slipping behind the container for cover.

"Everybody just stay where you are. I'll see what Inspector Sullivan wants us to do."

◆◆◆

My comm was going crazy. I had Kilgore and Josephson both trying to open a link with me. I opened the link with Josephson first.

"Sullivan, we're pinned down by a group of mercenaries. At least I think its mercenaries. They say when the freighters leave they'll pull out. They haven't used deadly force but they will if we don't let them go. What do you want me to do?"

The pup might not be outnumbered, but he was certainly outgunned and the officers with him were no match for hardened mercenaries.

"Just maintain your position. Don't do anything until I'm able to get there. If the mercs pull out and leave, let them. You're outgunned. Even if you weren't, you and the officers are no match for these guys."

I broke the link and shook my head. This was why I hate operations mounted quickly based on information I hadn't gathered myself.

I got Kilgore on the comm.

"Markeson's down. He's hurt bad, I've called for medics to get him to the hospital here. And Inspector, Colonel O'Donnell is here. He blew her away."

"As soon as the medics get there, get up to Josephson with your people. They're pinned down by mercs so be careful."

I broke the link and continued my march toward the two freighters. Red lights flashed over the airlocks as the engines of the ships started up. The plating underneath me shook as the locking mechanisms broke, allowing the freighters to drift away from the space station. Smoldering metal remained, showing where the crews had melted away the locking devices.

Above me, the other four freighters had broken their locks and were drifting away. I opened a link to Josephson.

"Talk to me."

"The freighters have managed to detach and are pulling away Inspector."

"The mercs?"

"They're pulling back. The mercs must have a ship of their own."

I broke the link and got the Navy pilot on the comm.

"Think you can mess with those freighters for a few minutes?"

He just laughed.

"What do you want me to do Inspector? Buzz 'em. Make 'em ram each other? Just give me the word."

"Just try to herd them and keep them from being able to create enough space to get vectors clearing the station."

"Roger."

I was missing something. The Colonel was dead. The mercenaries who had done the heavy lifting of hijacking the containers from the Brownstown base had demonstrated no inclination to hurt anyone unless necessary and were pulling out. A single Navy pilot didn't have a chance against them.

"Think, Sully, think," I told myself. Then it came to me. The man Josephson had spotted meeting Markeson in Brownstown.

I opened a link to the pup.

"Josephson, just stand down. Keep an eye on things, but do not, repeat, do not engage anyone. The mercenaries just want to leave. The freighters we can probably follow or catch at other ports of call. The Station Master has their flight plans."

I ran past the officers who simply watched me as I entered the elevator and took it down the main concourse.

Whoever was the real brains of this fiasco had to have an exit strategy. Things had gone south in a hurry. If the man Josephson had spotted was the brains, he would have considered the possibility of things going wrong at the station.

I just had to find him.

The elevator opened and I ran out into the crowded terminal to see the medics leaving with Markeson's body on a stretcher.

I nearly panicked. I had lost track of Sarah.

◆◆◆

Josephson just looked at the comm in surprise. It wasn't like Sullivan to toss in the towel like that. Mercenaries or not, Sullivan would have been blazing away.

He thought about disobeying his partner for all of one second. If he disobeyed and engaged the mercenaries and survived, he wouldn't survive the exchange with Sullivan when it was all over.

Pocketing the comm again, Josephson simply sat down and watched the freighters slip away. His heart skipped a beat when he saw the reckless Navy pilot maneuvering the shuttle they had arrived in with thrusters, acting like a herd dog he'd seen in school on a video, nipping at the heels of stray animals to return them to the safety of the herd.

Images of the carnage in the underground research center and the look of horror on Sullivan's face when they entered the "butcher shop," played through his mind. Sarah's tears of relief when Sully told her Ellie was not one of the victims of vivisection.

The injustice of it all enraged Josephson. How could people do this? How could they get away with it? He'd looked at the carnage and seen the hand of pure evil. He thought about the scientist he'd shot and to his surprise, he felt no remorse.

The sudden realization of this frightened him. He'd always followed the rules. He wasn't a rule breaker. In fact, he resented rule breakers. Decent people followed the rules and that allowed for society to be better for everyone.

Now he didn't know. He'd seen the arrogance and evil in the expressions of the scientists in that horrible place. In the past when Sullivan smacked someone around, it always bothered him. Now he understood the rage Sullivan felt, had to feel, after years of witnessing the depravity of humanity. Josephson knew at Sullivan's core he was a good man at heart. Sullivan wanted to help people, to keep them safe if he could.

It scared Josephson to his core to realize what he was capable of. That within him was the same potential to break the rules as the people who had butchered the helpless clones.

◆◆◆

I spotted him. He'd worked his way behind me, using the crowds of anxious and angry passengers as cover. In his right hand, he held a .42 caliber projectile weapon. Wrapped around the throat of a furious Sarah was the Sergeant's left forearm. She struggled, kicking the man in his shins and ramming her boot on the top of his foot.

He watched me and smiled, ignoring Sarah's efforts to escape his grasp. The smile vanished when she pulled the sleeve of his jacket up, exposing his forearm and sinking her teeth into his flesh. My cybernetic eye zoomed in on the tattoo on his forearm, a sniper's scope with a dagger bisecting it at a right angle. He was Army Special Forces. He'd done wet work.

Evidently, he didn't appreciate the bite and expressed his displeasure by slamming the barrel of his weapon into Sarah's temple. It was all I could do to control my rage. I felt I was reliving Maria's death all over again.

"If you value the life of your little friend, you're going to back off Inspector."

"Why? You can't possibly think you're going to escape. That you'll manage to get the cargo to your superiors."

"Oh, I'm no longer worried about that Inspector. Some operations just go bad. You're a military man I've been told. Contact with the enemy alters the plan instantly and irrevocably."

He reached into his pocket somehow with his gun hand, withdrawing a device I recognized all too well, a remote detonator. Placing it in his left hand, he began stepping back, dragging a barely conscious Sarah with him while pointing his weapon at me. Behind him was an empty concourse.

If I could get him to put Sarah down, I could end this without anyone else getting hurt.

"Inspector, you can relax. I have no charges planted on the station. I'm not a mass murderer." He lifted his gun hand holding the detonator, calling attention to the device. He smiled a sad smile as he spoke, "This device controls several functions. Allow me to demonstrate."

He glanced out the giant window of the space station. The Navy pilot was doing his best, but the freighters would soon be able to get underway. Without using weapons, there was no way he could stop them from departing.

"This function releases the containers," the dark haired man shouted as he pressed it. A gasp came from the few bystanders watching, the station police having cleared as many of the passengers waiting to board the *St. Gabriel* from behind me.

I watched as six containers drifted away from the container freighters and realized what was about to happen.

"This function," the deranged man announced, "eliminates the ability of you to track down my superiors."

A brilliant flash filled the darkness as the containers exploded into flames, vaporizing whatever was inside. With great certainty, I knew human lives had been snuffed out. Whatever was in those containers, I knew some of the space was dedicated to transporting clones.

A quiet rage filled me as I watched Sarah come to her senses. It wouldn't be long before she started struggling again. I doubted he would tolerate it this time.

I couldn't let him hurt Sarah.

"I'm a Marine. You're ex-Special Forces. You've done wet work."

He laughed. "Once a Marine, always a Marine. Your kind thinks you're special."

"We are. Let's settle this, soldier to soldier. Marine versus Army Special Forces."

He tilted his head to one side. Intrigued by my proposition.

"And just how would we do that Inspector?"

"Let her go. She has nothing to do with this. This is between us."

"And if I do?"

I holstered my weapon and stood with my great coat open, my hands at my side.

"You holster yours."

He laughed, a deep laugh from the bottom of his abdomen, filled with emotion.

"You must be a fan of ancient Earth movies. Space Westerns I believe they're called. The villain and the hero meet at high noon on the main hoverway and shoot it out."

"Sure, that's it," I said, measuring the distance between us carefully while calling up the specifications of his .42 pistol. I was just outside the range of the weapon, at least the range it could be considered accurate. I looked at his hips and noted he stood at a slight angle. I took two steps back and had my computer do the math.

"Let her go. Then let's settle this like soldiers, with honor."

I had him. He shook Sarah and elicited a groan from her. He dropped the detonator device and kicked it to the side. Then slowly, ever so slowly, he moved laterally to the inside wall of the concourse and gently laid Sarah down. As he moved back to his original position, she sat up, brushing her hair out of her face.

Childlike as ever, Sarah stuck her tongue out at him.

Slowly, the man holstered his gun in a service holster fastened on his belt.

We looked at each other, hands by our sides. One of us would be dead in seconds.

He drew quickly, aimed and fired. I drew quickly but did not hurry. I let my right eye do all the work and fired.

His .42 caliber round whizzed past my left ear and impacted harmlessly against the curving wall behind me. My. 50 caliber bullet impacted dead center in his right pectoral, nearly blowing his arm off.

I walked over to him as he lay bleeding out.

He grimaced as he looked up at me.

"Thank you Inspector. I was once an honorable man. You have allowed me to die the death of a soldier, with honor. My failure to serve the Colonel stripped me of my honor. The cause is better off without me."

He made a deep gasping sound as blood bubbled up from his lips, coating his chin as it ran down to his throat. It wouldn't be long.

"This is a quick, honorable death. The Society would not have granted me dignity in my death," he whispered.

A rattling sound escaped his mouth as his spirit left his body.

I didn't know how I felt about his death.

I felt slender arms slip around me and hug me tight.

"I want to go home Sully. Please? Can we go and eat at

Joe's? Please?"

What else could I say? There would be plenty of time tomorrow for paperwork.

CHAPTER THIRTY-ONE

A lot had happened in the past three weeks. First of all, the mercenaries made a clean getaway. I'm pretty sure they were responsible for the six hijacked containers and probably the dead railroad employee. There was no real point in pursuing them. I didn't have any evidence to convict with.

Kilgore didn't have any choice. With General Savier and this Colonel Sandra O'Donnell dead, he had to call the brass. Within forty-eight hours as scary a bunch of Military Intelligence types as I've ever seen descended on Beta Prime. Twenty-four hours later they were gone.

Along with what they believed was every scrap of proof clones ever existed on Beta Prime, along with any evidence of illegal activity violating the Anti-Cloning Treaty. Drives containing as much evidence as I could collect and hide had been locked away in a safe, the location of which only I knew.

Somebody had to pay for this. If nothing else, it was leverage. When I'll use it, I have no idea, but I have it for when the time comes.

It looked like Markeson was going to get away with whatever scam he pulled. Without the evidence of the illegal cargo, there was no way to prosecute the freighters, all owned by the same shipping company. The same company owned by the family of a late trillionaire by the name of Spencer Devereaux. A man, by the way, who had died in disgrace in our jail right here in Capital City.

One of Markeson's former associates as well I might add.

I went and visited Markeson in the hospital. That red head really messed him up. He had to have a new calf muscle regenerated and a steel scapula installed. We joked about having manmade parts. I think he knows I suspect him of being involved in this mess, but knowing and proving are two different things.

I'll say this for Chief O'Brian. He surprised me on this one. He backed me on everything, from start to finish. Covered for Markeson as well. Nobody on our planetary force got a single reprimand in our jacket. The Chief looks awful, but he didn't ask too many questions, just took the heat for us. Once he learned enough to have an idea of what had gone down, he just told us to do our jobs and leave the rest to him.

It bothers me though. I know a cover-up when I see one. All the government did was move the operation and cleanup its mess. They couldn't crush the people who uncovered what they were up to without the public at large getting wind of things. So we got a pass.

Makes me sick. We got a pass for doing the right thing, and Chief O'Brian loses a year or two off his lifespan from stress for backing his people, including Markeson.

This clone thing has me worried. I've read some of the logs I copied. Some of the clones cut loose on the civilian population had demonstrated signs of psychopathy. I'm pretty sure the clone I blasted when Father Nathan lost it was one. The scientists were tracking the clone, studying his behavior. There was no record of how many innocent civilians died as a result of this one psycho.

As hard as it is for me to believe, I'm convinced Sarah is telling me the truth. At least what she believes to be true. I have no doubt her sister Ellie exists, and I've decided to take her fears of being hunted seriously. Her ability to blend in and vanish is amazing. So is her ability to withstand the extreme weather of Beta Prime.

Great qualities for a soldier to have, making her a desirable piece of property for the wrong interested party.

Father Nathan and I haven't talked about what happened, but we're friends again. I guess he'll bring it up in the future and we'll have to hash it out. I'd be okay with things if he just left it alone.

I'm worried about Josephson. Shrinks make me a bit nervous. I don't really trust them. They want you to tell them all this stuff, stuff deep from inside you. The stuff that keeps me awake at night, things like remorse and guilt, the nightmares I have.

Stuff that can be used against you.

Despite all that, I've been making sure he sees the department shrink. I take him to the appointments myself. It irritates the shrink I won't go myself, but I make sure the pup keeps his appointments.

I might even have him talk with Father Nathan. He's a good kid, and if he sticks with it, Josephson is going to be a solid Inspector one day. I just don't want him to wind up like me.

Depressed and alone.

CHAPTER THIRTY-TWO

I watched Josephson enter Joe's and make his way over toward my table. He sat down and looked out the window, watching the people passing by on the cold streets.

"Inspector, would you be offended if I asked you a personal question."

I had an idea of what Josephson was going to ask. To be honest, I was surprised it had taken him so long to get around to it.

I just nodded.

"Sir, how do you deal with it? Just shooting someone, like when you shot that clone when we found Father Nathan or when you shot the guy who grabbed Sarah."

"Is it bothering you, the fact you killed that mercenary? That you shot that scientist?"

Tears welled up in his eyes as he nodded yes.

"If the mercenaries had just dropped their weapons as ordered, that man would be alive. You had no choice. That scientist, well, not the smartest thing to do, I'm gonna have to say. But that scientist was a stone cold killer, butchering people in the name of science so somebody could make money selling body parts. I'm not sure you should feel so terrible about that one either."

"But sir, I didn't think. I was just so angry. I mean, I know Sarah's a clone. She's...odd, I know, but Sarah's our partner, sort of. That could have been Sarah; you know how she goes on and on about the hunters looking for her. I just saw red."

"I'll agree with you, Sergeant. You shouldn't have done it. I'm just saying, it's not like you shot an innocent civilian or another cop."

He nodded, but my words seemed to make it only worse for him.

"How do you do it, Sir? How do you deal with it?"

He needed an honest answer, so I gave him one.

"Don't let my demeanor fool you. It bothers me, every time. Take that guy who drew on me in the concourse for example."

"Yeah, but he drew down on you Inspector. That and forensics says it was his weapon that killed the dead SP that started all this."

"It bothers me because I needed to protect Sarah. I baited him into doing it. As many people as that man murdered, and we'll never know how many clones were in those containers, I'm not sure he deserved to die like that. Josephson, I'll tell you this, what bothers me was what he said to me before he died."

The pup looked at me with his watery eyes. "I didn't know he said anything to you."

I shook my head in disbelief at the memory of the dying man's words. I'd replayed my recording several times just to make sure I hadn't imagined the incident.

"He thanked me. Before he bled out, he thanked me for giving him an honorable death, a soldier's death. He thanked me and then mumbled something about the Society wouldn't have done that for him."

We sat in silence, each of us alone with our thoughts.

"How do you thank somebody for killing you," I asked Josephson.

"Maybe he'd lost his dignity because of all of this. Dying the way he did, maybe you gave it back to him. That would be something," the pup offered.

"For him maybe, but I had to pull the trigger."

Josephson nodded. I doubt he understood, but he had his own demons to deal with. I certainly had enough of my own.

"Inspector, I'm going to go. I'll see you at roll call in the morning."

He stood to go. I reached out and stopped him.

"Don't lose your idealism, Josephson. It's what makes you who you are. Whatever you do, even if it means leaving the force, don't wind up like me. Promise me that."

The pup looked surprised. He smiled for just a moment and nodded. I hoped he understood what I was asking of him. I planned on reminding him. I'd see to it he got fired myself if that's what it took to save him from a fate similar to mine.

I watched him leave, waving to Joe, Ralph, and Alice as he left.

A few minutes later, Alice brought me my evening meal and sat it before me. "You okay Inspector?"

"I've had better days."

"I gather you can't really talk about it."

I just nodded.

"Sarah's had a hard time lately too. She hasn't said much, but I can tell."

"You've seen her?"

Alice nodded. "At the dormitory a few times. I think she doesn't want you to see her when she's upset. Sarah understands things in ways we can't. She knows you're having a hard time and seeing her upset would just make things worse for you."

"Not knowing she's okay makes things worse for me," I snapped, immediately regretting it. "I'm sorry Alice, this has all been just a bit much. Not being able to say anything makes it harder."

"It's okay. Just know you have friends and we're worried about you."

She meant well, but her kind words just made things worse.

"Any how," Alice said with a happy smile, "Sarah

39

stopped by after you had breakfast. She was in a good mood; wearing that snappy black greatcoat, you bought her. She said to tell you she'd be at roll call tomorrow morning. She's ready to go back to work."

Alice gave me one last smile before she left me to eat my meal alone.

Alone with my thoughts, thoughts like how did Kilgore know Sarah was a clone and Maria was her sister.

◆ ◆ ◆

Markeson tried to get comfortable in his bed. He decided being shot hurt, a lot. In the future, he'd be more sympathetic when one of his detectives got shot. Well, at least he'd act like it.

The doctors had been cutting back on his pain medication, and he was less than happy about it. A glance at the chronometer on the wall told him it would be fifteen minutes until the nurses changed shifts. Lech that he was, Markeson smiled at the idea. He was making slow but steady progress with the cute brunette nurse who had the next shift.

He turned his mind toward the events of the recent past. Shooting the Colonel had eliminated a very loose cannon that could have been trouble. Sullivan had cleaned up the remainder of the mess for him when he'd gunned down the Colonel's right-hand man. Even better had been the fact the Colonel's henchman had destroyed the evidence of smuggling for him.

Markeson couldn't have cleaned things up better himself.

The only thing worrying him now was the identity of the man who'd left him the cryptic warning on his bathroom mirror.

◆◆◆

Kilgore watched the Seabees finish filling in the open pit that had been the underground research facility. From his superior's perspective, things had gone pretty well. He'd found the illegal cloning operation. Whether or not it had been stopped was above Kilgore's pay grade. Who was behind the operation was an answer to a question he didn't know.

All things considered, it was a difficult op that had gone well, if only he'd not let slip the fact he knew about Sarah and Maria to Sullivan.

CHAPTER THIRTY-THREE

With ease, Sarah lowered herself onto the balcony of Sully's place. With an innocent grin displayed on her face, she bypassed his security system and entered her own secondary code into the lock.

It pleased her when the lock clicked. She liked having a code even Sully didn't know about. It allowed her to use the balcony to come and go and not the key Sully had given her.

Sarah enjoyed the warmth of the apartment for a few moments and then carefully shut the door to the balcony behind her.

A quick examination of the kitchen told Sarah it was time for a trip to the grocery store. She'd let Sully know at roll call in the morning. After making a sandwich and eating it, Sarah cleaned up the kitchen, leaving no trace of her presence.

She stood on the balcony and looked out at the lights of Capital City as she ate her sandwich. It wasn't home just yet, but Sarah decided she felt more comfortable living on Beta Prime than anywhere else she'd lived. Having finished her sandwich, Sarah set out to do what she'd come to do.

What she had done every night for the past three weeks.

Pressing her ear against the door to Sullivan's room, she listened to make certain he was asleep. Hearing the sound of gentle snoring, Sarah let her self in and moved to stand next to Sullivan's bed.

For nearly ten minutes Sarah watched the man who

both fascinated and frightened her. Twice now he had saved her life and risked his own to do so, the idea of which attracted Sarah.

Sullivan moved his head in his sleep, causing a lock of his hair to uncharacteristically fall across his forehead, covering part of the scar running vertically from his hairline down to his jawline, bisecting his right eye in the process.

Sarah carefully brushed the lock of hair back into its place and studied the scar once again. Many individuals would consider the scar ugly, even hideous. Sarah decided it gave Sully's face character.

It was proof he understood people suffered in life.

She smiled at Sully and turned to go. She paused at the door for one last glimpse. Sarah decided she liked Sully.

And then she was gone.

CHAPTER THIRTY-FOUR

For some reason, the stars seemed brighter this night. Ellie didn't like to look up at the stars too often, doing so reminded her of Sarah. Sometimes, like tonight, the temptation was too much, and Ellie would spend hours staring at the stars. Wondering where Sarah was, what she was doing. Sometimes it made Ellie angry, knowing Sarah was free, able to do what she wanted. Other times it made her sad. It was then Ellie would miss Sarah the most.

She would think of their short time together. The really good times in Ellie's short life had been spent with her sisters, especially the short time with Maria. It had been hard when Maria died and even more challenging when Ellie had to run, leaving Sarah behind.

When she did let herself think of Sarah, Ellie remembered things the sisters did together. Things like laughing, playing dress up, combing each other's hair and so often as sisters are wont to do, they bickered over the silliest of things. The best thing of all was sharing secrets.

Tonight she found herself missing Sarah more than usual.

For Ellie had so many secrets to share.

Want to learn more about Inspector Sullivan and the universe he inhabits?

For more information about Inspector Sullivan's universe, you can go to my author website and search the pages in the Universe of Thomas Sullivan page on the site.

The ultimate source of additional information on the good Inspector, his friends and dare I say, enemies, is my FREE fan newsletter, *The Inspector's Report*. *The Inspector's Report* will include short stories about the characters, backstory, excerpts and updates on when new Inspector Sullivan novels will be available.

Word of mouth is critical for the success of any author. If you enjoyed this work of fiction, please consider leaving a positive review on Amazon. Even if the review is short, one or two sentences, it will be a big help and appreciated. Thanks!

Other works of fiction by K.C. Sivils:

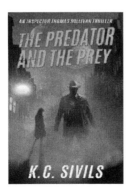

The Predator and The Prey

Grey Sky Blues

ABOUT THE AUTHOR

Author of over twenty non-fiction books, including an Amazon Best Seller, Sivils has now ventured into the realm of fiction with his Inspector Thomas Sullivan series. K.C. and his wife Lisa are the parents of three children. Sivils is a dog lover and a fan of Classic Rock bands like *The Rolling Stones* and New Wave rockers *The Cars*.

Science fiction and classic crime novels have long been favorites of author K.C. Sivils. The combination of film noir and science fiction in director Ridley Scott's adaptation of Philip K. Dick's sci-fi classic *Do Androids Dream of Electric Sheep* into the masterful Harrison Ford vehicle *Bladerunner* encouraged him to consume as much of both genre's as possible.

A fan of past noir masters such as Dashiell Hammett and Raymond Chandler, Sivils also enjoys the current generation of storytellers like Renee Pawlish and Matt Abraham.

Sivils has traveled extensively, visiting three continents, twelve countries and forty-seven states. An avid reader and fan of classic films, *The Chronicles of Thomas Sullivan*, reflects his interest in classic film noir movies and science fiction.

Last Train to Nowhere is the second installment of *The Chronicles of Thomas Sullivan* series by author K.C. Sivils. Author of over twenty works of non-fiction, including an Amazon Best Seller, *Last Train to Nowhere* is Sivils second work of fiction to appear in print.

For more details about the universe Inspector Sullivan inhabits (along with his friends and enemies) and to be notified of releases of future books in *The Chronicles of Thomas Sullivan*, please visit www.KCSivils.com. Sign-up for the FREE newsletter *The Inspector's Report* to receive details not revealed in the books along with the occasional short story about the characters.

Go to www.kcsivils.com/newsletter-signup/

42260502R00173

Made in the USA
San Bernardino, CA
08 July 2019